IN CONTROL

An Ivy Nash Thriller

Book 5

By
John W. Mefford

IN CONTROL
Copyright © 2017 by John W. Mefford
All rights reserved.

Second Edition

Sugar Hill Publishing

ISBN: 978-1-943774-26-5

Interior book design by
Bob Houston eBook Formatting

To stay updated on John's latest releases, visit:
JohnWMefford.com/readers-group

One

Perspiration gathered just below the eyes of Megan Espinoza. Even though she was known in her professional life for her calm under pressure—business colleagues had dubbed her the Ice Princess—there was no way to avoid sweating like a pig. Not with temperatures likely soaring above a hundred fifty degrees inside her car.

That's what happens, Megan, when you take a sweltering September day in San Antonio and cross it with a black Mercedes. Eh bien, c'est le prix à payer pour le succès.

The French phrase for *"Well, that's the price you pay for success"* just came to mind, harking back to her collegiate years.

Sitting in the parking lot at her son's elementary school, she cranked the air conditioner, attempting to keep her makeup from draining down her face. The airflow sounded like a stampede of cattle, but in mere seconds the stifling atmosphere was snuffed out by the dominant rush of cold.

She took a breath. Relief.

The groan of the Mercedes's four-hundred horsepower engine coupled with the state-of-the-art AC unit, drowned out the horde of kids that had just descended upon the elementary school playground next to the parking lot. After checking her makeup in the rearview, she leaned forward, trying to find the white and black Spurs jersey worn by her second-grade son, David.

"There you are, you little devil." She smirked, knowing he had a lot of his father in him. Charming, good looking, and a bit of a bad boy. The older bad boy had charmed the pants right off her when they both were attending San Antonio's Trinity University. Since then, she'd spent every waking moment either studying, working, or focusing on her family. Back in the day, it was just her and Carlos. They'd mated like rabbits night and day, surely breaking records of some sort. She could recall being so enamored with the man that his very essence nearly buckled her knees— which usually led to another round of hot sex.

She released a soft giggle, but not necessarily from reminiscing about the good old days. She'd always carried a hint of regret, although she couldn't bring herself to admit it until the kids were born. When she was young and smitten, and he was chiseled with a full head of hair, she'd always pictured Carlos as a future investment banker, or tort lawyer, or even a distinguished sales executive. But how was he using his high-dollar Trinity degree? He spent his days driving all over the area in a big, brown truck, wearing a brown uniform, delivering brown packages. It was demeaning, boring, and it paid like shit.

But Carlos disagreed. Admittedly, he'd never really found his passion—even if it could have been a single-minded drive to rake in the money—but always said his job was rewarding enough for him and, over time, would provide a decent retirement.

"Decent, my ass," she mumbled.

He'd routinely joke with her, saying, "What can brown do for you?"

It was difficult not to snap back, and she had on a couple of occasions. Resentment, if she really thought about it, was one of those things that never went away. It seemed to lurk near the surface, ready to pounce on any frailty of a relationship. But she would persevere…for the family. She always had. Someone had to.

She watched David grab a basketball and sink a shot from about ten feet out, then point at his jersey in a cocky fashion. *Just like your father. All that swagger.*

David's number-fifty jersey was the only clue anyone would need to understand for whom he was named: Spurs legend David Robinson. He'd been their first child and a boy, so she thought Carlos would want a Carlos Junior running around. Oh no. Carlos insisted that his son be named after the former Spurs center. She'd relented, as she often had early in their relationship.

And then came Annie. It had only been two years and three months, but so far the child had given Megan new hope that she and Carlos could produce something nearly perfect. With her momma's dark ringlets against her ashen face and her laid-back demeanor, Annie was a gift from above. Yes, Megan loved her son too. But she could already see his propensity for cutting corners. Of course, there was his smart-ass mouth, which had led to today's face-to-face discussion with the vice principal. But, like his father, it always came with a wink and a charming nod.

Oh brother. Her crow's feet might be coming out in full force between now and the time David graduated from high school.

With the temperature now at a perfect seventy degrees inside her lavish cocoon, she used her pick to fluff her curly hair in the right places. She reapplied her lipstick, which complemented her red and silver pantsuit perfectly. Her power suit. She was the vice president of Human Resources of a mobile home manufacturing company. She had a meeting in less than an hour with the COO and wanted to present herself in a professional manner.

She knew there was irony in the fact that she and the executive leadership team all enjoyed their lofty salaries and silver-spooned perks, while the product they built was marketed toward those who barely made above minimum wage. But what could she do to help them? Very little, she came to realize. Most of their buyers were people who lost the gene-pool lottery or had traveled a different path than she had during the thirty-four years of her life.

She'd worked her ass off to get where she was, routinely putting in weekends and long nights as she climbed the corporate ladder. She deserved her hundred-thousand dollar car. She'd single-handedly put the family on solid financial footing—no thanks to Carlos. Always looking ahead, she'd recently started working with a real estate agent to look for properties on the coast. Spend a few weeks on the beach, rent out the condo when they weren't there. Another win-win for Megan.

She caught herself smiling in the rearview as she shifted the Mercedes into reverse.

The stereo sound of her phone ringing made her flinch. The Bluetooth had sent the incoming call through her car speakers. She glanced at the sedan's control panel. The number wasn't in her contacts, but it did have the local area code, 210. She twisted her lips, contemplating punching the hang-up button on her steering wheel. After all, it was probably another phone solicitor. What did they want now, money to help underprivileged kids get braces? Or could it be someone from the office, an administrative assistant possibly, calling from a cell phone to give her an update on the upcoming meeting?

And then she felt that slight pang in her gut—the one she knew had a direct line to her motherly instinct.

"Oh hell's bells," she said, punching up the line. "Hello, this is Megan, can I help you?"

A scream pierced her heart. And then a female voice said, "We have your daughter."

Two

Megan slammed her foot on the brake at the same moment her heart slammed against her chest. A few seconds passed as she quickly replayed the words, "*We have your daughter.*"

"Who is this?"

"You don't need to worry about that."

Another scream. Without a doubt, that was Annie. A wave of emotion rushed up the back of her throat.

Keep calm, Megan. They want something; you want your daughter back. You can do this.

She swallowed. "Do not harm my daughter, do you hear me?"

A slight chuckle. "Do you think you're in a position to tell us what to do? I don't think so."

She dug her nails into the steering wheel, her entire body clenched into a knot. "I'm not telling you what to do. I'm asking…pleading for you not to hurt my little girl."

"Don't start blabbering. I can't handle that. Just do as you're told and Annie will not be harmed."

"I'll do anything. What do you want?"

There was a pause. She could hear muffled voices, at least one male. Were they all speaking English?

"Are you there?"

"Yes, I'm here.

We…I need for you to open your bank application on your phone and transfer fifty thousand dollars to an account I will send you through a text. Is that clear?"

"Yes, although I'm not sure I have fifty thousand that I can access right away."

"You do. Trust me."

She knew exactly how much money Megan had in her bank account? What else did this woman know about her and her family? Enough to take her daughter, obviously. She, or someone, must have snuck her out of the Crème de la Crème daycare. But how? Their security was rigid.

"No problem. I can do that. When can I get my daughter?"

The line beeped. She looked at the control panel and saw another call coming in. It was Carlos. She had to let him know what was going on. But if she switched calls even for a few seconds, she knew the people who had Annie might harm her…or worse. Her finger hovered over the button to switch calls.

"I'll let you know where you can pick her up once we verify the money transfer has been made."

The call from Carlos stopped beeping. She felt a tug at her heart. He should know, right? But it was too late. Dammit! "When do you need the money?"

"I thought you were a smart woman, Megan Espinoza. With your fancy title and luxury car, you have the easy life. The rest of us, not so much."

"What… I don't know what to say." For the first time in years, she felt exposed, belittled for her place on the income totem pole. But she didn't care; she only wanted her Annie back in her arms.

"Nothing. I will stay on the line while you transfer the money. Do not hang up. Do not try to contact anyone else. If you do, we will kill your daughter."

"Please don't!" she cried out as tears instantly pooled in her eyes.

"Then use your smartphone and send us the money. I just sent you a text with the account number."

She fumbled her phone, and it dropped to the floorboard. Scooping it back up, the phone felt like a hot plate in her hands. She could feel the sheer panic rippling through her body. She tried swiping the screen, but accidentally tapped her Facebook app. "Dammit!"

"Is everything okay?" The woman's pitch lowered. There was no sympathy in her words. She sounded more like a drill sergeant.

"I'm fine. Just give me a minute." She emptied her lungs, searching for the calm mental focus that she so desperately needed.

Another breath. With her dexterity under control, she tapped and swiped the screen as if she were playing the harp. In no time, she'd logged into her bank account, then switched over and found the text with the account and routing numbers. She copied them into the appropriate fields in the bank application, then tapped submit. A little virtual wheel started spinning.

"What's taking so long?"

"I hit submit. It's just taking a few seconds to go through."

Another scream, this one farther away from the phone. "Get her back in the van. Now!" the lady barked.

Megan stopped breathing for a second. Then she said, "What's going on? You're not hurting Annie, are you?"

No response.

"Hello! Are you there?"

A few distant voices and then the phone sounded like it had been tossed into a garbage disposal. She held her phone away from her ear. What the hell was going on?

Two beeps and the line went dead.

"Hello? You're still there, aren't you?" She desperately tapped her phone, hoping to find the call still open. But it had ended.

A punch to her kidney.

"No, no, no, noooo!" *You've got to maintain your composure. Annie is counting on you.*

She found the recent calls and tapped the call button. As she waited for the line to ring, she battled the urge to lash out.

"Come on, come on, come on…"

It rang. Just once. And then, *"I'm sorry, this number is no longer in service."*

She felt her phone slip through her fingers and bounce off her lap. Everything was a blur. She couldn't see the kids playing outside or feel the rush of cool air against her face. Her body went numb. She just sat there and stared at nothing. Time passed, but she couldn't tell if it was thirty seconds or thirty minutes. Her body had put up a wall. A defense system to keep her from breaking down, losing control of everything that made her human.

And then the wall slowly crumbled into dust. A throbbing pain took hold of her insides. It felt like a bear trap had clamped its razor-sharp teeth into her gut. Teeth that were laced with acid, born from the utter misery that had consumed her. She knew it wouldn't let go until her entire being was shredded into a million pieces. She couldn't stop it. Even worse, she didn't want to stop it. She had to suffer more than precious little…

A wailing sound split her eardrums—it was her own. She thrashed wildly, pounding her fist against the window, banging her head on the steering wheel. The devil had taken over her body, and she was just along for the tormented ride.

Her phone rang.

Three

She wiped her face and blinked, gaping at the control panel. It was Carlos.

Oh my God... Carlos!

She burst into tears. *What will I tell him?* She rocked her clasped hands in front of her face, hoping, praying that something would change. Everything she'd just experienced had to be a sick dream. Perhaps internal stress had built up to the point where she'd created some type of alternate universe, one that was designed to inflict the most pain. Just like when she'd cut herself over and over again while staring at her chubby body in high school.

"Stop it!" she yelled at herself, covering her face. "Stop making it about yourself, dammit!"

The phone continued to ring.

She couldn't bring herself to punch up the call. She kept replaying Annie's scream…the last thing she'd ever hear coming out of her daughter's mouth. Another wave of torment gripped her body. She started to cough, which morphed into a dry heave. She was losing control. She had devolved into something subhuman.

This wasn't happening. It couldn't be real, could it? Somehow, Annie would appear right there in her toddler seat in the back seat of her Mercedes.

She glanced over her shoulder. All she saw was Annie's stuffed animal, an alligator she'd appropriately named Allie.

She heard herself sniffle. Still staring at Allie the Alligator, she'd somehow calmed down.

The ringing phone shook her out of her trance. She couldn't put it off. She had to tell Carlos what had happened to their darling little girl.

She tapped the button.

"She's gone, Carlos. They took her, and I think they…they killed her." She exploded into tears just as she finished speaking.

"Megan, what are you talking about?"

Gasping to control her breathing, she couldn't respond. "I…I…"

"Megan, what on earth?"

"They took our Annie, Carlos. They took her, got me to send them the ransom. But they never gave her back. They said they would, but they just hung up on me. She's gone…forever."

"Baby, Annie's with me."

She stopped crying. She stopped breathing. Her heart wanted to believe what she'd just heard, but her mind wouldn't let go of what she'd just experienced…hearing her daughter's scream, dealing with the ruthless kidnapper.

"What did you just say?" Her nasal passages were completely clogged.

"I have Annie with me. I got off work early and decided it would be cool to have a little father-daughter time. We're at the park. She's running around, blowing bubbles."

"How…?" Her eyes came into focus, settling on the elementary school kids scampering across the playground. She even found David playing tag with some girls. She sniffled.

"Baby, are you okay? Did someone tell you they had taken Annie?"

Tears bubbled in her eyes again. "Put her on, Carlos. I need to hear her voice. I need to know she's okay."

Carlos called out for their little girl. A moment later: "Hi, Mommy. I'm blowing bubbles!"

Tears streamed down her cheeks. "I love you, Annie."

"Love you, bye."

Her heart was whole again.

Four

The cursor had blinked a thousand times. To be precise, it had blinked one thousand fifty-two times...and counting.

I forced my eyes to look away, settling on two drops of dried white paint on the taupe carpet in my new office. Actually, the first real office for my little firm—which I'd named ECHO—whose mission was to improve the lives of children, focusing on those who were at the greatest risk of harm or negligence. That mission had, over the course of the last several months, evolved into much more than I'd ever imagined, both in good and bad ways. The good? We'd reunited lost loved ones, rescued kids from abusive situations, and been able to root out some very nasty people.

The bad came in the form of risking our lives by crossing paths with those same nasty people. The worst of which was a man named Milton Weber, a crazed individual who'd stalked, abducted, and abused me. He had murdered countless others, all because of his obsession with me, wanting me to suffer. It had finally ended a couple of months back in his torture chamber, or as he'd called it, his fun house. He was finally apprehended by the San Antonio Police Department, but not before he had hurt two of my friends.

Stan, a burly detective and a huge supporter of the ECHO cause, had lost his arm. Cristina, my lone employee and one very street-smart teenage girl who'd been through her own turmoil growing up, had nearly lost a kidney. They were subjected to Milton's most gruesome torture techniques. I suffered my own injuries, which had also healed. The guilt I felt—whether well-placed or not—for allowing that monster to hurt my friends had torn a hole in my heart. On the outside, I did my best to hide what I was feeling inside—I knew it would only bring down those I cared about. For the most part, aside from a couple of transparent moments, I'd shown the world that I was all positive...there to support Stan and Cristina in any way I could.

The whir of skateboards brought my attention to the front windows. Two teenage boys with baggy shorts zoomed down the sidewalk, dodging an older man walking his dog. The man raised his fist as he yanked the dog chain to avoid a collision. I popped out of my seat, ready to yell at the kids, but they were out of sight in the blink of an eye.

That thought brought me back to my laptop and the blinking cursor. Using two fists to lean on my antique wooden desk, I quickly fell back into the routine of counting each flash. It was my coping mechanism. My delay tactic.

My phone rattled across my desk. I picked it up and found a text from Saul, the man in my life.

Have u done it yet?

It was submitting the state form that was open on my laptop. By clicking the red button, I would be formally starting the process to meet my birth parents. I'd been raised as a "system" kid, living in seventeen foster homes along the way. Most were complete nightmares. For years, I'd never considered wanting to meet my birth parents. They hadn't wanted me, so I didn't look back. Growing up, I was in a constant state of survival. Far too many nights I was solely focused on trying to avoid the lewd advances of drunk and high adults—in some instances I didn't succeed. Other times, I was scrounging for food in a home that wasn't fit for a dog. So, dreaming about Mom and Dad, a little brother or big sister, in a white picket fence home was so farfetched it had rarely crossed my mind.

But something had changed in me. And, surprisingly, it came after the latest near-death experience at the hands of Milton Weber. A feeling of wanting that unconditional love bubbled to the surface. It subsided occasionally, but would reappear in waves the more time I spent with Saul and his family. At times they could be an overbearing group, but I felt that bond between the kids and the parents. Just this past weekend, Saul and I finally agreed that I should follow my heart and begin the search. I had nothing to lose, right?

The door opened, and I flinched from the sound of metal scraping concrete.

"Hello, Ivy."

It was Mr. Roussel, the father of my best friend, Zahera. Wearing his combat boots and holding his Army beanie—even though he'd retired from the military years prior—he paused just inside the door. "Did you forget about our meeting?"

"No, it's fine. I was just in deep thought. Come on in. Can I get you something to drink?"

"Sure, I'll take a bottled water. You want to give me the grand tour of the ECHO home office?"

I fought back a laugh and waved him toward the back. "It will take all of about ten seconds." I walked into the main meeting room right off the front entry. He stopped, looked around, nodded. "Zahera had said this place wasn't fit for rats when you first grabbed the space. But this is nice. Real nice."

I recalled my friend's first time in the space. She was jumping on furniture to avoid rodents scampering across the floor. I explained to Mr. Roussel the transformation of the thirteen-hundred-square-foot office: new carpet, sleek but comfortable furniture purchased at an auction, a bunch of paintings donated by the art department at Trinity University, four cans of white paint, and a little bit of basic woodwork and plumbing by Saul to give us a functioning breakroom.

Mr. Roussel's deep-set eyes turned to the large window that faced east. A three-tiered water fountain sat under a tree, surrounded by flowers, bushes, and a bird feeder. A little bit of tranquility in the middle of the concrete jungle.

"This is a great setting. I'm sure it's nice to move out of the smoothie shop and into some real digs."

He was referring to our old office, a corner booth at Smoothies and Stuff. I showed him the breakroom, then handed him the water. I was reminded of how different he was from Zahera, both in terms of appearance and perspective on life. Zahera, a striking beauty, was a good three or four inches taller than her father, who was right at my height of five-six. He was a proud man, one who carried the burden of being a Muslim in a country that wasn't always open to his religion. Yet, after migrating from Canada—his family had French roots—he joined the US Army and served twenty-three years. Zahera said his time in the military had helped embolden his view of the world. Very black and white. Right and wrong. Nothing gray. And that lack of flexibility annoyed Zahera to no end.

From what Zahera had shared, her mother, who had died tragically years earlier by falling down a flight of steps, had served as a buffer between a militaristic father and his rebellious daughter. Since her mother's untimely death, there had been numerous battles with her father. She always classified them as speeches where he declared, "I told you so," most notably after her two quick marriages that ended in divorce. Those battles usually led to periods of silence between the two.

Now Zahera was engaged again, just a week earlier…this time to a former Navy SEAL turned security company owner. As in personal security, usually for the uber rich. The pair looked like red carpet royalty. Zeke had the looks of a James Bond type…the build, the set jaw, and cropped blond hair. She had the look of a Bond beauty, except she was no ditz and took orders from no one. As I spent time around the couple, beyond their obvious physical attraction to each other, they seemed to have this tremendous mutual respect. He never thought about telling her what to do, and she wouldn't have listened anyway. And vice versa.

Mr. Roussel gazed around the room, and I took that as the cue for us to discuss the reason behind his visit. "In your email this morning, you said you wanted to talk about me possibly helping you with an urgent family matter." While my intuition had been peppering my mind with possible theories of what kind of family matter might require my involvement, I'd been too busy to dissect it too far. Well, that, and I'd been preoccupied with filling out the Texas Central Adoption Agency form. Dammit, I still hadn't clicked submit.

I extended my arm toward one of the white leather seats around the oval glass table. He held up a finger, took a couple of chugs of water. As he sat down, I reached over to a side table, picked up a coaster, and slid it toward him. He set his water down and brought his fingers together. They were calloused—Zahera would probably draw irony from that, saying it matched his personality. But I tried to maintain an open mind.

"Ivy," he said, looking me squarely in the eye, "I need for you to do me and Zahera a favor."

Father and daughter were on the same side of…something. If nothing else, my curiosity was piqued. I gave him a single nod. "That being…?"

"I need for you to investigate Zeke Moffett."

I went mute.

Five

Our stare-down lasted for a good minute. A bird fluttered into the window, and I turned my head. Then Mr. Roussel broke the awkward silence.

"You are thinking about it, which is a good sign." He drummed the tips of his fingers together while showing what I'd call a professional smile.

"Good for who?"

"Whom," he said.

There he goes with his corrections. I tried not to let my inner-Zahera come out. "Your daughter, my best friend… Is she aware that you're asking me to investigate her fiancé?"

He scratched his neck, then went right back to his finger exercise. "She's aware of my…reservations. And I think, to a degree, she is in agreement, but you know her, Ivy. She is stubborn. Or should I say stubbornly blind? Especially when she thinks she's…" He cleared his throat and raised his hands to form air quotes. "…in love."

A rush of adrenaline sent my pulse into overdrive. I knew it was nothing more than my protective instinct. To protect my best friend. "Mr. Roussel—"

"Armand, please. We're both adults."

Like I needed that acknowledgment. "Zahera is thirty-two years old. She admits that she hasn't always made the best decisions. But who hasn't screwed up? We're all only human."

"I couldn't agree more."

I did a double-take. "Okay…"

"You are her friend. She has colleagues that work for her in her medical practice. We all have roles in her life."

"She's a damn good friend. I would do anything for her." My tone was far more defensive than I'd intended.

"Zahera's mother is no longer with us. So, as her father, my role is to not simply agree with every little whim—"

"You're calling her engagement to Zeke a whim?" The air conditioner hummed in the background, but I still felt a line of perspiration down the middle of my back.

He leaned his forearms on the table and lowered his voice. "Ivy, please, I'm not trying to agitate you. I love my daughter. I'm only trying to do what is best for her. I'm sure you can see that, right?"

He wasn't winning me over. In fact, I could feel my mental heels digging in. I matched his lower tone and then some. "I can't betray my friendship with Zahera because you're afraid to let her live her life."

"Who said anything about a betrayal?"

"I'm assuming you'd want me to conduct any investigation without her knowledge?"

"Unless she flat-out asks you if you're investigating Zeke, then you won't be lying."

Leaning back in my seat, I chuckled, shaking off a what-the-fuck moment. Armand could have a second career in politics. "This…" I waved my finger between us. "It isn't happening. In fact, the moment you walk out of here, I have every intention of calling her up and letting her know what is going on."

He just sat there, nodding, drumming his fingers. I could still taste my words, and they were sour, even a little vindictive. I blew out a breath. "Look, Armand, I respect your desire to keep Zahera safe. I get it. There's got to be a self-help group you can go to, or a book you can read. I'm probably not the right person to do this kind of work anyway."

"Do you care about Zahera?" A hint of emotion crept into his tone.

"Of course. Like a sister. Well, like a sister who's the opposite of me." I tried to laugh, but I never got there, and he certainly didn't reciprocate. He just sat there and stared me down. This went on for another minute. My focus was beginning to drift. I had background checks I could be doing for a local private school— ECHO was on a monthly retainer with them. And I still had to make a decision about submitting that form to signal that I wanted to meet my birth parents.

Wait. Was I already backtracking? *Stop it, Ivy. Don't make excuses against taking that next step. You're a grown-ass woman.*

"I'm sorry, Armand, but I have a lot of things I need to get done before the end of the day." I began to push up from the chair.

"Zeke might be mixed up in an international drug ring."

I froze and read his face to see if he might be joking. What was I thinking? This man didn't joke. He recited facts, or at least facts as he saw them.

I slowly dipped my body back into the cushiony leather. "If you're trying to shock me into listening a few more minutes, it worked. Tell me more."

"I have a friend who used to work for the FBI. We go way back to my early days in the Army, when we both were stationed in South Korea."

"The thirty-eighth parallel," I said.

He nodded. "Bart and I share the same values, and he knows how much family means to me. He did me a favor and reached out to a buddy of his still working at the FBI to do a complete background check on Zeke. The kind that uncovers every dirty little secret."

I swallowed back a dry patch in my throat. "And that's when you learned about this possible connection to…what did you call it? An international drug ring?"

"To be specific, Ukrainian."

My neck felt stiff, and I started to rub it. Not surprisingly, it didn't help alleviate the strain. "If you know all of this, what do you want me to do?"

"The intel has a fifty-percent chance of being correct. They talk in those terms. I need to know one hundred percent either way before I speak to Zahera. Anything less, and she'll laugh me out of the room."

"You know your daughter well."

"Indeed."

"Look, if Zeke is mixed up in something illegal, I want to know. I want to keep Zahera out of harm's way. Two things don't make sense to me though. First, if you have your own little intelligence-gathering posse, why not just let them finish the job? Second, I'm not a covert spy, or whatever would be required to get the information you want."

He looked off for a second. Then he turned back to me and said, "Bart suffered a heart attack last week. He's in ICU and he may not make it. I don't know the name of his contact at the FBI. Even if I did, I doubt he'd return my calls. That group is rather tight-lipped to outsiders."

I nodded. "Which takes us to the second point. I want to help, Armand, but I'm not trained to do this. Don't you have other friends from your military days who would be better suited—"

He shook me off. "They're all off playing golf or traveling with their wives. They are far removed from their former lives."

I got up, walked into the breakroom, and grabbed my own water. I had taken a large chug by the time I reached the table. "A Ukrainian drug ring. It just sounds too bizarre."

"Does it? As you know, Zeke hasn't always played by the rules."

He was referring to the event where Zahera and I had first crossed paths with Zeke. He was running security for a wealthy entrepreneur named Dillon Burchfield, who was acting like he'd been set up on a sexual assault charge, all while hiding behind his adorable little girl and his contrived persona of being someone who raised millions to fight drug addiction. Dillon even went so far as to hire an old high school buddy to shoot him in the shoulder for no other reason than to evoke public sympathy. Zeke, convinced that his client was innocent, played along with the charade. Dillon was guilty on that charge, however, and a hell of a lot more. Zeke came clean on his part, saying he felt remorse for believing him. Beyond that, Zeke seemed like a stand-up guy. But I didn't know much about him.

"You have questions about Zeke, as I do," Armand said.

"But this whole fifty-percent thing. I don't even know what that means."

"It means his name was found in a communication."

"A communication." *Talk about vague.* "I need to see it, in whatever form that might be."

A smile finally appeared. "I don't have it; I've never seen it. Bart just told me about it. But I do have a name I can share with you. Someone who was in the same communication and is the one tied to the drug ring." With the ease of a blackjack dealer, he slid a card across the table, but he didn't remove his hand. "Once I give this to you, we have a deal, yes?"

He was teasing me. At the same time, he was pushing me into a corner. I liked neither. "No."

He began to slide the card back to his side of the table. "I can't play games, Ivy. I guess I'll start searching for someone who will do it for the right price. They may not be as careful with the information, and it will be difficult to trust them. But I can't stop until I know for certain. I hope you understand."

The poker game was on. I had to call his bluff, but not in a way that would embarrass him.

"Stop, Armand."

The card started moving in my direction again.

"No, stop all of this." I glanced out the window at the water cascading over the sides of the stone fountain, contemplating how I could take this case and not tell Zahera. Then again, even if I didn't take this case, Armand had planted a seed of doubt. Zeke and an international drug ring? If I went to Zahera with what I knew right now, she'd rip me a new one for believing her dad. And then what? She'd marry Zeke, if for no other reason than to spite her father. I'd be in the middle, trying to convince her that she or someone needed to find out the truth.

She and Zeke had talked a great deal about traveling. In fact, they'd taken a quick trip to Montreal a few weeks ago. Surely, that wasn't connected to any of Armand's insinuations. Or was it?

"You are a thinker, Ivy. And that is why I'm glad you are Zahera's friend. She acts too irrationally, too emotionally. You think through the consequences."

I lifted an eyebrow. "Right, and then I make stupid decisions. Please, don't patronize me."

"My apologies."

I could feel his eyes on me as I scanned the room—my neck feeling like I had a metal plate screwed to my spine. In reality, I was searching for some sort of sign that would point me in the right direction. Right for Zahera's safety and well-being. Right for my conscience. Were the two goals even achievable?

A popping sound followed by a crash jolted me from my seat. I turned toward the front room and heard someone yell, "Motherfucker!"

It was Cristina.

Six

Cristina was on her backside, moaning, when I swung open the front door. I saw blood trickling down her forehead. But it was the black Mercedes sitting on top of a bent street sign that had me most surprised. Its front wheels were still spinning.

"Are you okay, Cristina?" I moved to her side and noticed Armand's black boots rush out the door.

"What happened? How badly is she injured?"

"I'm…fine." Her voice sounded like a creaking door. With her eyes squinted shut, she turned on her side, ran her hand up to her back. "That bitch in the fancy car better run for cover. I'm gonna kick her ass as soon as I can walk."

"Don't move, Cristina. Let me call the paramedics."

"I'm already there," Armand said, pulling out his phone and tapping the screen.

"I don't have insurance," she said, opening her eyes. "Wait, are you Zahera's dad?"

"I am," he said, then walked toward the curb while glancing at the car. I heard him say, "Yes, there has been a crash at…" and then his voice dissipated.

I began to pull my eyes back to Cristina when the front door of the Mercedes flew open, smacking Armand in the face, launching his phone into the air. He stumbled backward.

"I want to speak to Ivy Nash. Now." A woman crawled out of the car. Her twisted skirt was hiked up to her thighs, and her smeared makeup made her look like she was a walking, talking impressionist painting.

"You just ran into my friend, dammit. You could have killed her." I stood up and met her eye to eye. I was nearly knocked back by the booze on her breath.

"Actually, she didn't hit me." Cristina was sitting up, her arms folded over her knees. "She scared the crap out of me, and because I might have been moving a little too quickly on my skateboard, I lost control and rammed into the fire hydrant." I followed her finger pointing over my shoulder.

"Seriously?" I jammed my fist on the side of my hip.

Cristina climbed to her feet as the woman straightened out her skirt.

"Anyone see my phone?" Armand asked.

"No," I said without turning around.

"Cristina, you should be wearing a helmet. I've told you a dozen times."

She held up a finger, grimacing as she tried to twist her torso. "More like a hundred times. But you know me, I've got a thick skull."

"That's for sure. And what about your kidney? If you damage it again, you might lose it."

"I'm sorry," the woman said before Cristina could respond. Resting a hand against the side of her car, it appeared she was using it to keep from tipping over.

Cristina waved a hand in front of her face. "Whoa, lady. It's obvious the sun didn't just get in your face. You've been hitting the sauce a little early in the day."

"I…" The woman looked off. She didn't even make an attempt to fix her hair or makeup. I noticed one of her heels had snapped off.

"Are the cops and paramedics on their way?" I asked Armand.

"They will be as soon as I find my…"

I turned to see Armand on the street looking into a sewage drain. He glanced up and me and shook his head. "You might want to make the call."

"Are you Ivy?"

I turned to see a single tear rolling down the woman's face. It created a new trench of smeared mascara. Her eyes were filled with sadness, and almost instantly my impression of her switched from rich, privileged lush to a woman who was desperately trying to keep it together. I raised my hand. "That's me."

"Please don't sing us this sad song because you've got a drinking problem," Cristina said.

I turned and gave her the eye.

"Okay, okay, I'll back off." She threw her hands in the air. Armand walked over to Cristina. "Let me take a look at that head wound."

I was slightly shocked to see this side of Armand. But maybe he had more in common with his doctor-daughter than I'd thought possible.

"Ouch," Cristina said as Armand gripped her head.

They began to talk quietly, and I took a step toward the woman, extending my hand. Her grip was firm, as if she was used to holding her own in a handshake contest. "I'm Megan. Megan Espinoza. I understand you—" She clipped her mouth shut. For some reason, she couldn't get the words out.

She took a long swallow and appeared to fight back more emotion. I didn't know if that was the booze rearing its ugly head or if there was something really there. I noticed a sizable diamond on her ring finger. "Can I call your husband or friend to come pick you up? Well, unless the cops turn up. Then they might need to pick you up from the police station."

She crossed her arms, her eyes staring off into the distance. I wasn't sure she'd heard me.

"Megan, this is serious. You destroyed property, banged up your nice car, and caused my friend to crash." I looked over my shoulder to see Armand walking from the office, holding wet paper towels, Neosporin, and bandages.

"You found the first aid kit. Thanks, Armand."

"No worries. I think she'll be fine. Not sure about the kidney though. She might need to go the hospital to get it checked out."

"I'm fine, Colonel. Just let it be and get me cleaned up," Cristina said with her usual attitude. I gave her the eye again, and then she said in a much nicer tone. "Please."

I flipped around to Megan, who pulled out a crumpled picture and held it inches from my face. It was an adorable little girl cuddled up with a teddy bear. It had to be Megan's daughter. She had cute ringlets framing her round face.

"She's darling," I said, my body growing tense. Questions pinged my mind, and all were concerning the safety of her daughter.

Her arm began to tremble. Then she quickly covered her mouth, but it wasn't enough to stop the sobbing.

I touched her elbow. "Megan."

She didn't respond. She looked straight ahead, as if I wasn't there.

"Megan," I said, louder.

I could sense Cristina and Armand pulling up near me. "Is she having a nervous breakdown?" Armand asked.

Megan held up the picture again, allowing Armand and Cristina to also look at it.

"Who is that?" Cristina asked.

A quick shake of my head. I wasn't sure Megan could hear anything, but I didn't want to upset her further. Something had happened to the little girl. And that had to be why she'd shown up at the ECHO office. Her drunken, reckless state also added to my concern that the child might have been harmed. Or worse.

"It's my daughter, Annie." She swiped at her nose and tried to control her breathing. All three of us nodded without saying a word. A grieving mother was on the verge of going somewhere none of us could imagine.

"Tell us, Megan. Why are you here? Is your daughter okay?"

"Through luck or the grace of God, Annie is okay," she said.

"Good." I took a breath; my shoulders dipped a couple of inches. "Now, can we get to why you're looking for me?"

"Because the monsters that took my little girl—or should I say *pretended* to take my little girl—they need to rot in hell. I want you to find them. And I want you to kill them. Whatever it takes. Kill those bastards."

We moved the discussion into the office.

Seven

A uniformed officer showed up at the scene. I walked outside and talked to him while Cristina and Armand got Megan comfortable in the ECHO meeting room with a non-alcoholic beverage.

"What the hell happened here?" He snapped off his mirrored sunglasses while eyeing the Mercedes.

Ten minutes earlier, I would have gladly asked the cops to cart Megan off. But given what she'd shared—someone had apparently faked her daughter's kidnapping—I knew her mental stability couldn't take any additional stress. I was willing to fudge the truth to give me a few minutes alone with her. I figured that if after further assessment I could see that she was lying or delusional, then I would sever any ties with her and make sure she got home without operating a vehicle.

"It's one of my clients, Officer."

He leaned around me, looking to the front door that had the name of the firm, ECHO, painted on it in white. Under that was our new tagline: *Where kids always come first.*

"I don't understand," he said, twirling his glasses.

"She's very emotional. Something happened to her daughter and—"

"That's why she needs to work with the police, not some amateur private eye. No offense, mind you."

Offense taken, but I rolled with it. "I believe she has spoken to the police." She hadn't told me that, but if she hadn't, I'd make sure she did once I got back inside. "She really needs someone to talk to right now."

"Are you some kind of shrink too?" He arched an eyebrow.

"On some days, I guess I play that role. You probably have some of those days as well, where sometimes people can't take any more bad news and they just need to talk."

He nodded once, but I could see that he didn't want to be associated with the likes of me, so I quickly got past it. "We've called a tow truck and any bill for replacing the sign can be sent to my office. I'll make sure she pays for it."

"Well, I guess that would save me some paperwork. When will the tow truck get here, so we can make sure no one else gets hurt?"

"Within fifteen minutes." Another fudge, but I'd get Cristina on it right away.

He nodded. "I'll put in a call to the city roads crew and make sure they replace this sign within the next day." He slid his glasses back on his head. "My shift ends in a few minutes, then I'm headed to Ernesto's to meet my boys for a couple of beers. I can already taste the beer. It's been a long, hot day."

I gave him an approving smile, then we parted ways. As I opened the door to the building, I spotted a business card. I leaned down, picked it up.

"Petro Udovenko. That's how you pronounce his name," Armand said, just stepping to the threshold of the door.

"How's Megan?"

"She has calmed down. Cristina is talking to her." He glanced at the business card, then back to me while patting his front shirt pocket. "The card must have fallen out while I looked for my phone. I guess this means you're taking the case."

"I never—"

"You'll ensure that Zahera isn't about to marry a ruthless, lying piece of scum?"

He was stubborn, but I shifted gears. "What if somehow I find something that proves Zeke is mixed up in this Ukrainian drug ring? Are you going to talk to her, or do you expect me to do that as well?"

He touched his hand to his chest. "If you do this, I will be forever in your debt. And, as her father, I will have to be the one who shares the news. Trust me, it's not something I look forward to."

"Trust." I flapped the card against my hand while glancing up the sidewalk. I spotted a couple of people gawking at the Mercedes. "Now I'm starting to feel another wave of guilt."

"Ivy, there is no other way. I haven't slept more than a couple of hours a night since I learned this news. As distasteful as it might be, this is the only way. Could you live with yourself if six months down the line Zahera is either injured or caught up in an international investigation of her husband's so-called business dealings? She could end up in prison in some Third World country."

I turned back to Armand. "I don't want to lose her as a friend."

"She might get angry at first, but she will thank you. Or, if you find nothing, she'll never know."

"That doesn't help me with the guilt factor."

"Forget I said that."

His ability to flip his moral switch surprised me. Mr. Black and White? I was beginning to have my doubts. But I knew that didn't change the facts: Zahera might very well be walking into a marriage that could get her arrested, or even killed. I loved her too much not to try to find out more information.

"I might have more questions for you," I said.

"Anything. You're the professional. I'll give you anything, as long as it helps get to the bottom of this and keeps my Zahera safe. And I will pay you the top rate."

I wasn't sure how I felt about that, but for now I agreed, just to be able to move on. We shook hands, and he thanked me six times before marching off.

Still muttering the name Petro Udovenko over and over, I walked to the opening of the meeting room. Cristina, with two bandages on her forehead, was flipping through a magazine with her legs on the table while Megan was face down on the table.

"Is she…?" I pointed at the woman, who was a hot mess.

Then I heard a loud snore.

"I went to the can, got out, and she was sound asleep." Cristina held up the magazine. "Did you know that parenting magazines are clueless about how kids really are?"

I rolled my eyes, and we waited for our client to wake up.

Eight

Megan snored for an hour straight. While we waited, Cristina called for the tow truck. When Megan finally sat up, she had a huge red mark on her forehead. Cristina stared directly at it, while I averted my eyes. "I won't bother getting out my mirror," Megan said, running her fingers through her hair. "I probably look like I should be in a Halloween haunted house."

She wasn't far from the truth, but as she hopelessly wiped dried makeup from under her eyes, some changes had already taken place. She was calm, composed, and speaking without slurring her speech. Now, I figured, we could make some headway into this trauma.

"Not to be redundant—I'm not sure what you recall—but I'm Ivy, and this is Cristina. We are ECHO."

She sighed while trying to smile. "I'm quite embarrassed about my behavior. I do recall most everything, at least I think I do," she said, placing her palms on the table. She looked toward Cristina. "Thank God you're okay. I'm truly sorry if I hurt you or scared you into crashing your skateboard."

"No probs."

"Your daughter, Annie. She's okay?" I asked.

A deep nod. "Thankfully. I'd never experienced anything like this before, and even after I found out it was a hoax, I completely broke down and went straight to the bottle."

"Are you...?" Cristina asked hesitantly.

"I'm what you call a corporate drinker. I go to all the happy hours—mandated, voluntary, with the executives, my colleagues, or the lower-level employees. I do it all. I fool myself into thinking that I'm playing the game, moving up the corporate ladder. But I'm really just giving myself an excuse to drink. And after Annie's life flashed before my eyes, I just...couldn't deal with it."

Her voice ended in a whisper, her eyes focused on the glass table. Cristina coughed, and she came back to life. She then described the kidnapping hoax. Even though I'd asked her to try to stay with the facts, she veered into her emotional reaction at least a dozen times. It was completely understandable.

"When I finally heard Annie's voice on the phone, it was surreal. I wanted to believe it was her. But part of me thought my mind was playing games—that I'd just made it all up as some type of coping mechanism so I wouldn't have a breakdown."

She thumbed a tear in the corner of her eye. "Damn, I never knew how much I loved her until I thought she'd been taken from me."

I nodded as the wheels turned in my head. I was stunned. Stunned to hear that instead of racing to the park to go hug her daughter, be with her husband, spend time with them, Megan had instead turned to booze. "You reported this to the police?"

"Of course. I spent two hours there before I went to the liquor store. Detective Stan Radowski was assigned to my case."

I could feel Cristina's eyes on me.

"What?" Megan asked. "You know him?"

I nodded. "Stan and I worked together when I was at Child Protective Services. To be honest, he's a great detective, and a better friend."

I thought about how far he'd come since having his arm amputated a couple of months earlier. After feeling like his life was over—who wouldn't?—Stan had pushed himself through rehab and gained decent control of his right-arm prosthesis. He'd been learning to do everything, not only with just one good arm, but with his left arm. He had been right-handed. He even dedicated himself to becoming certified with his pistol while using his left hand. On top of that, he'd recently started working out. His cousin Nick, an FBI agent up in Boston, had challenged him to train for the Boston Marathon.

"Did you know he uses a prosthesis? Well, of course you do. I'm sorry," Megan said. "He's a little slow."

Cristina arched her back. "Do you have a problem with that?"

"Cristina." I shook my head at her defensiveness, then turned to Megan. "We're all rather protective of Stan, after everything he's been through."

"I understand. It's great that you have so many close friends. I'm not sure what those really are. All of my relationships are fake, outside of what I have with my kids, especially my little girl."

"You're married?" Cristina asked.

"Yes."

I waited for more, but she didn't offer anything. I didn't ask a follow-up question. For now, I only needed to understand what she wanted from me.

I set my forearms on the table. "I know this might have been the worst day in your life."

"And then some."

"It sounds like you've come to realize that you have a drinking problem, and I'm guessing you're going to try to deal with it."

She clasped her hands on the table, then pressed her fingers together, as if summoning the fortitude to declare war on her issue. "Yes, I have that as a goal. But..." She seemed to be considering her choice of words. I stayed silent, and thankfully, Cristina followed my lead.

"The people who did this…they need to be punished. I want you to find them, and then give me five minutes in a room with them. That's all I'm asking."

My first thought was that she had no idea what she was asking. She was still fuming. She was essentially asking me to be her vigilante hunter. I couldn't agree to that, no matter how much I hated those same people for even thinking they could harm her daughter.

"I'm sorry, Megan, but that would be against the law. And even worse, you don't want to be in a room with the folks who did this."

"Believe me, yes I do."

She held my gaze, and then her jaw flinched slightly. I said, "I don't want to belabor this point, but even if I was inclined to hand these people over to you, it's against the law. So, if that's why you came to see me, then I think our meeting is over. I can call you a cab." I began to rise out of my chair.

"Please don't." She held up a hand. "I'm sorry. I'm just upset. I'm letting my anger take over all of my thoughts. These monsters are worse than terrorists. They destroyed me, all because of greed."

I remained standing. "It's horrible. I hope the police catch them and they spend a lot of time in jail," I said, walking toward the breakroom. "Do you want a bottled water?"

"Sure. That would be nice. My mouth is a bit dry."

"Hey, while you're in there, I'll take a Coke," Cristina said.

I returned with two bottled waters and Cristina's Coke. We spent about thirty seconds chugging our drinks.

"I get the feeling you don't have a lot of confidence in Stan and the police. He might only have one arm, but his mind is still intact. He's a bulldog of a detective, and he knows when and how to use the resources around him."

"He might be the greatest American hero, but you should have heard what he and some other detective told me after two hours. A guy named Moreno."

"Omar Moreno. I know him." I didn't like him, and he felt the same about me. For Stan's benefit, we'd learned to coexist.

She went on to say that she had learned this same hoax had been played out at least a dozen times in Texas, mostly in San Antonio or Austin. She was told that their best hope was getting the FBI to add technical resources into some type of joint task force, which had yet to be formed.

"Interesting," I said, twisting the bottle on the table.

"I know Detective Radowski was trying to give me hope, but it smells of bureaucracy. And I don't want to wait three years for them to come back and say they ran out of money, or the leads dried up. The time to catch these piranhas is now."

"Agreed."

"Then will you do this for me?"

"I'm not a vigilante hunter."

She waved a hand in front of her face. "I wasn't being serious. I only want justice served. And to keep them from ripping another family to shreds."

I locked eyes with Cristina. She took in a breath, then nodded. We had the same thought—Megan was fighting through a lot of issues, the kind that end relationships, ruin lives. But at least this episode was brought on by something so sinister and mean that it was hard not to feel sorry for her. And to turn down her request to go after the people who would undoubtedly strike again would be tantamount to personally witnessing a crime and not doing a damn thing about it. I couldn't live with myself, and it appeared Cristina couldn't either. I turned back to Megan. "Realize that I consider Stan part of my extended team. He might help quite a bit. Hell, the cops could still find these people before we get close."

"I'll cheer if they do. I just can't sit around and do nothing. I'm sure you'll share more than the police, and my guess is that you won't have all the restrictions and procedures to slow you down."

She wasn't wrong on that thought. I leaned forward in my seat, pausing an extra second to see if I might have an epiphany telling me to decline the case. It never came.

"You'll take the case?" For the first time her voice carried hope.

It would be our second case that seemed to fall outside of our niche. But I figured we had to adjust to the market.

"We'll take the case."

"Perfect. Thank you."

I offered to call her husband or a cab, but she refused. She said she wanted to walk home to give herself a chance to gain perspective on what was important in her life. It sounded noble. I shut the front door and turned around to see Cristina at my computer.

"Are you about to do what I think you're about to do?" Her big, brown eyes had doubled in size.

She'd seen the online form. I rested both hands at my waist and considered my options. Get into an endless debate with Queen Rebel herself—which would assuredly do nothing to enlighten me any further—or I could simply make the decision for myself, and own it. I walked behind my desk, where she grudgingly gave up her position, and I grabbed the mouse and clicked submit.

"You really want to test those waters? Look at the train wreck that was just in here. Look at my mom. You can't pick your family, Ivy. There's probably a damn good reason why you've never seen them."

I knew the response she was expecting me to provide. It was embedded in the corner of my mind. But after twenty-eight years, I'd finally been able to look beyond the spontaneous reaction of resenting someone I didn't know. If anything, seeing these parents in pain over their kids, even their grown-up kids, made me want to reach out even more. I couldn't keep it buried any longer. For a while now, I'd felt this seed of hope sprouting. Hope to find one or both parents still alive. And even greater hope that they cared to know that I existed at all. I was taking a risk, opening myself up to being hurt by someone who may not give two shits about me. But there was that little seed of hope.

I knew that while I waited for an official response from the Texas Central Adoption Agency, I'd probably regret clicking the submit button a dozen times. That was why I didn't debate the action a few moments ago. I could talk myself out of anything.

"I'm not going to get my hopes up," I said, organizing my desk just to keep myself occupied. "But there comes a time in your life, when you just have to know. Even if I get hurt in the process."

"Damn, you're stubborn."

"Are you serious? Just wait until you're out of college and you work with a teenager." I closed up my laptop and shoved it into my backpack. "By the way, how's school going?"

"Eh. Boring and a waste of time. But I'm pushing through it."

"Good to hear. Still on pace to graduate at the end of this semester?"

"As long as I pass geometry. It's kicking my ass."

I threw my backpack over my shoulder. "I know you can win any ass-kicking battle."

"You know it."

I certainly did.

Nine

The fluttering of the cash-sorting machine. The slurping of liquid circulating through a maze of tubes. The whir of the occasional helicopter landing and taking off in the middle of the forest. The growling generators that kept the entire operation moving forward, twenty-four hours a day.

The sounds of money.

Standing just outside his personal tent in the shade of the tall pines, Petro Udovenko took it all in. If anything could warm his sixty-year-old heart, this had to be it. He puffed twice on his cigar—a Cuban Partagas Serie D with a blended woody finish—and let his thoughts wander, searching for a time in his life when he'd felt more accomplished. He recalled the day he walked through the doors of the local recruiter and volunteered for the Red Army as a pimple-faced eighteen-year-old. Not two months later, he was trudging through the rocky terrain in the hills of Afghanistan, fighting a war that no one in his homeland thought they could win. But defeat wasn't a term that the military leaders would ever utter. Not publicly.

His first lesson in survival came on his third night. He'd fallen asleep while leaning against a large boulder when the first enemy bullet cut through the flesh on his thigh. A moment later, dozens of mujahideen forces descended upon their camp. With pain rippling through his body, he froze for a moment. He didn't want to die, not at such a young age, before he'd achieved anything in his life. He wondered if he'd be forced to kill to stay alive, and if he had that kind of rage inside of him. Maybe they would take him hostage, trade him for one of their own.

The decision was made for him. A bearded man jumped him from behind, nearly slitting his throat. He didn't think; he just reacted. And at six-five, two hundred twenty pounds, his response was immediate and thunderous. He flipped the man over his head, punched him in the throat, and then used his own knife to stab him in the gut. With the knife still inserted, he looked the man in the eye—the full moon illuminated their space as if someone had snapped their fingers. Then he used the knife to shred the man's insides, pretending he was shaving the skin of an apple, just like he'd done as a little kid in his hometown of Pripyat. The man gurgled blood and died in seconds.

That night had confirmed two things for Petro. First, he would do anything to survive in this harsh world. And second, he'd enjoyed it. Ecstasy. Petro's comrades later celebrated his first kill, saying he'd finally popped his cherry. Deep down, he knew he was a natural-born killer.

That was the beginning of what could only be called an extraordinary career, one that had involved its fair share of killing, but also so much more. He could envision some deep-pocket producer making one of those Hollywood movies about his life. But who would believe it? He'd fought in wars both warm and cold, developing skills that would not only save his life but also reap major rewards for the cause he'd pledged to support.

The cause of Communism. What a joke. It was nothing more than a failed attempt to brainwash the masses into believing everyone should sacrifice for the good of society. The messages always implied that material goods were wasteful, when money and effort should be focused on supporting the cause. If nothing more, the Communist regime was a propaganda machine. That was evident in how the people rarely rebelled, helping the message spread like wildfire.

Meanwhile, the upper echelon would snub their noses at the very message they propagated. He'd seen generals and party leadership say one thing to the public, or the rank-and-file of the military, and then turn around and travel in a private jet to a lavish vacation home on the French Riviera, where gluttony was the norm. He'd seen it with his own eyes, having accompanied one such general as part of his logistical support and security team. He could still recall standing guard next to the infinity pool where the general, whose enormous belly hung over his thong bathing suit, lounged on a cabana mattress while six women pawed at him like he was Adonis. The pungent mixture of sweat and tanning lotion had soured his stomach. A waterfall of perspiration poured off the general, but that hadn't stopped the scantily clad woman from rubbing up against him, feeding him fruit and drinking bottles of champagne that cost upward of a thousand euros.

It was at that moment when Petro Udovenko made a life-altering observation: he would no longer surrender his thoughts and aspirations to the bullshit messages from the elite who ran the party. He would learn the necessary skills, soft and otherwise, to enable him to succeed. Not success the way an average person would judge it. But success in terms of how these self-righteous bastards lived their lives—he would be one of them and, at the same time, not. He vowed to attain influence, power, and money to give him anything he wanted.

After several formal military roles, at about the same time as the fall of the mighty Soviet Union, he'd moved on to more engaging careers, ones that put him first, not last. And he flourished. Since then, he'd outsmarted greedy leaders and even greedier criminals, survived coups, and chased more than a few women.

Ah, the women. He could write a novel about all of his conquests. The great beauties of Europe, some of whom were runway models, girlfriends of prime ministers, and even one who was connected to what had been called the Russian mafia.

Fucking amateurs.

He took another long puff of his cigar and watched his team of scientists and production assistants carry out their roles. They were like ants. They did what they were told. They didn't question authority, and they were reliable. It had taken a while to find the right mix of contractors. Some had perished in the vetting process. But that was the way of business.

Other people outside of his immediate team had tried to suck up to him, to manipulate him into making certain decisions— changing distributors to one of their cousins, suggesting price breaks as a way to expand their drug network's footprint. He prided himself on never falling prey to even the most seductive manipulation. He made decisions based upon the possible return on investment. That was it. He could recall only a couple of instances where emotion came into play. But those situations were personal. No one would ever influence the direction he chose in those cases.

He knew that it took a rare person to think in those terms. He was one of those rare people.

A blur of movement captured his attention, and he stopped breathing.

Ten

He shifted his eyes to the station where young men packaged the heroin and then stamped the baggies with their logo—yes, branding, even for illegitimate businesses, was so very important to the long-term growth of his empire. The young man, with a soft, pale face and bones protruding through his white T-shirt, couldn't be any older than fourteen. He had tripped while carrying a basket of heroin packages over to the larger distribution bin.

Petro very quickly knew this was a possible sign of desperation. Well, that and utter stupidity. He puffed twice on his cigar and watched the boy intently. The boy pushed up to his knees, scrambling to clean up the mess he'd created. There had to be dozens of baggies scattered everywhere. The boy was slick, he could see. Very slick.

Once the baggies had been put back into the basket, he walked straight for the brown bin.

"Halt." Petro's baritone voice turned heads and scattered birds in the surrounding trees. Walking with a slight limp, he made his way over to the work area where he could see bewilderment in his workers' eyes. They were all wondering who had drawn his wrath.

His director of operations, Mirkov, ran up next to him. "Petro, please tell me what is wrong. I will fix it right away."

"Let me handle it, Mirkov."

"But, Petro, this is why you pay me. To do the difficult task of keeping everyone focused on their one job. To keep the machine moving twenty-four hours a day."

Petro stopped, turned, and peered at the shorter Mirkov. "I will handle it. You can watch. Everyone can watch. It will be a good learning opportunity."

Mirkov's eyebrow twitched. Petro knew Mirkov was puzzled...and concerned that he'd found a flaw in Mirkov's operation. Even more concerned about how Petro would respond to this issue. With all eyes on him, Petro plodded across the flattened grass. As he passed each employee, without looking directly at them, he could see their shoulders relax. They knew they had been spared his fury. One by one, they were being eliminated from the pool of suspects. He could hear their deep exhales of relief.

"You," he said, marching up to the boy who held the basket of heroin baggies.

"Yes sir." The boy arched his back, standing at attention as if he were in the military.

He rested his hand on the boy's shoulder. He could see black shadows hovering under the boy's eyes. His voice filled with compassion, he said, "I saw you fall to the ground. Did you skin your knee?"

He watched the boy turn, and a few people broke out in smiles. They'd rarely seen the softer side of Petro. "I'm okay," the boy said, now struggling to hold up the heavy basket.

"You can be honest. You hurt yourself, no?"

"Well, maybe a little."

Petro followed the boy's eyes downward to see blood soaking through his white pants. "Mirkov, get this young man here a new pair of work pants. And while you're at it, make sure he has antiseptic and bandages."

The boy smiled, rocking from side to side. "Thank you, sir, Mr. Udovenko."

Mirkov opened a plastic cabinet and riffled through it. When he found a pair of white pants, he held them above his head. "You can go into your tent to change," he said to the boy. "Be quick. We don't want to fall behind on our daily productivity goal."

The boy walked toward the large bin to dump his haul and then go change his pants.

"Hold on there," Petro said.

The boy froze with his basket leaning against the bin.

"Do you know the value of the product you have in your wicker basket?"

His eyes got wide.

"Do you?"

He shook his head. "No sir. But I will learn. Mr. Mirkov can teach me, right?"

Mirkov mumbled something, but Petro ignored it. "The value is based upon how many bags are in that basket, as long as the amount of heroin is the same in each bag, isn't that correct?"

The boy looked off for a second. "I suppose so. Yes sir."

"I assure you, Mr. Udovenko," Mirkov said, stepping forward. "We measure each bag on three different scales to ensure its accuracy. Our QA process is unmatched, sir." Petro nodded, glanced over at the weighing station, and then back to the boy. He took a long drag on his cigar and let the smoke drift into the boy's face. The boy tried not to choke, but after a few seconds it became futile, and he coughed.

Some of the men nearby laughed. Petro caught them in a steely glare, and there was silence. He turned back to the boy.

"If we're to believe Mirkov, each bag is precisely the same size. What's the market price today, Mirkov, for one baggie of our finest product?" he asked without taking his eyes off the boy.

"That depends on the city. Paris is one price, while here in Ukraine, maybe Kiev, would be less."

His eyes stayed on the boy as he snapped his fingers at Mirkov. "Let's take Paris."

"Umm, probably two hundred euros, maybe more during peak travel seasons or near the holidays."

"Two hundred euros," Petro repeated. "So, does anyone here know how many baggies fit into the basket?"

"Maybe a hundred?" one person said from the crowd.

"Anyone else?"

Everyone, including the boy, shook their heads. With his hands on his knees, he bent over to stare the boy in the face from six inches away. "One hundred twelve."

"Thank you for that information, Mr. Udovenko." The boy blinked several times.

"Count the baggies," he said.

The boy stopped blinking. In fact, he didn't move at all.

"I said, count the baggies. I just want to make sure we're all respectful of how much money we're dealing with here."

The boy set the basket down and started counting the baggies, placing each one on the ground.

"I can't hear you," he said.

"Five, six, seven."

He turned to the workers, who'd shuffled closer. "Everyone count with the boy."

The group formed a tight circle around the boy and recited each sequenced number out loud. Petro walked around the workers, blowing smoke into the crowd every few steps.

"Seventy-nine, eighty, eighty-one…"

As he made two more rotations, he looked beyond the inevitable ending to this ordeal. His operation—dubbed Big Bear—was beginning to expand beyond the European borders. With his new contacts, he hoped to break into more lucrative markets. He had one score to settle, and he could envision the scenario in which he'd be able to exact revenge, wielding his own version of justice for a wrong that had been perpetrated against him many years earlier.

The group finally reached one hundred, and Petro wedged his way into the center of the group, next to the boy. "Keep going," he said.

"One hundred one, one hundred two." Petro moved his arms up and down to the cadence of the crowd as if he were directing a symphony. With his eyes looking not at the boy but into the faces of the crowd, they chanted, "One hundred eleven," and then stopped.

Petro put his hand to his ear. "Tell me there is one more baggie."

A few brave souls shook their heads.

He glanced down to see the boy with his hands to his face, whimpering like he'd just lost his best friend.

"This boy is a thief." Mirkov broke through the pack and pointed a finger at the boy. "Give us the baggie. Now."

The boy reached into his pocket, removed the baggie, and held it above his head without looking up. He began to cry even louder.

Mirkov took the baggie, then backhanded the boy across the face. The boy fell from his knees to the ground. Blood trickled out of his nose. "You are fired. You will get your things and leave at once. And if I ever see you on the street, I will personally kill you. Do you understand me?"

The boy sniffled, and looked up. "Yes."

Mirkov looked to Petro. "We will not tolerate this type of incompetence and deceit." He clicked his heels and extended his hand that held the baggie of heroin.

Petro blew out a puff of smoke, then pulled his Makarov pistol from his side holster, turned and fired a single shot into the back of the boy's head.

A grunt, and then he went limp. "That's for the deceit."

Gasps sounded from all around him as Mirkov nodded and then broke into a smile. "Nice, boss. I should have thought of that myself."

"Yes, you should have." Petro raised his pistol and pulled the trigger. Mirkov tipped over like a tree, hitting the ground with a thud. "And that was for incompetence."

He walked back to his tent and finished his cigar. He had plans to make. And nothing was going to get in his way.

Eleven

I flipped through a trashy magazine while trying to ignore the overwhelmed mother on the other side of the waiting room. Not just any waiting room, but the waiting room for Zahera's OB/GYN practice. It wasn't time for my annual exam. On my way out of the ECHO office, she'd called me over to discuss something very important: her pending wedding to Zeke Moffett.

The timing couldn't have been worse. And not because I'd told Saul I'd meet up with him for dinner. He was a big boy, and he respected my friendships. And he was ultra cool about the unpredictability associated with my job, my passion. My angst, of course, was that her father and I had just entered into an agreement for me to dig up all the dirt I could find on her fiancée. In the first few minutes after Armand had left the office, I'd convinced myself that I wasn't "digging up dirt," per se. But I knew that would be how Zahera would interpret my actions, regardless of how I described it. If she found out.

According to Kelly, the office manager, Zahera was still playing catch-up after an unexpected delivery early this morning. *Sucks to be her*…well, except for the high six-figure income.

I flipped another crinkled page and sighed for about the hundredth time since I'd sat down.

"I can't help it if you keep changing your mind." The woman across the room grunted as she rocked a baby she held in the nook of her arm and tried to console her toddler, a little girl who was whining about not having the right kind of snack. "Dammit, Brit, just take the snack. Mommy got no sleep last night."

With food stains smeared across her face and white shirt, the girl opened her mouth and let out an ear-piercing shrill. The woman, who looked to be at least eight months pregnant, tried reaching for Brit, but the little girl shook her hand away and waddled toward me.

I wasn't sure what to do. Reach out and grab the little girl? That might upset her. And even though the mom looked like she needed the help, she might go ballistic. For a quick moment, I raised the magazine, hiding my face. But her next scream seemed to rip right through the pages. I placed the magazine on the chair next to me and tried smiling at her.

Another scream.

I'd lost my magic touch with kids, or at least this one. Looking for an escape, I lifted from my seat and walked to the receptionist's window. A shapely woman in blue scrubs was on the phone. She held up a finger. I turned back to the circus behind me and felt badly for everyone involved.

"I wouldn't trade spots with her for a million bucks."

I turned to see the receptionist flipping her pen between two fingers. I nodded. "Can't disagree with you on that. Is Zahera ready for me yet?"

She put a hand to her face. Was she smirking?

"Did I miss the joke?"

"No. I just—"

Just then, the main office door opened from the hallway, and a man wearing a red tie marched in. He scooped up Brit, who immediately stopped screaming, and then walked over to the pregnant woman. They spoke quietly, then in a matter of seconds, were out the door.

"What was that all about?" I asked.

The nurse grinned. "That was supposed to be Zahera's last appointment once Mrs. Donahue's husband arrived. Maybe they'll call back and reschedule."

"Cool. Well, not so much for them, but can I run back and talk to Zahera?"

I'd already shifted to the interior door, anticipating a quick nod.

"Well…"

"Well what?"

"She's…a bit indisposed."

I wasn't following. "I need more words."

Just then, Kelly walked up behind the receptionist and handed her a couple of folders. "Hey, Ivy, you still waiting on Queen Z?"

I couldn't contain my laughter. "Haven't heard that one before."

A woman probably twenty years older than any girl working in the office, Kelly had pizzazz. She arched an eyebrow. "Neither has she. Let's keep it that way for now, if you don't mind. I like my job. Well, on most days."

Turns out I wasn't the only one keeping a secret from Zahera. "No problem. Any idea what's holding up Queen Z? She summoned me over to talk wedding plans."

"Come on back," Kelly said with a smile.

"But, Kelly, don't you think we should wait?" The nurse gave Kelly a knowing nod, but I didn't think Kelly noticed. Maybe she didn't care. She ran the place, so I followed her lead and met her on the other side of the interior door.

Her yellow and white flowery skirt flowed behind her as she swiftly made her way down the maze of hallways. I had to skip to keep up. "I think she's finishing up some paperwork." She knocked once on Zahera's office door and opened it.

All I saw were white butt cheeks.

Twelve

After a few minutes for the loving and horny couple to get dressed, Zeke opened the door. His cheeks—the ones on his face—were abnormally pink. I didn't know if that was from overexertion or embarrassment.

"Hi, Ivy…again."

"Sorry for just barging in," I said, taking a step inside the door.

Zahera adjusted her considerable bra and then fanned herself. "Wipe that image from your memory bank," she said with a wink.

That might not be as easy as she thinks, but I said, "It's wiped."

Zahera checked herself in her portable mirror. "Zeke just flew in from Canada, right, sweetie?"

"Yep. Toronto."

"It's been a few days since we've seen each other." She walked over, wrapped her arms around his shoulders, and kissed him on the cheek. Even though he had muscles on top of muscles, he smiled like a school kid.

"Four days and nine hours to be exact," he said, popping both eyebrows.

She patted his face. "Isn't he adorable?"

"Just like a puppy dog," I said.

I thought about the first time Zahera and I had met Zeke. Zahera's attraction to him had been instantaneous. I realized I was dealing with two lovebirds, but I couldn't help but think of the real Bond's natural charm with women. Zahera certainly seemed smitten. I just didn't want my best friend to get hurt because Zeke had a woman in every port, so to speak.

Zahera smacked her fiancé on his backside, then moved behind her desk and glanced at her computer monitor. "So you're going to meet me at the tux store later?"

"It's a date," he said, pulling out his phone. "Remember, I'm flying out later tonight to Mexico City. I have a meeting early tomorrow morning."

"Toronto. Mexico City. Your international business is really picking up for your security firm," I said.

"Funny thing, it's all referral business. I guess once you make it into the right circle of people and they have a good customer experience, then they spread the word to their friends. It's kind of like a stock tip, except any 'insider information' in my business won't get the SEC up your ass."

I instantly wondered if his circle included Petro Udovenko, the name of the man Armand had shared. While I knew I had homework of my own to learn everything I could about Petro, convincing Zeke to open up would get me there a lot faster. But he was a former Navy SEAL and basically in the business of concealing information, per his client's wishes.

"I can relate, at least a little bit on the word-of-mouth references going a long way to build a business. I know that ECHO is nothing compared to your firm—"

"That's nonsense," he said. "Don't underestimate the service you provide for this community."

I was taken aback by Zeke's compliment and lost my concentration. But to avoid an awkward silence, I just said, "Uh, thanks."

"Well, I'm off. Need to run by the house, wash up, repack my bag, and then... What did I need to do? I can't seem to recall." He twisted his lips and looked to the ceiling.

"Very funny, Zeke. Did you bang your head while you were...?" Zahera pressed her mouth shut as her eyes got wide.

"I guess I'll leave on that note. See you soon, Ivy."

And with that, he was out the door. Zahera's smile suddenly went flat. She picked up a pen and clicked it a few times.

"What's up, Z?"

"Nothing."

"That's means it's something."

She didn't respond, but she did click the pen another ten times.

"Do you want me to guess?"

Five more pen clicks. I followed her eyes to where her framed medical degree hung from the wall.

"Z, you're the one who asked me over. I thought it was to talk about wedding stuff. Is there something going on here at the office?"

She shook away her trance. "Sorry, no, yes...Oh, I'm such a scatterbrain."

I walked over and put my hand on her shoulder. "You're anything but. You're probably the smartest person I know."

"I know, but..." She looked at me and then cackled a few seconds. Her confidence wasn't lacking. But that was typical Zahera.

"What's going on?" I asked again.

"It's Zeke." Her eyes found mine, and I felt an extra zip in my pulse. Had she just been playing the role of the happy fiancé in front of Zeke? Maybe she'd discovered something about his other life, the one that somehow connected him to the Ukrainian drug boss. I braced myself for the worst. Or maybe it would be for the best.

"What about Zeke?"

A sigh, then she rested both hands on her desk. "I don't know what to do, Ivy."

I rubbed her back. "What did he do?"

She flipped her head toward me. "I'm hoping no one."

I was sure I looked confused. I certainly felt it. Then the comments started connecting. "Are you thinking he's…you know, with another…?" I didn't want to come right out and say it. Uttering those words was like jinxing a pitcher who had a no-hitter going into the ninth inning—something Saul had taught me after watching more baseball games over the last two months than I had the previous twenty-eight years of my life. If you said too much about it, then it was more likely to screw everything up. In this case, literally.

"No." She exhaled a long breath. "Well, I can't say I haven't thought about it."

"Why? What's making you go there? Lipstick on his collar? Suggestive text messages?"

"What? None of that."

"Then what, Z?" I could hear an irritation in my voice. Before she could respond, I said, "Hey, I don't mean to press you or anything. It's your life, your business."

She turned, ran her fingers through her hair. "I think I'm worried that I'm going to lose him, Ivy."

"But you have no evidence that there's another woman in his life?"

She cocked her head. "Hell no. If there was, I'd kick his ass."

"You're not making a lot of sense."

She puffed out a breath. "I know, I know. I'm just…"

"In love?"

"Yeah, that's it."

"And you're feeling vulnerable, so you start imagining the worst."

"Damn, you're good."

"I took a lot of psychology classes in college."

"I'm glad one of us has their head screwed on right," she said.

I almost laughed, but I held back when I could see she was serious.

"I've locked my keys in the car twice in the last week. I wake up at night in a cold sweat—"

I smirked at that one. "Was Zeke in the bed with you?"

"No, traveling again."

Interesting.

"Ask the girls here at the office. I'm just not completely myself."

I shook my head.

"What?" her voice sounded like that of a little girl. "Don't make fun of me."

"I said it earlier, Z. You're in love. Embrace it."

A smile escaped her lips. "I've been married twice before, and I can honestly say I've never felt anything like this. It's great, but it's also unnerving at the same time."

"You're a lucky girl. What can I say?" My happiness for her quickly shifted to guilt. And I wondered if I should just open up and tell her what her dad had shared with me. That was what friends did, right?

Are you nuts, Ivy? She'll never speak to you again, and it will probably lead to a huge fight with her dad. And then Zeke will get involved, and you'll never learn the truth. You took the case to learn the truth, before Zeke hurts Zahera, if that's where everything is headed.

"There is one thing that I can't get past, Ivy. As long as I'm spilling out my soul to you and everything."

I tilted my head, waited.

"My dad. He doesn't think I should get married to Zeke. Thinks it's too quick, I'm not ready, and Zeke's too much of a jet-setting playboy."

"He told you all that?"

She puffed out a breath. "You know him. Straight to the point. Doesn't mince words."

I could feel my throat get tight. "Since when do you listen to him?"

"I know, right?" She put a hand on her hip and flipped her pen to the table. Then she turned to look at me. "Two failed marriages. That's my resume."

"But you don't care what he thinks...well, not about that stuff."

She pursed her lips.

"You do care what he thinks."

"I wish I didn't. But..." She paused and looked off. "Two marriages that didn't work out."

"You just acknowledged how different it feels with Zeke."

"I know," she said softly.

"Is this really what's driving your anxiety? It's not Zeke possibly cheating on you; it's more about your—" I stopped, not sure how to say it.

"Go ahead and spit it out. I've got Daddy issues. And I'm pissed at myself for it."

I'd never seen Zahera this emotional about so many things. Love and family pressures obviously were at the core of her sensitivity. Her dad could be a real ass. Yet, I also knew that he cared for Zahera deeply; so much so that he'd convinced me that the ties between Zeke and this Ukrainian drug lord were a real possibility. And if I were to ignore his request to investigate the connection and something were to happen to Zahera, then I'd never be able to live with myself.

"Z, we've all got issues. Just some of us are better at hiding them."

She reached over and gave me a hug, then held both of my shoulders. "Sorry if it's all about me right now."

"You're getting married soon. I get it."

She smiled, but it didn't carry over to her expression.

"I forgot to ask. Do you have a date for the wedding?"

"New Year's Eve."

"Really?"

"Is there something wrong with that date?"

"No, it's just that there's a lot going on at that time of the year."

"Eh. Remember, it's number three for me."

"You wearing white?"

"Me and white don't go." She looked at her watch. "I've got to handle a little internal HR issue before I run a couple of errands and then meet Zeke at the tux shop. He's getting a personal fitting from the owner. Zeke apparently knows him from some job several years ago."

"Which rental place is it?"

"They only do custom apparel. It's for the uber-rich. Run by a guy named Vladimir Medvedev."

A Russian name. I chewed on that nugget all the way over to Saul's place.

Thirteen

"**D**o you want a cigarette?"

Staring out Saul's apartment window to a myriad of lights flashing against the dark sky, I shifted my eyes over to Saul, who'd just crawled back into bed.

"You know I don't smoke." I playfully tapped his bare shoulder, but felt the curve of his muscle and kept my hand there. He might not have that James Bond aura, but under his cheap suits—he could only afford the two-for-one specials often advertised on TV—he was a real man. It wasn't just the size of his deltoids or pecs; it went way beyond that. He'd always treated me with respect. The way he looked at me, the way he talked to me, the way he encouraged me to follow my passion…it was all so uplifting. He made me feel better about myself. It was selfless. It was Saul.

"You kind of have that glow going on," he said, gently rubbing my thigh. "You up for a doubleheader?"

I snickered. "Wow, your, uh, appetite is certainly healthy. Did you take a blue pill when I wasn't watching?"

He took my hand and kissed it. "I don't need any blue pills when you're around."

"Are you taking that line from your old single-guy playbook?"

"I guess that was pretty cheesy, huh?"

"Uh, yeah. But in twenty years or so, you might just need that little blue pill."

He didn't respond for a few seconds. I turned to look at him. "Did you fall asleep?"

"No, it's just that you mentioned something about the future. And you usually don't talk about the future and us in the same sentence."

"I don't think I mentioned us. If I did, you can strike it from the record, counselor." I leaned over and poked his ribs. He grunted out a laugh, and then he found my tickle spot—the top of my knee. We kicked and laughed for a good minute. Then I went back to looking out his apartment window. We'd promised each other not to put labels or a timetable on our relationship. I knew that I didn't do well when I felt pressure from a partner. I'd push him away, or I might pull him too close. I'd grown up thinking that dependency on someone else, even if they professed to care about me, left me exposed. To the point where it seemed like my skin had been peeled from my body and every little breeze of air would send a shiver up my spine.

But now that Zahera and Zeke were getting married, "couple" labels were being thrown around a lot. I could almost predict the questions Saul and I would field at Zahera's wedding. *Have you guys been thinking about your future? Is this wedding getting you in the mood to finally settle down together? Ivy, you're not getting any younger...don't you think it's time you prepare to have kids?*

I pushed the sheet off my legs. "I'm getting hot."

"What's up, Ivy?"

"Eh."

"Something's really up. Tell me."

I grabbed his hand. "I just don't want things to change. I like what we've got."

He nodded. "Is Z's wedding freaking you out a bit?"

"Eh."

"You can say yes. It's just me."

"Okay. Yes. But it's not because of you. It's me. I know I just need to get over myself."

His phone buzzed on the side table. He scrambled to pick it up.

"Something from your asshole boss, Herbert Ross?"

"No."

That was abrupt. A normal girl sitting in my position—literally and figuratively—might start feeling a bit insecure, wondering if Saul had another woman on the side, someone who wasn't afraid of labels and such.

"You going to keep me guessing?"

He sighed, tapped the screen, and then set the phone on the table, his eyes staring straight up to the ceiling.

This was the point at which I might normally bail. Think the worst. Close up my emotions. Pick up my stuff and walk out the door. Like a little kid who didn't get her way.

I had to grow up eventually.

"You don't have to tell me who that was, Saul, but you're upset. Can I help in any way?"

Was that so tough, Ivy? Well, that depends on how he responds. Another sigh, then he turned his head to me. "Wait, are you thinking I've got another woman on the side?"

"Did I say that?" My response had more attitude than I'd intended.

"No, but I could tell."

I took in a breath. "Like I said, you don't have to tell me anything. You ask if you can help me when I've got stress going on. I was just doing the same thing. But maybe you don't want my help. Or you don't want me to pry. I'll stay on my side of the net." I pulled up the sheet and turned on my side, away from him.

His hand touched my hip. "Don't pull away. I like it when you care."

Relief. I chided myself for thinking the worst and turned to face him. "Do I need to provide a leading question and then you can just let it all out?"

"I'm just nervous, that's all."

"About?"

"My bar exam. I'm not sure I passed."

"What does that have to do with the late-night text message?"

"I set up this auto-message feature that keeps me updated on anything related to the exam. Like when the grades are posted."

I sat up. "I'm confused. Did they tell you something about your grade?"

"No, it was just a reminder that the grades will be posted within forty-eight hours."

I rubbed my hand across his chest. "I have confidence in you."

"That makes one of us."

"Come on."

"I'm serious. That test kicked my ass."

Like everyone, Saul had his moments where his confidence bucket seemed to have a leak. "It's over, Saul. You took the test. You studied like a crazy man for weeks and weeks. You can't ask more of yourself. I'm proud of you for just making it this far."

The lighting wasn't great, but I could still see his frown. "My parents worked really hard to put me through school. And I've been taking it up the ass from Ross and the other partners at the firm just to keep a job in the field as a legal assistant. If I don't pass this test, I will have let my entire family down, and my future will be nothing more than being a lackey for Ross. I'm not sure I can handle either."

"Saul."

He stared straight up.

"Hey." I turned his face in my direction. "It's going to work out. I know it's going to work out. You are brilliant, and I believe in you."

"Thanks." He cracked a smile and sat up. "You never told me how things went with Z's dad."

I puffed out a breath.

"He is high stress, isn't he?"

"And then some."

I glanced out the window, questioning whether I should share the entire saga about Armand twisting my arm until I'd agreed to look into Zeke's connection to the drug lord. Hell, I couldn't put it all on Armand. He was convincing, but I was the one who'd said yes. And I was also the one who felt like a load of bricks had been strapped to my back—stress bricks.

The old Ivy would go on lockdown. What Saul didn't know wouldn't hurt him. And I was a mature adult who could make decisions on her own without approval from him...whatever this was with Saul.

But ever since I'd survived the last abduction by Milton, who'd undergone something close to twenty surgeries to conceal his identity, Saul had made me promise just one thing: share with him anything I was working on that involved dangerous risks. While I could argue that over half my cases could be labeled as a dangerous risk, he said he'd leave it to me to tell him when something crossed that line.

He kissed my shoulder. "Are you off in la-la land again?"

Get right to it, or I'll talk myself out of it. "Armand wants me to investigate Zeke."

No immediate response. I turned to look at him.

"You're kidding," he said, his forehead crumpled.

I didn't smile. I couldn't smile.

"You're not kidding?"

I shook my head, rubbed the back of my neck. He moved my hand and took over the rubbing duties. "I know there's a story there."

"A big one."

I told him how Armand's connection at the FBI had been at least temporarily severed, but not before he'd found some evidence to suggest Zeke was tied to a Ukrainian drug lord.

"I never thought about Ukraine being a haven for drug production. I thought that was left to our neighbors in Central America."

"I think you're missing the headline here, Saul."

"Sorry. Are you're freaking out because Armand asked you to investigate the fiancé of your best friend?"

"I'm freaking out because I took the case," I said, head down.

A slow nod. "And you're telling me this because you think there's a potential risk to your life."

"Honestly, I don't see how it can go there. It's not like I'm jumping on the next flight to Kiev to begin an expedition into the mountains to find this guy's drug operation. He's a world away. I just want to know if Zahera could get her heart broken when she realizes that she married an international drug smuggler and could unknowingly place a target on herself."

"You're putting her life over your life."

"Saul."

"No, I get it. I just wish you'd put your life first, for once."

"Can you please not go there?"

"Sorry."

A moment of silence. My thoughts danced around to everything that I'd experienced during the last few months.

"You're feeling guilty," he said.

"Yep. But if I'd turned him down, then what would I do? Either way, with him sharing this with me, I'm screwed, at least in terms of my relationship with Zahera."

"As one smart person told me, 'It will work out. I have faith in you.'"

"So you do listen to me," I said with a raised eyebrow.

He picked up a pillow and playfully smacked me upside the head. Before he could get in another blow, I barreled into his chest and held down his arms. Then I gave him a kiss.

"Hey," he said, suddenly serious. "Did you have time to submit the form to the state adoption agency?"

"Buzzkill," I said, climbing off of him.

"Sorry."

I put my finger to his lips. "Stop saying you're sorry. You care. That means everything."

"Care's my middle name."

"Funny. Not."

"I'm assuming you haven't heard anything back?"

"Don't you think I would have told you?"

"You know it might take a while. The slowly churning wheels of government agencies."

"If you're trying to cushion the blow of getting no feedback so far, thank you. Part of me might be curious: is it because they hate me, or is it because one is dead and the other is fishing in Alaska and could care less? I'm basically going to put it in the back of my mind. If I get word from the state, great. If not, then I guess it wasn't meant to be."

He held up his fist, and I popped it with mine. Then I threw back the sheets and climbed out of bed.

"Where are you going?"

"My brain has started cranking, and it won't stop until I get some work done."

"Do you mind if I try to get a few hours of sleep?"

"You're the one with the corporate job, so you need the sleep. Someday soon, though, you'll have your own law practice, and then you'll work long hours because you want to."

"Only if you'll visit me and we can have sex on the big meeting table."

I put my hand on his package. "Dreams do come true."

He got to his knees and gave me a kiss, his hands starting to move up my thigh.

"Later, big boy. For it to be a dream, you have to be asleep."

He chuckled, then rolled over and closed his eyes with a smile on his face. I padded out to the living room and jumped on my computer. I had to find out if my best friend was about to marry a very bad man.

Fourteen

The arm prosthesis made Stan sweat even more than usual, so he threw it to the couch and we walked out the front door.

A bird chirped from a tree limb hanging over the front steps of the modest, Tudor-style home in the historic King William District of San Antonio that Stan shared with his wife, Bev, and their son, Ethan. He said it reminded him of some of the small New Jersey towns, where some of his family lived.

I reset the timer on my watch. "You ready for a good run this—"

"Hold on." He held up a finger on his left hand, but I could also see the nub on his right arm move. I tried not to stare. He disappeared inside for a moment.

I was anxious to pick Stan's brain on a couple of topics, the fake-kidnapping case involving Megan Espinoza, and the search for dirt on Zeke, something that I'd need to keep discreet. At the same time, I didn't want to add any extra burden to his life. I'd have to be careful how I approached the topic. At least on the fake kidnapping case, I hoped he'd see me as a benefit to his investigation. We'd worked in that capacity in the past. Of course, that was before his arm was amputated. His outlook on life since then seemed to be less jovial, more about surviving every day. It made sense to me. But I knew that was no way to live.

I spread my feet, leaning forward until I could feel my hamstrings stretch. I thought about the previous late-night search for information on Petro Udovenko. I learned he was a former member of the Soviet Union's Red Army more than three decades earlier. Since then, there was no evidence to suggest he was even alive. But I knew my method of retrieving information was limited. I needed access to data only people in our intelligence-gathering community would hold. Stan had a cousin who worked for the FBI out of the Boston office. Nick Radowski was a leaner version of Stan and more self-disciplined on the eating front. He'd actually turned into a marathon runner in the last year or two. Something about being ribbed by his longtime partner, a snarky female agent named Alex Troutt—Nick's words, not mine.

I met Nick a few months ago when official FBI work brought him to San Antonio. His case overlapped with my ECHO business, and we ended up working together to capture a predator. It felt like we'd worked well together, had a pretty good connection. Would he give me a few minutes of his time to at least offer some options on how I could find out more information on Udovenko? That was what I wanted to bounce off Stan. I was hoping he'd see that part of the discussion as a distraction from his real job.

Even though I knew the pace of our jog would rival that of a tortoise, I continued to stretch as multiple birds chirped overhead. Through the dense foliage, I could see a few wispy clouds that would likely burn off, leaving us with another blue-sky day. At least this one was supposed to stay under a hundred degrees.

While Stan had yet to actually state that he hated running or otherwise working out, it was obvious that exercise was not something that Stan enjoyed. But running in this heat might be on par to Stan being forced to eat kale every meal for a year. Born and bred in Brooklyn, Stan was a meat-and-potatoes man. Well, that and any junk food he could get his hands on: donuts, candy bars, greasy burgers, you name it. But he was working on it.

At least three times a week, I'd shown up no later than seven a.m., and we'd go on a jog. His goal was to run in the Boston Marathon next spring. To make that happen, he had to run a marathon in Dallas by December, where he would hopefully qualify for Boston.

Given where he was in his training, that was no more than a distant dream. And, frankly, one I wasn't sure he really wanted. Every day since Stan had lost his arm, he'd accepted one challenge after another during his recuperation. He wasn't the kind of guy to back down, but I'd also seen his frustration redline on more than one occasion. I couldn't blame him. In fact, every time I saw him struggle to function in life with only one arm, it just added to my guilt. My stalker, my monster, had done this to him. While Milton Weber had avoided a long trial by admitting everything he'd done and was now safely tucked away in prison, the wake of his destruction was something that would never go away. He'd killed countless people and maimed Stan—all because of his twisted vendetta against me.

"Okay, I guess I'm ready now," Stan said as he popped back out of the house.

I noticed what looked like donut crumbs in his mustache, but I chose not to point it out. "Everything good?"

He glanced at the door as he slipped a headband over his coarse head of hair. "Ethan had one of his episodes. But he finally calmed down."

Ethan was autistic and, like some kids on the spectrum, experienced times when he couldn't deal with certain stimuli or other people. Then he would lose control, throw a tantrum. To me, Stan and Bev were heroes in the way they handled Ethan, but I could see the stress it caused both of them.

"I'm sure you'll feel better after a good run."

He grunted, and we walked down the steps, then headed north on Madison.

"Oh, your shoe's untied," I said, coming to a stop after jogging past just one house. He stopped and tried to use the drawstrings on his shoe specifically designed for someone with one usable hand.

"Dammit all to hell," he said.

"Got a problem?" I said, reaching my hand toward his shoe.

"I got it. It just takes me longer."

I gave him all the time he needed to use his one good hand to untangle the laces and pull the drawstring taut. He'd actually become pretty good at using his prosthesis, but he'd left it on the couch. As he stood up, I took in the Stan Radowski workout attire: a blue Dri-FIT shirt that made him look seven months pregnant, a pair of baggy basketball shorts that had me wondering if he had an ass, and a shiny pair of green and blue running shoes with white athletic socks pulled up to his knees.

We jogged three blocks to the end of the street, then turned left onto Turner.

"Not sure I can make it much farther," he said, huffing out each word.

We'd only jogged about a quarter of a mile.

"Let's try to make it to the park up ahead."

A loud grunt, but he pushed forward, and about ten minutes later, we made it a full half mile. Leaning against a tree, he gasped for air for a good five minutes. Then he went straight to the water fountain.

"You going to make it, old man?"

He turned his head and gave me the eye.

"What? You're older than me."

He wiped his mouth, stood up. "It's not my age. It's this." He grabbed a chunk of fat at his waist.

"Stan…" I bit the inside of my cheek.

"What?" He splayed his arms—rather, his arm and his nub. It looked kind of funny. Did he see me smile? His eyes shifted to his right arm, then looked back at me.

I was just about to apologize when he let out a loud chuckle. I started giggling, and in no time, we were both crying from our fits of laughter.

"Oh damn…I needed that," he said, wiping tears from his face.

"Glad I could get you there," I said.

"And then some. Oh my."

Fifteen

We began to walk through the park, trees providing decent shade, so we weren't pouring with sweat. My love of parks had waned since I was abducted by Milton earlier in the year. I used to think that every park had at least one place that was its serenity. Now, I wondered the opposite: where was the most secluded location that offered the best opportunity for a psycho to kidnap you, or even kill you?

But with it being in full daylight, I was able to keep my pulse in check. My eyes, though, darted around like I was being hunted.

"I hear you got a visit from Megan Espinoza."

"You knew? Do you secretly work for the NSA?"

He tried to arch an eyebrow, but his headband had both eyebrows already there.

"Word got around the station very quickly after the responding officer returned from the ECHO building, where Megan's car apparently had mowed over a street sign."

"Oh, that. Megan's got issues, without a doubt. But I think they'd still be mostly invisible had she not been victimized by the people who pulled off this fake-kidnapping escapade. Even hours later, I could see that she was still reeling from the possibility of losing her daughter, Annie."

He shook his head, his lips pursed. "It's the worst fucking thing you can do to a parent, outside of actually taking their child. The way Megan described the call…it literally made my heart race. I really felt for her, and that's saying something, given my tendency toward skepticism."

We came up to another fountain, and Stan stopped to drink more water. It was as if his body had been put through a three-hour boot camp instead of a snail-like, fifteen-minute crawl. "Is Megan…" he began to say, water drooling from his mouth. He wiped it away. "Is Megan hoping you can find these hackers before the cops can? Feel free to jump in and help. I got no ego. But it won't be easy."

I put my hand on his back and immediately regretted it, with the sweat and all. "You used the term hackers."

"So far, we've confirmed more than a dozen cases like this. We've brought in local FBI support to help us track their online presence. The thought right now is that it's a small group of people who are nothing more than computer hackers. They search for data on possible targets, then use certain technology to pull off the life-like call, where you hear your kid screaming or whatever. They might even employ one or more real actors."

"Hackers. Never thought about that angle. Any idea of their location?"

"About two hundred. The tech guys were able to pull some packet information from a cell tower before it disappeared into never-never land and the IP bounced around the entire planet. These people aren't just one step ahead of us, they're about ten miles ahead of us."

"Did you share this with Megan?"

"I told her we had indications that the group could have ties to the computer hacking industry, but I'm not sure she heard me. She was very emotional, almost belligerent. But we let it pass because we knew what she'd been put through. You know how it goes, the hacking theory is just that—a theory, until proven or disproven."

"Makes sense," I said, my eyes aimlessly scanning the dirt as ideas bounced around my mind. "I guess the question is: why her?"

"Huh?" a distracted Stan asked.

I followed his eyes to see him staring at two kids no taller than my waist who were standing next to a woman and gasping and pointing at Stan. She was trying to keep their hands down, but it wasn't working. The nub had apparently frightened them.

"Hey, Stan. Let's head back to the house."

He didn't move. He just stared. I could hear the kids mumbling their fears to their mother. I looked into Stan's eyes. They were flat, as if he'd been punched in the gut. I could see his pain, identify with his embarrassment—the sense of not feeling like a complete person.

I turned, tapping him on the shoulder. "What do you say we go back to your house, and then after you clean up, I'll run you by Smoothies and Stuff? They have this great new—"

"I'm not a little kid, Ivy. I can handle it." He turned and started walking. Out of Stan's view, the mother and I traded glances. She shrugged, as if she had no control over her kids' emotions. I knew she didn't, but the timing sucked.

I caught up with Stan, who said, "Hey, if I happen to find anything on this Espinoza case, I'll be sure to share it with you."

He suddenly started jogging, although it was no faster than our walk. I kept that to myself and started jogging at the same slow pace.

"You want me to do the same, right?"

His eyes looked straight ahead.

I acted like he'd responded. "That would be cool. Thanks." I thought of another angle. "What if we agree to share everything, because, of course, that will only catch these assholes even faster. But we can put a wager on whoever gets there first."

"You want to bet on who solves the case quicker?" He chuckled. "The shit you think of…" he said, his voice trailing off. Then his voice came back to life. "What would we put on the line?"

"I don't know. Money, a good dinner…"

"A trip to the World Series?" He glanced my way with a grizzly smile on his face.

"So that's what you want."

"Maybe. What about you…*if* we were to do this?"

I could sense he was into it. Getting him focused on something, anything other than feeling like a freak, was my goal. It was working, so far. "Let me think that one over," I said.

We jogged another ten minutes. About a hundred yards away from his house, he took off in a sprint, or what should be called a Stan sprint. "What are you doing?"

"Kicking your ass," he yelled over his shoulder.

I laughed so hard I didn't catch up until he'd reached his mailbox. "Didn't know you had such a competitive streak in you," I said.

"I think you woke it up with your wager idea." His sweatband did little to slow perspiration rushing down his red face. "I might be…" He took another couple of breaths. "I might be broken, but this old guy still has some fight left in him."

He sounded like he felt he was on his last leg of life, which was ridiculous, so I focused on his positive energy. I would have put my arm around him then, but the task was just too gross. And I wasn't exactly feeling fresh.

Stan huffed and puffed for another couple of minutes, giving me a minute to think through our next step for finding the fake kidnappers. The government agencies appeared to be very focused on tracking the hackers. Good for them. Cristina and I would never match their resources, although Cristina wasn't exactly a technical neophyte. Still, I wondered how the hackers knew about the Espinoza family. Did they have access to tax returns? Maybe they simply searched through hundreds or even thousands of returns to find someone with a young child and a family whose income was in the top five percent.

"Stan, can you get me the names of the other victims of this fake-kidnapping crime?"

"Uh…"

"Remember, if you want to make this a wager, we did agree to share our information. It's only fair, especially with all the resources at your disposal."

"Resources. I know you PIs like to think we can just kick up our feet and let the wheels of the investigative machine do their thing, but it doesn't work like that. Hell, I have to beg and plead to get the pens and notepads I like to use."

I considered reminding him that was probably because his method of documentation was antiquated—notepads used from cop shows in the 1980s.

"I bet you've figured out a way around that."

He smirked. "I did get to know the guy in purchasing. He likes these brownies that Bev makes. Seems to do the trick."

I nodded. "You see? You do have all the resources you need, even if they're Bev's homemade desserts. So, the names of the victims?"

"I still don't know what I'm getting into. If I somehow lose this wager, either by luck or some technicality—"

"Technicality, my ass."

"I'm just ribbing you, Ivy. What would I be on the hook for?"

"If you want a trip to a game in the World Series, which I know you're assuming would include the Yankees…"

"They only trail the Red Sox by two games. I got this feeling this could be their year."

"Okay. I'll try to think of something comparable and let you know. So, the names?" I knew he was being hesitant because of his natural instinct to keep official information inside the department. It seemed like we did this song-and-dance routine every time I tried to inch my way into a case. But I'd always tried to provide value for Stan and the SAPD. Ask for a favor, give a favor.

"Let me get into the office, track down the names, and figure out a way to get those to you."

"Cool. Thanks." I reached over to touch his elbow in appreciation, but he'd already pulled the bottom of his T-shirt upward to wipe sweat off his face. I was both blinded and repulsed by his white, hairy belly.

"For the love of God, Stan, can you cover up your Jabba belly?"

For a moment, I was mortified that I'd voiced my thoughts out loud, more or less. Thankfully I hadn't. It was Nick. He was standing at the top of the front steps.

"What are you doing here?" I said, a smile splitting my face.

Still looking svelte as ever, Nick hopped down the stairs with the ease of a tap dancer. "Big boy here didn't tell you I was flying in?"

Stan stretched his shirt over his belly. "Didn't know you'd be here this early."

Nick gave me a half-hug. "I took the red eye. Last second change of plans."

"Did an investigation bring you back to the land of never-ending heat?" I asked.

"Not officially. This is more of a working vacation, but I can work remotely for a few days, and then spend my time busting his balls a little bit. It's time to get in shape, cuz. We've got a marathon to get ready for."

Stan ripped off his sweatband and threw it at his cousin. Nick nimbly moved out of the way. Then, Stan hopped forward, trying to rub his sweat on Nick. But again, his cousin was too quick.

"Skinny fucker," Stan grunted.

Nick and I both laughed, then he said, "This is going to be a hell of a week."

Sixteen

Gathered around the kitchen table, the three of us gabbed nonstop until Bev waltzed in and gave us the signal to quiet down, saying Ethan was tired after his episode earlier and had conked out while playing some online video game in his bed. Though the whites of her eyes were covered with webs of red lines, she looked put together as always—the opposite of Stan—even if her figure wasn't that of a model. She wore flowing dresses that fell to her calves and walked with a quiet grace. Part of me wondered if she'd been into ballet as a youngster, although she was very top-heavy, so it was hard to say. With her beehive hairdo, she kind of had the vibe of a "homemaker" from the days of black-and-white TV. I'd seen repeats on cable from a show called *Father Knows Best*. The name of the show was enough to make me gag. But Bev had it going on, her own style, her own way.

"Can I make you some eggs and bacon?" Bev asked, a well-worn, cast-iron skillet in hand.

Nick hopped from his seat. "Beverly, you are so kind. But I stopped at the organic store on the way in from the airport and got some basic things to get us started on our new training regimen."

Stan glanced at his wife, then shifted his sights to Nick. "A diet. It's called a diet, Nick."

"Diets are temporary. What's needed is a life change."

Stan held up his nub. "I've already had one of those, dude. Do I really need another?"

"What's your last name?" Nick said.

"Radowski, asshat. Same as yours."

I couldn't stop a grin from spreading across my face. No one smiled, so I kept my mouth shut and let the two cousins fight it out. I was pulling for Nick, but I had to act neutral.

Nick pointed a finger at his larger cousin. "Radowskis don't just throw in the towel. We don't let outside things dictate how we live our lives. Remember your great-grandparents that came over from Poland?"

"Yes," Stan said, grudgingly.

"They preached to their kids that to live a better life, you had to make a better life."

"You think I'm throwing in the towel?" Stan said, a quiver in his voice. "I get up and go to work every day. I figure out how to get shit done with one good arm and a club attached to the other one." He smacked a hand to his nub.

Bev sniffled. "You know I'm so proud of you, Stan, don't you?"

"Sure I do, sweetie. No one else seems to have any compassion, that's all."

"Dude, you know I support you," I said.

"Well, okay. That's true, I guess."

"Stan…" Nick stared at his cousin.

Stan adjusted his jaw, his eyes scanning the Formica tabletop. There was silence for more than just a few seconds. I could feel the tension, and I wondered if my questions for Nick should wait until later in the day.

A second before I was about to push up from my seat, Nick came at him again. "Stan, I know you were dealt a bad deck of cards. Getting your arm amputated sucks. But I understand it's healed, and you've done well in your occupational therapy. So, it's now time to focus on living a long life, to see Ethan grow up, to maybe look ahead and do some traveling with Bev. Life goes on, my man, and it's time to fucking step up."

"Oh yeah?" Stan turned and looked at his cousin, his eyes on fire. Worried that the cousins might start a fistfight, I was on edge, prepared to move quickly.

Stan nodded his head a few times. Was he wondering how many shots he could get in with his one arm, or simply trying to calm himself down so he wouldn't create a scene?

Finally, Stan said, "You're right, Nick."

I smacked my hands on the table. Everyone looked at me, but I didn't say a word.

"Yep, I said Nick was right. I'm a grown man. I can admit when I need to be knocked upside the head, figuratively speaking, of course."

Bev gave her husband a smooch on the cheek. "Okay, how can I help?" she asked.

"You're the key to making this work, Bev," Nick said, pulling out three sacks from the fridge. "We need to purge this house of all the crap food that's in here. Everything. I can give you a grocery list to restock with the right stuff."

She put her hand on the counter. The idea seemed to fluster her.

"It'll be okay. Promise you," Nick said.

He quickly divided up the contents of the bags into four bowls and handed them out.

"Granola, blueberries, and raspberries," Stan said, feigning enthusiasm. "Yummy."

Beverly took in a spoonful. "Not bad. Good taste. I could stand to lose a few pounds. Would you like to see me in a bikini again, Stan?"

Everyone laughed. Well, everyone except Stan, who said, "Come on, Bev. That's private stuff. Besides, I like you just the way you are."

"You're sweet, but if Nick is going to show us how to do this, then I'm going to do my best to follow the program. I could use more energy, and haven't we talked about taking one of these walking vacations through Ireland?"

Bev hugged Stan's shoulders, his shirt still a darker shade from his sweat-fest.

"I don't know. That might be pretty fun." Stan took a bite of his fruit and didn't grimace. Then, when Bev left the kitchen, he quickly changed the subject to Zahera's fiancé. He winked, which was the signal for me to query Nick about the alleged drug kingpin and Zeke.

I paused, unsure how to raise the topic without immediately getting shut down. Nick was cool, but he definitely wasn't into breaking FBI rules. I just hoped I could get him to bend a little.

"What's on your mind, Ivy?" Nick began to riffle through the fridge, tossing every fattening item he found into the trash.

I took in a full breath. In that moment I decided that full transparency was the only logical path if I expected any help from the federal agent. Nick knew both Zahera and Zeke, at least a little bit, and he certainly understood my desire to keep Zahera out of harm's way. I told him the story from the moment Armand had entered the ECHO office until the time I'd read the name of the possible international drug leader on the business card.

"And so, even though I know Zeke, I don't *really* know him. I just need to figure out if there's any way he could be connected to this—"

"What did you say his name was again?" With the fridge door still open, he stood upright, facing me.

"Petro Udovenko. Like I said, it's only a name. I did some research last night and not much came up. Looks like he used to be in the Red Army. But who knows? It may not even be the same guy."

Nick shut the fridge door and sat down at the table, his hands clasped in front of him. The lines around his eyes were more pronounced, which seemed to add a good five years to his age. "If anyone you know is mixed up with Petro Udovenko, then the sphere of danger for a lot of people, not just Zahera, is real."

I poured myself more water.

Seventeen

Nick munched on granola, his eyes peering into the ceiling. "So Armand was a career military guy and knows someone named Bart, who knows someone in the Bureau."

"That's what he told me."

Stan arched an eyebrow. "Sounds a little too much like Deep Throat."

We both turned to look at him.

"You know," he said, sitting straighter in his chair. "The code name for the secret source for Woodward and Bernstein in their Watergate investigation."

"We know," I said.

Nick jumped in. "Stan, this Udovenko guy is bad news."

"Why isn't more coming up on him, then?" I asked.

"Because, as much as he can control, he chooses it not to be there. He apparently likes to live in the shadows. And as a result, his drug network is vast. But he didn't get there by holding bridge parties. He's as coldblooded as any cartel leader from Latin America. In fact, he's known to be far more ruthless than the Russian mafia. They pretty much steer clear of the guy."

I felt a dry patch in the back of my throat. I gulped down some water. "How do you know about him?"

He traded glances with Stan, then looked at me. "I'm sharing this because I trust you won't go running to the media or the bad guys."

"It's just us sitting here, dickwad," Stan said, popping a blueberry into his mouth.

Nick rolled his eyes. "In Boston, we've found evidence of his heroin on the streets."

"How do you know it's his heroin?"

"Good question. Many times the big traffickers are so bold that they put a logo on the baggies sold on the street. They see the users as a customer, just as any business would. What better marketing tool then to include a graphical representation on the bag? It's obvious but subtle at the same time. People have an amazing high, then wake up and see the empty baggie. They want more, so they go find the dealer who gave them that brand of heroin."

"What's his logo?"

"A bear holding a red sickle. So, it's kind of a cross between the old Communist hammer and sickle and a Russian bear."

"If you ask me," Stan said, his spoon scraping the bottom of his bowl, "it sounds like it has a double meaning. It's brand awareness for the drug users, but it's also a warning to any other drug traffickers, or maybe even law enforcement, that he'll strike back if they try to stop him."

Nick nodded. "It very well could be, Stan." Nick's eyes went to Stan's bowl. "Your body must have been craving real fruit."

Stan set his spoon on the table. "Okay, so tell me that was just the first course of the meal. Are you going to make some pancakes, or maybe get fancy on me and make some Eggs Benedict?" He licked his lips like he was Scooby. "Add plenty of hollandaise sauce, now."

"You're kidding, right?" Nick said. "We just went through what would have to be called an intervention and here you are ten minutes later thinking you're going to get Eggs Benedict. Do you know how many calories are in hollandaise sauce?"

Stan's face went blank. "Dude, I was joking. Man, you're gullible." Stan laughed so hard his belly jiggled. Then he grabbed a pinch around his waist and laughed some more. "Oh, damn, I crack myself up."

Stan's laughter filled my heart. It had been a while since I'd seen him so relaxed. He and Nick could bicker like siblings, but he also trusted his cousin. And it appeared that Nick's presence calmed his nerves, made him believe that he didn't always have to be the strong, tough guy.

The laughter ended. Each of us were looking away, as if something more pressing had fought its way to the top of our minds. For me, I knew exactly where I needed to go. "So, Nick, any thoughts on how we can verify if Zeke is connected to this guy?"

"No idea what we would learn, but I certainly know where to go."

"Cool. I'm all ears."

"The thing is, I'm not sure if she'll play ball," he scratched his chin. It looked like the guy had just started shaving.

"Who is...she?"

"My partner, Alex. She's running lead on this investigation by herself, at least in the FBI house, because she was out a while and I'm carrying a huge caseload. Too much detail for you, I know. But I think she'll share my opinion that to keep the public safe, we—those of us around this table—need to know some of the details."

"Won't it help that you know Zahera, and that your own cousin, a detective with the SAPD, knows Zahera?"

"It won't hurt. I'll put in a call here in a bit, and then I can let you know."

"Then where do we go?" I asked.

"One step at a time," he said.

"But don't we need to figure out where this Petro guy's home base is and then determine a way to bring him out of the shadows and try to catch him? You know, cut the head off the snake?"

Nick pointed a thumb at me, while turning to look at Stan. "Does she ever stop moving?"

Stan shook his head. "She's got more energy, more drive, than ten detectives."

"You're not thinking like a PI who's simply trying to help keep your friend safe. You've got the mindset of a federal agent, as if you're on a mission to bring down bastards like this Udovenko fellow."

Stan popped him on the arm. "Don't you remember me telling you when you were here a few months ago? She needs to get her ass into the police academy."

"Why stop there?" Nick said, turning to me. "Why not aspire to work for an agency where you could have the most impact?"

I felt my face flush. I'd never put a single thought into doing what Nick suggested. Bigger stage, bigger impact? Hmmm. But it would also be a much bigger bureaucratic machine. No words came to mind. I flipped my hands to the ceiling.

"Kind of reminds me of someone I know," Nick said, scratching his chin again.

"Who's that?" Stan asked.

"Uh, no one you know. It's just uncanny."

"Guys, hello. I'm right here."

"You should be flattered," Stan said.

"Thank you for talking about me in front of me. How's that?"

"I get your point," Nick said.

I lifted from my seat, found my bag, and pulled out my phone. Nick and I traded phone numbers.

"Where are you off to in such a rush?" Stan asked, as I walked toward the back door.

"To talk to Cristina so we can prepare to start research on the names you're going to send us." I winked.

"Right. I guess that means I need to get off my fat ass and get to work." Stan pushed up from the table. He froze the moment he stood up, grabbing at his hamstring, his eyes bulging out.

"Oh crap. Did you pull a muscle?" I asked.

A slight pause, his face now turning red. I took a step back toward him. "Stan?"

Nick leaned over and shoved his cousin, forcing him to use his legs to regain his balance. "You're full of shit, Stan Radowski. You're just trying to get out of the new training program."

Stan sighed. "Can't blame a guy for trying."

"I saw you do the same thing when you were nine years old, trying to fake being sick in order to get out of going to Mass."

"It worked, didn't it?"

Nick smiled. "You're going to be a fun student."

They started to laugh, but I quickly shut them down. "Can you get me those names within the hour?"

"I'll do my best, Ivy. The contest is on, I guess."

"I already have a theory, so you might want to get moving."

"You shitting me?"

I winked again and walked out the door.

Eighteen

I clicked refresh on my browser and went back to the hard copy I'd just printed. It was the list of names that Stan had emailed of those who'd been victimized by fake kidnappings, purportedly just as Megan Espinoza had experienced yesterday.

"I've never heard of some of these Podunk towns," Cristina said from the other side of my desk at the ECHO office.

"They're all here in Texas. Let's create a map to give us a visual, and then assign each a number based upon the chronological date of when the crimes took place."

"I'm all over it. Just give me a couple of minutes," she said, hunkering behind the new laptop I'd bought her.

"Is it strange working with a fifteen-inch screen as opposed to your phone?"

She used her forefingers to jab a few keys. It probably felt foreign to not use her thumbs as she would on her phone. I decided not to bring up the fact that if she would learn how to type—the old-fashioned way—she could probably crank out seventy or eighty words a minute.

"Eh, not really," she said. "I have to use one in my animation class at school."

Of course, this delighted me to no end—her going back to school to get her diploma. A few more credits this semester, and she'd have her degree by Christmas.

With her eyes still focused on her laptop screen, she said, "I see you smiling."

"Who, me?" I put my hand up to my mouth to cover my grin.

She rolled her eyes. "You know I could quit any day."

She was only trying to draw me into a debate. "That would be the right move. Quit just a couple of months before you can get your degree."

"Just saying."

"Oh, I know. *Just saying*," I said in a mocking voice.

"You're getting too good at that."

"Learning from the best, sweetie."

Cristina's round, dark eyes peered above the lip of the laptop. She said something, but my sights were already glued to my computer screen. A message in red text had finally appeared: *Currently, neither of your birth parents have submitted the proper forms to show their desire to meet you.*

I could feel my heart flutter. Closing my eyes for a moment, I filled my lungs with air, trying to maintain my composure.

You should have gone with your instincts, Ivy. Protect yourself, first, foremost, forever. If your parents gave a damn about you, they would have never given you up.

I opened my eyes and found more text on the screen in a smaller font.

Please do not be alarmed or upset. Oftentimes, parents who give up their kids for adoption feel embarrassed or ashamed by it. As a matter of policy, we will try to communicate to them your desire to meet. We cannot promise this status will change, but we do encourage you to continue checking back for status updates.

Best wishes,

State of Texas Central Adoption Agency.

"You didn't hear a word I said, did you?" Cristina said.

"Huh? Sorry. I was just distracted." I anchored my chin in the palm of my hand, but I could still feel a quake deep inside me. "You were saying?"

Cristina turned her head. "I saw your lips moving. What are you reading that's so important?" She got up, moved around the desk. I tried covering the screen, but she moved my hand and read the message.

"Oh...Ivy. I don't know what to say. I'm sorry."

"No need to apologize. You're not my birth parent." I picked up a pen, wiggled it between two fingers and studied the victims' names on the paper again. What did I expect to find, a misspelling? I couldn't deny that I simply wanted to crawl into a ball and cry my eyes out.

I felt a hand on my shoulder.

"Hey...it's me, Cristina," she said in her most comforting voice. "It's okay to be open with me. I've seen and felt all sorts of crazy shit. You're disappointed, right?"

I swallowed back emotion while searching for some perspective. "I'm sure they just went on with their lives. It's been twenty-eight years. Why would I think they'd hold some type of everlasting bond with someone they never knew? It's unrealistic. I think I need to get out of la-la land and get back to the work in front of us. I have a feeling Megan is going to be asking for an update very soon."

Cristina stood there, her arms crossed against her chest, as I shuffled papers to organize my desk.

"Is there a reason you're looming over me? You're acting like a prison guard."

"This isn't normal, Ivy. You shouldn't be taking this news so nonchalantly." She moved around to the other side of the desk where I could see her.

If she only knew what was churning inside of me. But I knew that sharing everything I was feeling, getting myself all worked up, wouldn't change anything. And what would it bring? Temporary empathy? It would only make me wallow in self-pity. I didn't need that, and I certainly didn't want to drag Cristina into another Ivy drama.

"I'm just a normal girl going through normal, everyday stuff, Cristina." I could feel her staring at me, then she moved back to her laptop.

A few seconds passed. "How's it going with graphing the victims on a map?"

"Making progress. Just a little slow today."

I craned my neck and spotted her mouthing words. It was her dyslexia. She'd admitted months earlier that one of the reasons she never enjoyed school was because of how slow she was to complete her work. It made everything much more difficult to finish, especially in the assigned time.

"Do you need my help?"

"No, I got it."

I realized that something had changed. She hadn't complained about her reading issues since she'd restarted school in the summer. Was there any way she'd been lying about attending school? I knew she'd enrolled initially because of the case we'd taken on. I hadn't seen a report card or actually gone to the school to see her sitting behind a desk. Yet, I had seen her carry around a new backpack. What else would be in there besides books or notebooks?

Who was I kidding? Cristina answered to no one. Her independence, her ability to rely on no one but herself to survive, was inspiring. But her stubbornness to do things her way in her own time was almost legendary. Could she have gotten tired of me hounding her to go back to school? So much so that she decided to put on this little charade…anything to keep me off her back? I decided to give her a little pop quiz.

"I appreciate you diving in to work on this case. But I can take over if you want."

"I'm good."

"You don't have any homework?"

"I usually get it done in class. Most of my teachers are pretty cool."

"How many credits do you have left before you graduate?"

A pause. She was thinking about it, and my suspicion meter edged higher. "Did you hear me?"

"Yeah, just focusing here. You know, I'm trying to get this shit done, like you asked."

"I know. Thank you."

I looked at my laptop screen to see the same message I'd read earlier. Obsessing over it wouldn't do me any good. I clicked the browser shut. Picking up my phone, I considered texting Saul, knowing it might be easier just to communicate the news through words on a screen. If we talked about it in person, I knew I might break down. Might? Hell, I knew for a fact I'd break down. He'd console me, comfort me. Who could ask for anything better, right? But I didn't want to be in the position, again, to garner anyone's sympathy. I just wanted to live my life and do my part to help make this world a better place for kids of all ages. That included the kid of Armand Roussel—Zahera. And the kids who could have been kidnapped. A thought swept through my mind: was there any concern that these apparent computer hackers might someday actually abduct a kid? To at least remind everyone to take them seriously?

"Motherfucking piece of shit."

And I couldn't forget about the kid sitting across from me, cussing like nobody's business.

"Something wrong?"

"Just lost all of my work. No worries."

Another muffled expletive, then she said, "Okay, now we're making headway."

I had to jump on the positive wave. "You were reminding me how many credits you had left to graduate."

"Oh really? I thought you were just hounding me again."

If she'd looked at me, she would have seen me roll my eyes. I persevered. "Seriously, I have a bad memory."

"Could have fooled me."

"You're taking that animation class. That's probably pretty cool."

"Yeah, because it's all about graphics. No words. My dyslexia didn't go into hibernation, although I gotta admit, it's a lot better."

I sat up. "Really? Why do you think?"

"This teacher. She's pretty cool."

"What class?"

"ILA."

Kids used acronyms for everything these days.

"I can tell you're stumped. For you old people, that means English."

"Ah. Thanks for the interpretation." I instantly recalled my senior English teacher, Mrs. Foster. She'd been a positive influence in my life. She had the kindest eyes, yet I could always feel this quiet inner strength from her. I'd never seen that in a woman before. I'd read books about strong, smart women, but she was the first one with whom I'd connected. She gave me confidence in myself, in being open to learning, figuring out who and what I wanted to be. If Mrs. Foster hadn't come along, I doubt I would have had the fortitude to get myself through college. I hadn't touched base with her in years. Didn't we have a class reunion coming up in November?

"If you don't mind me asking, how has your teacher helped with your dyslexia?"

"She's given me some exercises and stuff to help, but more than anything she's just patient with me. Really calm, and…I don't know. Just acts like she believes in me. I know that sounds stupid."

"Far from it. Sounds like a cool teacher I had in my senior year."

She raised her head above her laptop. "Yeah, but did your teacher allow you to listen to audiobooks as an assignment?"

I looked to the corner for a second. "I'm not sure those were invented back in the days of horse-drawn carriages."

"You said it, not me," she said dryly.

"No, really. She's the bomb?"

"First, if you're trying to act young and cool, we don't say stupid phrases like that."

"What's second, smartass?"

"That I'm finally done with the homework you gave me. Want to take a look?"

I walked around to her side of the desk as she angled her screen upward. All I saw was a hand shooting me the middle finger. Cristina smacked the table three times, trying to speak, but she couldn't because she was laughing so hard.

"Very funny, Ms. Tafoya."

"Now you sound like a snooty old teacher," she said through a laughing gasp.

It took her another ten minutes to calm down and create the graph. We analyzed the data for another hour, but weren't able to derive any noticeable pattern.

"We were lost before we even started!" Cristina exclaimed, leaning back in her chair.

"No, we're just not seeing the right data. We need more information. Different information."

My phone buzzed, and I saw a text from Zahera.

"What's up?" Cristina asked.

"Zahera is throwing a celebration party at her condo."

"For what?"

"She's had her practice for four years. All the girls from the office will be there, and we're invited too."

"I'll pass. I'll just hang out here and stare at this information and maybe something will come to me."

"You can bring your computer, set it up in the kitchen or maybe one of the back bedrooms. That'll be good. We can do some multitasking. I need to talk to Stan about getting more data anyway."

"Dude, it's not my kind of deal. Too much giggling and shit. It's for women who went to college."

I shut my laptop and grabbed my purse. "You're going tonight, and you're also going to college."

"Pfft."

"I thought you felt inspired by your ILA teacher? Without even meeting her, I know she'd want you to go to college."

"Maybe. But Mrs. Foster wouldn't force it on me. She'd just let me figure it out on my own, you know?"

I grabbed Miss "You Know" and walked out of the office.

Nineteen

Slack-jawed, I watched two women wearing silk pajamas beat each other with pillows while they juggled glasses of champagne. I was standing next to Cristina just inside the front door of Zahera's high-rise condo. Cristina and I turned to look at each other at the same time. "I have no words," she said.

"It can't all be this bad. Follow me." Bruno Mars music grooved through ceiling speakers as we weaved through bunches of balloons and streamers. Most of the furniture had been moved out, and in its place were massage chairs, as well as stations set up for manicures and pedicures. Moving through the dining room we walked into the kitchen. Zahera and three other ladies sat in lounge chairs, wearing mud masks with cucumbers covering their eyes.

"Seriously?" Cristina giggled.

I elbowed her just as Zahera sat up. "Hey guys. Haven't I been saying we need to have a spa day? Well, I brought the spa to us. Just find an open station and treat yourself."

"Uh, I'm not—"

I stepped on Cristina's foot. "Thanks, Z. We'll take a look around and just get comfortable."

"Sure thing."

"Hey, we have some work stuff that needs some attention. Mind if we set up shop somewhere…if you have some free space?"

"Guest bedroom. I have a desk back there, and it's even quiet. *Mi casa es su casa.*"

I wasn't great at Spanish, but I understood Zahera's basic message. I turned to head back across the condo when I heard someone hollering.

"We turned four today. Woo-hoo!" The lady who worked the front desk at Zahera's practice bumped into my shoulder, sloshing her drink over the side. "Aw, damn. I guess I'll have to go get another Screaming Orgasm."

Some female voice yelled, "That'll be your first, Nancy Klein."

Every girl in the room cracked up. Everyone except Cristina. Nurse Nancy, who had cotton balls between her toes and was walking on her heels, finally noticed Cristina's blank stare. "Can I get you something, honey? A Shirley Temple maybe?"

Cristina shifted her eyes to me. I only had a few seconds before she would say something that might lead to an unnecessary spat. I hooked my arm around hers and pulled her out of the kitchen. "See you gals in a bit."

The second we exited the room, Cristina said, "Damn, that bitch should be thanking you."

"Come on, Cristina. She's just—"

"A cutesy girly-girl."

I was almost stunned that she hadn't come off with a rash of cuss words. "Aw, come on. It's not so bad. I thought it would be much worse."

"Where I come from, it doesn't get much worse."

I escorted Cristina through the throng of ladies, spa personnel, and a couple of bartenders. I saw Kelly, Zahera's office manager, lingering near the large bank of living room windows. She held up her glass, and I gave her a quick wave in return before she continued to converse with two younger girls from the office. From my two-second perspective, she appeared to be forcing an interest in their conversation. But neither seemed to catch on to her disinterest. It was probably a generation-gap thing.

As soon as Cristina and I turned down the main hallway, the noise level dropped in half. The guest bedroom was immaculate as always. So many shades of off-whites and tans, but somehow perfectly blended to soothe your senses. I picked up a waft of lavender as Cristina plopped her computer bag on the desk.

"Don't scratch it." Somehow Zahera, or maybe her interior decorator, had been able to pull off placing an impeccable, cherry wood antique in the middle of a contemporary setting. It worked, and I sure as hell didn't want to damage it.

"Chill," she said, carefully placing her laptop on the desk. "Is that better?"

"Much." I thought back to our conversation at the office and all the old high-school memories that had subsequently flooded my mind on the ride over to Zahera's. "Your English teacher—"

"ILA."

"Yeah, whatever. Mrs. Foster. You're going to die when you hear this, but I'm almost certain she was my senior English teacher."

Cristina slid into a rattan chair, grimacing a bit. "Not likely," she said, logging into her computer.

"Why would you say that? Sounds like she is just as positive and encouraging as she was to me, and that's a great thing. If you don't mind, I might drop by your school and say hello."

She turned to look at me. "First, please don't come to my school...ever."

"Why not?"

"Because everyone will think you're my mom, or older sister, or aunt. And it's just not something I want to deal with."

I wouldn't make that promise. If I wanted to catch up with my old teacher, I would. That lady truly had changed my perspective on what I could do with my life. It had been far too long since I'd seen her, to thank her for how she'd inspired the person I'd become. "You have a second reason?"

"It's not the same woman."

"Why are you so sure?"

"My teacher just got out of college in the last two or three years. I think she's twenty-six or something, which in my book is still old, but not ancient."

A tinge of disappointment washed over me. Then I had a thought. "I wonder if she might be related."

"It's possible, I guess. Mrs. Foster talks about her parents all the time. I think they had a big anniversary recently. Oh, she talks about her brother too. He has autism and all, but they seem like a pretty close family."

I nodded.

"Dammit, Ivy. I didn't mean to bring up family stuff after the rejection note from the adoption website."

I thought I could be direct, but Cristina's form of bluntness could win awards. "I'm cool." I walked to the door. "I'm going to mingle a little, get a drink. Can I bring you something?"

"Food. But give me some time to study this graph I put together. Sometimes if I'm in the zone, I can find crap that even surprises me."

I liked her confidence and told her that I'd bring her a sampler plate in a few minutes.

Twenty

After dropping my purse on the bed, I walked back into the living room. Kelly swooped in just as I felt my phone buzzing in my pocket. "Please take me away from all this inane conversation. They're so young and immature; I'm just not sure I can take it any longer."

She tipped back a flute of champagne and drained the glass. It appeared she could hang with the younger girls. But was she basically saying that I looked to be closer to her age? Surely not, right? "You know I'm the same age as Nancy and the others. Or at least in the same range."

She touched my arm. "Oh dear, I offended you. Believe me, I only wished I still had everything that you've got."

I shrugged. "Uh, thank you." I looked for a bartender, but she squeezed my arm and I turned back to her just as she laid her palm to my face.

"Not a blemish on your buttery skin. Your blue eyes are simply luminescent. And I can tell you work out. Wow, it must be nice to be in your twenties, yet I know that you've lived a hard life. I can feel wisdom oozing from your pores."

Feeling awkward about her praise, I gently removed her hand from my face. "Thanks again," I said, padding away.

I found a bartender and ordered a lemon drop martini for me and a Coke for Cristina. She'd appreciate the jolt of caffeine. As I headed for the long table of food laid out by the entertainment center, I felt my phone buzz. I plucked it from my pocket. A text from Nick.

Sorry about delay, Ivy. Was forced to join long conference calls. I just reached out to my partner, Alex. Turns out she's in Lyon attending meetings on her investigation. She'll call me tomorrow. I'll let u know if and what she can share about Zeke.

A quick glance over my shoulder to ensure the ladies nearby didn't have wandering eyes, then I thumbed a response to Nick.

Thanks for reaching out. If you think it will help our cause for me to speak with Alex, let me know.

From the blinking dots on the screen, I could see he was typing. Then his message popped up.

She's a bit of a spitfire, but thx for the offer. I'll contact u tomorrow. I'm taking Stan out for a late-night walk.

I responded with: *Thx for pushing Stan. He needs a big brother...or cuz right now.*

I heard a "whoop" and then an arm smacked the back of my head. "Oh, Ivy, did I hurt you?"

It was Nancy, who'd fallen to the floor. Two other girls helped her up. She was officially the drunkest person at the party.

"Sorry about the drunk punch to the head." Zahera, with her face now clear of the mud mask, had snuck up from the opposite side. "Hey, is that a text from Stan's cousin, Nick?" She dipped her head closer to my phone. I pulled it to my chest.

"Wait, is he in town?"

"Uh, yeah. Just visiting."

"Are you hiding something from me?" She playfully tried prying my arm away from my chest. "Ivy, what are you doing? We share everything, right?"

"It's nothing, Z. We're just talking about how to get Stan motivated."

Realizing it would only create more suspicion, I released the tension in my arm and read Nick's latest text—the only thing showing on the screen: *It will be good for both of us to jog with Stan. Talk to u tomorrow.*

I could feel my shoulders drop in relief. "Nick's not holding back. He's even got Bev involved. Earlier, I watched him clean out the family fridge of all the bad food."

"I bet that was fun…or gross. Was there anything left when he got done?"

I chuckled. "He was going to give Bev a new list of groceries to pick up, and I'm thinking it's all going to be organic."

Zahera brought a hand to her face. "Tough love from his cousin. This will be great for Stan. Hell, it will be entertaining for us to watch this transformation."

"For him to lose the weight and be able to run in the Dallas marathon by December, it might take a miracle. But we need to support him."

Another "whoop" from behind me, and I turned to see Nancy dancing…with her drink. "Hey Zahera, when are the strippers showing up?" She yelled above the thumping music, suddenly blaring twice as loud.

"Strippers?" I whirled around and asked Zahera. "Remember, we have a seventeen-year-old in the back bedroom."

She rolled her eyes. "Nancy doesn't know when to stop. She was that HR problem I was telling you about. Never knows when to shut her trap." Zahera moved in and took Nancy by the shoulders.

"What?" She hiccupped, then cackled at herself as Zahera guided her to the couch. "I still got plenty left in me. Who's up for a game of charades?"

I tuned her out, but was thankful that something had drawn Zahera's attention away from my text messaging with Nick. The thought of her seeing Nick's original text, especially the last part— *I'll let u know if and what she can share about Zeke*—it made me wince.

I sipped my martini until the glass was mostly empty, then grabbed a plate and loaded it with something from every offering: shrimp cocktail, nachos, even a cucumber sandwich. I found a can of Coke in an ice bucket and said, "Excuse me," about a dozen times on my way to the guest bedroom. I pushed the door open, and Cristina startled from my abrupt entry, putting a hand to her chest.

"You scared the shit out of me." She was on her knees next to a brown satchel and dozens of folded papers.

"What is this?" I motioned at the mess on the floor. "What are you doing?"

All color had left her face. "You won't believe the shit I just read."

"Read? Are those personal letters, Cristina?"

She held one up in the air. "You have to read this letter."

"Why? That's none of your business, or my business."

"Ivy, this is about Zahera's dad."

I put down the food and Coke and locked the door.

Twenty-One

Before I could get two words out, Cristina jabbed her finger into a piece of paper while holding it inches from my face.

"Who wrote it?" I asked.

"Zahera's mom. Did you know her name was Simone?"

"She's French or French Canadian like Armand. This is just wrong, Cristina." But I found myself taking hold of the letter and scanning the handwritten note. "You're acting like this is something scandalous."

"Second to last paragraph from the bottom."

I ran my finger down the page until I found the paragraph and read it to myself: *How on earth do you expect me to respond to this news you sent me through a written note? You didn't even show me the respect of telling me in person.*

I lifted my eyes for a second. "Does she ever share this news she's talking about?"

"Keep reading."

I did just that. *I'm sure you want to know what I'm thinking or feeling as I sit and write you this note. Maybe you are eagerly awaiting my response from your army bunk at Camp Ederle. But perhaps you are outside staring at the majestic hills of Vicenza, Italy, your arm wrapped around the woman who stole you from my heart.*

I stopped, reflexively grabbing at Cristina's arm. "No. This can't be."

"It is. It happens all the time, Ivy. Can't trust men. Well, I think I can trust Leo."

I did a double-take. "You're seeing the Hollywood actor? What's up with you not sharing things with me?"

"We see each other when he comes into town to check on his sister, Nikki. He's cool, and I'm cool with him. Nothing to share."

For now, I couldn't focus on her dating games. With my stomach in knots, I went back to the letter. *If you see splotches on this letter, know it's simply my tears. My heart is broken and I am not sure it will ever mend.*

I glanced up at Cristina, as random thoughts rattled in my mind. But they came at me so fast, it was impossible to make sense of anything.

"What are you thinking? Where do you think Zahera got these letters?" Cristina asked.

I answered her question with one of my own. "Do we know when this was sent?" I flipped the pages, looking for a date.

"Pulled it out of this envelope. It's a little blurred, but I can make out the month and the year. May of 1990."

I looked off as air emptied from my lungs. Cristina was right; this type of stuff happened every day. But for some reason, I'd viewed Armand as someone who would not be tempted by another woman. And I'd made that assessment, even though I'd never met Zahera's mom. Integrity and commitment were at the top of his attribute list, or so I'd convinced myself.

"I feel kind of bad for snooping and all…" Cristina said. "I read a couple of other letters too. The first one was real sweet; Simone was sharing how much she missed her husband and how she dreamed of them being a whole family again."

I closed my eyes for a moment.

"Are you okay? I mean, I guess Zahera knows, right?"

"How did you find these letters?"

"They were in this satchel; one stack had a rubber band around it, and then there was this other stack that was wrapped up in a plastic bag."

I spotted an empty plastic bag under her knee. "Where are the letters?"

Her head seemed to sink into her shoulders. "They're all around us. I picked up the bag and they all fell out. I'd already taken the rubber band off the other stack. I know I shouldn't have done it, Ivy. I'm sorry for snooping. What should we do?"

Flapping the letter in my hand, I said, "I wonder how Zahera came to have these letters. Maybe she got them after her mom died, maybe before?" I shrugged in answer to my own questions. "But there were two different stacks. I'm just wondering if this was in one pile, and maybe some of the other letters, the sweet ones you mentioned, were from the other pile."

"It's possible, I suppose. Or it could be divided by date, or by who sent them."

I put a hand on her knee. "You found letters from Armand?"

"Yeah, a few." She picked up pile of disorganized letters and let them fall through her fingers. "They're somewhere around here."

I heard some giggling outside the door, and I stopped moving. It didn't sound like Zahera, but the last thing we wanted was for her to walk in on us right now. "This is nuts, Cristina," I whispered, then paused another second. The giggling ladies must have walked to the bathroom. "I know you meant no harm, but we are really prying into an area that is none of our business."

I started stuffing the letters back into the bag. Then I stopped. Without the letters being put in the two proper stacks—separated by whatever method, which we did not know—she'd still know that someone riffled through her stuff. I rubbed my temple.

"I've got to stop doing this. I need to tell her the truth."

"Hold up." Cristina's lips moved for a second as she read another letter. Then, as if my words had just registered, she jerked her head up to look at me. "What did you say?"

I'd said more than I should have. Armand had entrusted me with the task of learning more about Zeke. The less Cristina knew, the better, if for no other reason than it seemed the betrayal was less extreme if fewer people knew about it. "It's nothing, I'm just pissed at myself for being interested in this—"

"You're not going to believe this."

"That was your opening line when I walked in here. I'm not falling for it again." I opened the satchel. "Let's just throw all of the letters in here, and then after all the girls leave, we'll both tell Zahera what we did. She might get upset, but it will be out in the open, and we'll all get over it."

"Yeah, yeah, whatever. This…this letter is…" She let it fall out of her hand as if it were on fire.

I snatched it from the floor. "I refuse to read this, Cristina." I pushed it into the bag.

Cristina countered that move, quickly pulling it back out. "This is different, Ivy. Much different. Read it." Her eyes were wide, unblinking.

Without saying a word, I took it from her hand. "Where?"

"Start at the top. It doesn't take long."

I took in a breath, and after three words, I could feel an extra weight on my chest. *I have cheated.*

Twenty-Two

I looked at Cristina, who said, "Keep going. It's… I don't know." She ran her fingers through her hair as I went back to reading the note:

I thought those words would never apply to me. I have thought about you every day that I've been gone, over eleven months, on this tour. Every thought has been filled with love and adoration. I have missed our late-night talks and our early-morning walks. You are the light of my life. You, along with Zahera, fill my heart with goodness and hope.

I realize you may not want to hear this, and you may not even believe it, but I was set up. A man who befriended me at a local bar in Venice, just twenty kilometers away from our base, has betrayed me. I know, you are probably thinking I did the same to you. I did. But he is the reason why. How did this happen? I visited his bar, both with colleagues and by myself several times. We talked about life, sports, and even some world politics. One night he introduced me to a young lady and told me I could have her if I defected to the Soviet Union. I laughed in his face; I knew he was joking.

But he wasn't. He was a Soviet spy. KGB. He drugged my drink, and when I awoke I was without clothes, lying in bed next to this woman. He showed me pictures of us doing things. And he said he would tell everyone, including you and my superiors, unless I defected to the Soviet Union.

I gazed at Cristina, my heart no less than a drum roll against my chest. She shook her head, and I read more of the note.

I am telling you now so that we will not have this hanging over our marriage. My guilt is immense, but to perpetuate the lie would be selfish. I tell you the truth, hoping that you will forgive me.

He went on to say he was sorry a hundred different ways, and I skipped to the last paragraph.

And finally, I want you to know that I would never betray our country. I told that to this man as I punched in his face and ripped up his pictures. I found his Soviet ID card and his name is Anton Kovalchick. I'm only telling you this in case something happens to me. If it does, it was probably fate, for somehow allowing myself to be unfaithful to the woman I love. Please know that you will always hold the dearest place in my heart.

Forever yours,

Armand

Cristina started yapping immediately. I nodded, not really listening as I tried to align my thoughts on what, if anything, all of this meant. Armand had come to me, asking me to look into a possible connection between Zeke and an international drug lord. Do the letters change any of that? Technically not, I told myself.

Armand, like any parent, was worried about the safety and well-being of his child, albeit one who is thirty-two years old and not exactly a slacker. He'd been framed. At least that was his claim. Was this Anton fellow even real? Could Armand have made up the whole story after the fact, to justify his cheating? Guilt could seize control of even the most disciplined mind and guide it to do some strange things.

I pushed out a breath—it felt like the weight on my chest had doubled in size. Why was I still feeling like there was something in those letters that would change my dealings with Armand?

I felt my body shake. I looked down to see Cristina tugging on my arm. "Houston, are you with us?"

"Yes, sorry. I'm just thinking everything through." The last thing I wanted was to bring Cristina into this potentially dangerous mess…well, further into this mess.

"Did you hear what I said?"

"Can you repeat it one more time?"

A loud sigh. "These letters. What do we do? Should we share this with Zahera like you were thinking earlier, or try to cover our tracks?"

More giggles from outside the room.

"Just throw them in the bag for now," I said, suddenly nervous someone might walk in on us.

I got up, walked over, and put my ear to the door. I heard the giggles dissipate and turned to see Cristina stuff the last of the letters into the bag. She didn't appear to be trying to keep them organized. "Seriously?"

"What? I'm nervous someone will walk in."

I rolled my eyes, while my head still spun with this new information.

"By the way, I actually studied the data of the kidnapping victims."

Finally, we had some hope on at least one front. When focused, Cristina was quite sharp. "Cool, what did you figure out?"

"*Nada.*"

"What? I thought you said you figured it out?"

She stood up and took another quick glance at her laptop. "I only said I studied the data. I can't piece together a pattern if I don't have enough information."

"True." My eyes drifted to the detailed crown molding as I thought about our options.

"So, is the data fairy going to leave it under our pillows tonight? I'm stuck if we don't get something more."

"I think we need to do a deep dive on each victim," I said. "Find out where each parent works, ages of each kid, where they go to school or preschool. If possible, we need to try to find out where they shop, whether they're part of the same tennis club or poker group. I know it will be doubly difficult, but knowing health history would be invaluable."

"Why their health history?"

"If it's ultimately about how the hackers got their personal data, maybe they've all been to the same hospital or same doctors' group. Or heck, even the same pharmacy...anything else we can think of. Some of this might be really tough to find, but if we can somehow capture this kind of data, then we can see where the overlaps are between families. Hopefully."

"Okay. I'll start the process. Might take a while to figure all of that out for each of the fourteen families. And in the end, we still may not find what we want. Megan will be all down your throat by tomorrow at the latest."

I could picture it in a nanosecond. "Let's split them up. Can you get started tonight?"

She nodded. "I didn't want to take part in this spa stuff anyway."

"You're right, dammit. I'm sorry for ignoring your desire to participate. Let's get you all dolled up." I reached for her hand, but she quickly backed up a step.

"Can't you tell when I'm serious? I'd rather have my legs broken than hang out with the girly-girl squad."

I realized then that I was reading everything wrong. "Geez, okay. My mind is just a blur right now."

Cristina put her computer in her bag, then hoisted the strap over her shoulder. "I'd rather get to my place and start work on the research. And given what you think is needed, it might require me to make phone calls during the business day. So, I'll need at least through tomorrow, maybe longer. Maybe much longer."

"Thanks for being so diligent, Cristina. Let me know where you are in the morning. Now, let's make a quick appearance, and then we can get out of here."

I opened the door and saw Nancy jump. She'd been eavesdropping.

Twenty-Three

While part of me wanted to rip into her, I stayed nonchalant. "What's going on, Nancy?" Wasn't she shitfaced about fifteen minutes earlier?

She swallowed once, her face and neck completely pink. "Uh, I was just wanting to see the rest of Zahera's place. I like to see how the rich folks live."

Her eyes shifted from me to Cristina.

"Well," I said, extending my arm, "The room is all yours."

She peeked inside and nodded. "I can see from here." I noticed her usual perky, jovial expression had gone away, then I turned back to see the brown satchel just sitting on the floor next to the desk, partially ajar. It was an open invitation for someone to start snooping, just as we had. But at least we cared about Zahera and wouldn't use anything we learned against her or needlessly spread gossip. I walked over and casually picked up the bag. Cristina's eyes watched me, but thankfully she didn't draw attention to what I was doing.

"Zahera is one lucky lady," Nancy said, as we walked past her. The comment had a bite to it, and I couldn't stop myself from turning around.

"Z's worked her tail off to get where she's at. She's a great role model for young girls, for not letting society determine what is or isn't possible. She's unique, but very self-made."

"I don't disagree. But to have this kind of wealth, on top of her good health—she's fortunate, let me put it that way."

The seed of jealousy seemed to have taken root in one of Zahera's employees. I knew to move on. "We need to get out of here, so we're going to go say goodbye. Talk to you later."

Just as we entered the large living area, Kelly approached us. The music was strangely muted, the party less raucous. "Is Zahera back in the kitchen?" I asked, already moving in that direction.

"She left."

I stopped so quickly that Cristina ran into my back.

"Sorry," she said, stumbling to the side.

I twirled around, gazing at Kelly, who'd started picking up cups, plates, and bottles and throwing them in a trash bag. "Where did she go?"

"Off to Toronto," she said with the swat of her hand. "I'll clean up everyone's mess, just like I always do."

Toronto? I expected to hear she'd gone to the grocery store or something. I caught up to Kelly. "She's leaving the country…without telling me?"

The moment the words left my mouth I knew they sounded like I was her mother. Kelly didn't seem to notice or care. In fact, she seemed annoyed.

She shrugged, pressing her lips together. "I had no idea this was going to happen, and it didn't look like she did either. Zeke just swooped in here and said he wanted to take her away on a surprise trip to Canada."

I moved right in front of her to stop her movement. "Zeke?"

"Who else would it be?"

"I don't know. But for him to take her without telling anyone, that's just—"

"He is her fiancé, Ivy." She held my gaze for a second, then went back to picking up trash. "Apparently, her parents lived near Toronto years ago. Anyway, she was on cloud nine. She scooped up her things and left—of course, not before asking me to take charge of cleaning up."

Oxygen flooded my brain as I tried to rationalize what I'd just heard. One day, Armand is asking me to investigate Zeke's ties to an international drug leader. The next day, Zeke is taking Zahera out of the country. Was it just a coincidence?

I remembered that Zeke had recently been in Toronto. Then in Mexico earlier today. And now, no more than a few hours after arriving home from Mexico, he wants to take Zahera to Toronto? And she goes? Without saying goodbye? Just like that?

Strange, strange, strange.

"This is nuts," I said, tugging on my ponytail. "I mean, this borders on being irresponsible."

"Believe me," Kelly said, continuing to load the trash bag with anything that wasn't currently being used. "I know it's inconvenient. I've got to reschedule appointments, find a backup for her, and keep the office staff working efficiently. Everything falls on me. Always does," she said with a loud sigh.

I looked up to find Cristina staring at me. I felt like she was reading my mind. She knew something was up. I pulled my phone from my purse, then spotted Nancy marching through the room, her arms swaying back and forth. She had a sort of frustrated grimace on her face. Maybe she was nothing more than a mean drunk. Or maybe there was something else going on with her.

My eyes on Nancy, I leaned toward Kelly and said, "Sorry about the load Z put on you. But hopefully you'll get some help around the office."

Kelly caught me looking at Nancy. Her voice low, she said, "That girl is on an emotional roller coaster. I can't rely on her to do anything, but Zahera is always wanting to give her another chance."

"Surprises me that Z would hand out so many extra opportunities. I thought she ran a pretty tight ship."

"I just think Nancy has her fooled. The girl might be bipolar. One moment, she's bouncing around like she was just asked out on a date by the Prince of Wales; next, she's seething with anger." She took a breath. "This last time, I don't know how Zahera didn't fire her."

I raised a brow, waiting for more info.

"We found evidence that she'd been trying to sell information about our patients to a pediatric group, giving them the opportunity to put the hard sell on these families."

I felt a sharp prick at the base of my skull. "And you didn't fire her?"

"Believe me, I wanted to. Selling confidential patient data is against the law. I think Zahera was about to fire her, but after she met with Nancy personally, she decided against it."

"Do you know what changed her mind?"

Kelly swatted a hand in front of her face. "She gave her some sob story about her family. On top of that, she said something about how she never actually took money from this pediatric group. She even told Zahera that she'd let her take a look at her bank account statement. It was all nonsense. She lies constantly."

As if the police had just raided the place, ladies stampeded out of the condo the moment Kelly asked for more help. I looked around for Nancy, but she was long gone.

Cristina tugged on my arm until we reached the dining room. "Something's not right, and I want you to tell me what's going on."

"Actually, I just learned something rather disturbing. Not sure it's directly related to our fake-kidnapping investigation, but this gives me an idea of where we should focus our time in trying to find the common thread among the victims."

"That's cool, but there's something else going on, Ivy."

"What?" I tried to blow her off. "Let's help Kelly clean up, and then decide if we're going to call Z or wait until she's back in town. Actually, I forgot to ask Kelly when Z is expected back." I tried to turn around, but Cristina took hold of my wrist.

"First, you tell me why you're so paranoid about Z's safety."

Dammit, she must have overheard me talking to Kelly. I know I'd sounded upset about Zahera taking off with Zeke.

I put on my best performance and gave her a bewildered look. "I think you're watching too many teenage soaps. She's my friend and I was surprised she took off for another country without telling me. Just not like her."

She moved so close to my face I could see a few extra hairs between her eyes. "You know you need to do some plucking, right?"

She gritted her teeth. "No more delays, Ivy. You're hiding something from me, and it's big. You can't get out of this until you tell me what the hell is going on."

She had me cornered. I had to tell her everything.

Twenty-Four

What or who was in Toronto? That question kept me awake a good part of the night. Well, the first half of the night was taken up by Cristina berating me for not telling her about the investigation I'd taken on from Armand. While I tried to convince her it was to protect her from a dangerous drug lord, she scoffed at it, saying, "You're trying to protect me from the *risk* of being hurt. On top of that, this guy is in Ukraine, and he doesn't give two shits about me anyway. We agreed to run this ECHO business together, not just together when you feel like it."

I told her she'd made a valid point, and then I held up two fingers and gave her a make-believe Girl Scout oath, promising I would tell the truth going forward. She rolled her eyes, which was her way of accepting my apology.

It was just after morning rush hour, and I walked into the ECHO office following an early-morning workout with Stan. We'd jogged a solid mile without stopping, and then he did twenty sit-ups. While he wrenched his body with each surge upward, pausing at least a few seconds between the last five sit-ups, he persevered with only minor grumbles and complaints.

Progress.

Nick had every intention of joining us, but was forced to go into the San Antonio FBI office for a confidential meeting. He promised he'd head straight over to my office afterward, and by then, he should have heard back from his partner, Alex.

I grabbed a water and stood in our conference room, staring out the large window. A couple of birds were washing up in the fountain as the eastern sun glistened off their wings. Seemed like a good way for a couple of friends to cool off.

That thought sent me right back to my best friend, Zahera, and what was going on in Toronto. I strolled into the front room and removed my phone from my purse. I saw one brief text from Cristina saying she'd be in the office mid-morning, but no messages or calls from Zahera.

Was that really surprising, Ivy? Zahera's on a romantic getaway with her future husband in a bustling city where she has some roots.

Those roots, of course, were her parents. The same two people about which I'd read intimate details of their lives last night at Zahera's place. Twelve hours had since passed, yet I still felt this odd sense of betrayal from Armand. Of course, he didn't have to share the scandalous information with me. Still, I felt like there was some connection, with no real basis for that feeling. An affair by Armand twenty years ago—big deal. It certainly couldn't have anything to do with Armand's concerns that Zeke was involved in some bad stuff. Two separate subjects: one which was my business, because it was a case, and one which really wasn't. But at the same time, both felt painfully personal.

I wondered if Zahera was aware of her father's infidelity. Had she read the letters?

Armand mentioned that this KGB spy, Anton Kovalchick, was the one who'd set him up in an effort to coerce him to defect to the Soviet Union. More questions pinged my mind. What information or skills did Armand have that made him a target to defect? I think I recalled Zahera saying his area of focus in the army was communications. That seemed vague, at least to me. My investigative instincts wanted to find out what he did for the Army…specifically.

I reminded myself one more time: it shouldn't matter, if the whole scandal had no connection to this drug lord or Zeke.

Another moment later, I found myself wondering how Simone must have felt, half a world away from her husband, reading about how he'd cheated on her. My sympathy turned to anger. Anger at Armand for cheating on his wife, to being even angrier at him for creating this conspiracy story involving the evil empire.

I looked off as I recalled one part of the letter. He said one of the reasons he'd told his wife Anton's name was in case something happened to him. As if he almost expected it would. By rejecting their attempt to lure him into the Soviet web, perhaps he was fearful of a reprisal from the Soviet Union or their intelligence agency, the KGB. Or perhaps he was concerned about how this incident would be viewed within the army ranks. This Anton guy supposedly was going to use these pictures to get Armand to defect. Had he followed through on his threat after Armand had assaulted him? Surely he had other prints, or at least the negatives. Weren't film cameras more popular in the late 1980s?

I had so many questions I wanted to ask Armand. Maybe I would. I wondered if some of the answers might be buried within the trove of letters. We had ended up walking out of the condo last night with the satchel full of letters, not wanting Nancy Klein or anyone else to stumble upon the personal information.

The anxiety of the entire ordeal made my eyes hurt. I could actually feel a tiny throb behind them. I chugged some more water then lifted the phone, willing it to somehow let me know that Zahera was safe and having fun. Of course, I could just send her a text myself. Check in. If something happened to her and I hadn't tried to reach out, I'd never live with myself.

Of course, even if she answered, there's no way to know if she was the one really typing the text.

Dammit, Ivy, you've been watching too many spy movies.

Then again, Zeke did have that James Bond appeal. Given his role as the owner of a private security firm, he could easily have a fascination for living on the edge, putting himself in a position where he came perilously close to felons. Some people skydived for an exhilarating thrill; maybe Zeke got the same high by cavorting with a known drug kingpin.

I'd just talked myself out of and then back into being bat-shit worried about Zahera. I squeezed the frame of my phone until my knuckles turned white.

Metal scraped concrete. The sound was all too familiar—the front door had just opened—but I still sucked in a quick breath and jerked my eyes upward. It was Nick.

"Need to fix that door, don't you?" he said.

"That can wait." I pointed at the empty chair across from my desk. "Let's talk."

Twenty-Five

Nick was dressed in a conservative, if not boring, suit. Shades of gray, from the coat and pants to the drab tie. And a bland, white dress shirt. As he placed his computer bag on the floor, I caught a glimpse of something green under his coat.

"Are those suspenders?" I put down my phone.

"Yep. Got them from—" He suddenly clamped up. "Just a friend."

That was awkward. Could be an ex involved, so I steered clear of that topic. He removed his coat, draped it over the back of the chair, then loosened his tie and unbuttoned the top button on his shirt.

"Comfortable?"

He took a seat and paused. "Almost." He unbuttoned the buttons on his sleeves and rolled them up to his elbows. "Damn, I'll never get used to this Texas heat. Even in September, it's a beast. Glad I'm in decent shape, or I'd feel like, I don't know…"

"Stan?"

He smiled then pushed out a breath, resting his elbows on the edge of my desk as if he were waiting to be served the first course of a meal.

"Now, are you ready?"

He patted his front pocket and saw that it was empty. "What time do you have?"

I looked at my laptop. "Close to eight thirty."

"How close?"

"Six minutes. Why?"

He leaned over and riffled through his computer bag. "Can you get me a water? My tongue feels like it's been baked in an oven."

"No problem." I walked around the desk and back to the breakroom. When I opened the fridge door, he yelled out, "Can you make it two?"

I got three, knowing I'd need another one myself. I walked out and set his two bottles on the desk. Hovering over his phone that was sitting on the desk, he used his two pointer fingers to type something.

"Is that a text to Alex?"

"No, something back in Boston that's unrelated. But I am expecting her at any moment."

I gave him a minute to take his first swig of water.

"What has she shared with you so far?"

His lips went straight. "Uh, not much."

I blew out a disgusted breath.

"Hold on. It's all very reasonable." He paused a moment, looking to the front door, then toward the back of the office. "We're all alone?"

"There might be a couple of mice roaming around. But we're the only humans, yes."

"As I mentioned, Alex is in Lyon." He paused for a second, then said, "Lyon, France, is the headquarters, or the General Secretariat, for INTERPOL." Another pause. "INTERPOL is the—"

"International Police Organization, blah, blah, blah. I get it."

"They also have seven regional offices across the world, as well as an office at the UN in New York and the European Union in Brussels. Their reach is far and wide, with a major focus on crime and corruption."

I nodded. "So if Alex was sent to INTERPOL, this means that Petro Udovenko is drawing major attention around the globe."

"He sure is, with the heaviest focus in Europe. But as I mentioned, he appears to have already found a foothold in the northeast with his heroin. Haven't been able to nail down his trafficking path. Not yet, at least."

"Is that one of the goals for Alex in Lyon...to collaborate on a plan to take down Udovenko's drug cartel?"

"Look, there's only so much we can share, even with Stan's blessing and the fact that I trust you."

I clasped my hands. "So after all this, you're going to go mute on me? You came over here just to tell me that you're going to hide behind the great FBI shield?" I shook my head and looked out the front windows.

"Just give me a second, will ya?"

"I'm listening," I said, my gaze focused outside, where a mom was struggling to convince her son to hop into the car seat. Two red faces, and their mouths were moving nonstop. It looked very intense. I swung around to face Nick. "And?"

"I had to provide that caveat, because we...I mean, Alex, can't provide details of operations in play. We do that and people could get killed."

"But what *can* you tell me?"

His phone buzzed. He looked down.

"Is that your partner?" I knew I sounded impatient. I was.

"Yeah. Alex. She was hoping she could call me, but she's stuck in meetings, so she'll have to text."

"I'm confused. I thought you'd have information about Zeke and his possible ties to Udovenko."

"Early this morning I only had time for a quick conversation with Alex, to let her know what we're asking and why. She's the sole representative from the FBI. I should probably be over there with her. We had no idea she'd be this immersed in...in..."

"Bureaucratic bullshit."

"Thank you."

"I can relate. I'm all too familiar with it through my former job at CPS."

"I've learned to deal with it. Alex, not as much. But she's having meetings with police, military, and intelligence officials from something like nine different countries. Many of them don't speak great English, so there are interpreters involved in every conversation. She said it's tiring as hell, and it just slows down the process of sharing information and collaborating on next steps."

"Well, I'm glad she's over there and I'm sitting in my little San Antonio office."

Nick wasn't paying me any attention. With his phone still flat on the table, he was typing a text, using his two forefingers again. He looked like a toddler pecking away on a keyboard.

I strummed my fingers on the desk.

He tapped the send button, then looked up. "I told Alex that I'm at your office and wondered if she'd been able to find any data tying Zeke Moffett to Petro Udovenko."

"You punched all of that into a text? I thought you typed about ten letters."

He smirked. "I did. She just knows what I'm thinking."

His phone buzzed. I tried to read the response, but it was too small and upside down.

He twisted his lips.

"What now?"

"She said it's complicated."

I sighed. "What the hell does it take to get a straight answer out of this woman?"

"Stan was right."

I could feel my eyebrow arch. "Right about what?"

"That you had a fiery side, especially if it was something you were passionate about. Other than that, you were pretty laid back," he said with a Brooklyn-laced chuckle.

I couldn't help but crack a smile, although it was brief. "Back to Miss Complicated."

He was already typing. Stan with just his one hand could type faster. Without taking my eyes off of Nick and his phone, I cracked the seal on my water and drained about half of it. He was still pecking away, so then I strummed my fingers on the table again.

"There," he said, tapping send.

"And?"

"I asked her if she needed more information or if she needed more time. Give her a minute. She hates texting as much as I do."

"Good gosh," I said, looking out the front window again. "Where's Cristina? Her thumbs move a hundred miles an hour. She could act like our court reporter and bang out these messages in two or three seconds."

Nick shrugged, then took a moment to drink more of his water. His phone buzzed. "Okay, she's saying that she personally found Zeke's name in two different confidential memos."

I could feel my throat tighten. I drank more water. "Is she really saying that Zeke is guilty of being in cahoots with Udovenko and his drug cartel?"

"You're jumping to conclusions. She's still typing."

I could feel my armpits get sticky. I flapped my arms a couple of times, and Nick gave me a strange look. "I feel like I just ate ten jalapenos."

"My face lights up like Rudolph's nose. I'm a wimp when it comes to hot spices. And Antonio gets pissed."

"Who's Antonio?"

He pressed his lips shut, then looked off. His phone buzzed, so I turned my attention to more relevant matters than the fact that I'd just learned Nick was gay.

"What did she say?"

He pushed a breath out through his nose, then tilted the phone upward. "It's a long one."

"Go ahead. I can handle compound sentences."

He gave me the eye, then said, "She said the two memos were between INTERPOL and the Ukrainian security service, something called the SBU. Apparently, so much of the memos were redacted..." He looked up. "That means—"

"I'm not FBI, but I'm not an idiot. They marked out a lot of the words in the memo."

"Right. Anyway, even with an interpreter, it was difficult for Alex to understand the purpose of the memos. And she's yet to get a straight answer on why Zeke's name is in them."

I didn't move. I was stuck in neutral, unsure what my opinion should be.

"I know it's confusing," Nick said.

"Do you think it has to do with the language barrier?"

He lifted one shoulder. "That would be the easy answer, yes. But sometimes, I think officials try to hide behind the language issue just so they don't have to explain how their country does business, which we might find...uh, troubling."

"In what way?"

"Every country is set up differently, even if they are purported to be a democratic society. In some instances, different intelligence or police agencies might not like to share how much power they actually wield."

"It could be embarrassing?"

"It could take the focus off the main point of the investigation. So, some things are left unsaid by all parties. But if there's anyone who will ask the question no one wants to ask, it's Alex. She's got a pair on her that..."

"Is that locker-room talk, Nick?"

"Sorry."

I winked. "No worries. This Alex person sounds pretty cool." A sudden urge to pee came over me. I asked Nick to try to get some idea from Alex on when we could expect an update, and then I ran off to the restroom as he warned me that the wheels of international diplomacy rarely moved at a quick pace.

Twenty-Six

During my few moments alone, I further considered what we'd just learned. And a growing unease washed over me. As I walked back to the front of the office, I said from a distance, "Thing is, Nick, we've learned that the possibility of a connection between Zeke and Udovenko is—" I broke off when I saw Cristina next to him with a phone in her hands, which wasn't surprising really, except that it was Nick's phone. Her thumbs moved at breakneck speed.

Nick looked up. "She just walked in and saw me struggling, then asked if she could help. At this point, why not?"

I patted Cristina on the shoulder as I made my way around my desk.

"You were saying?" Nick said, then chugged more water.

I glanced at Cristina and then back to Nick. "I'm surprised you're letting her on your phone. But I guess she told you that she's now in the loop."

"*She* is standing right here," Cristina said, her eyes still on the tiny phone screen as she typed away. "Just because I'm typing doesn't mean I can't hear."

"Teenagers. They take multitasking to a completely different level," I said.

She finished, then set his phone on the table with a thud.

"Careful," I said. "It's not a brick."

"Feels like one." She set her backpack against my desk, glanced at Nick. "You might want to think about an upgrade, dude."

Dude. Nice.

He splayed his arms. "It's government issued. What can I do?"

"So, back to the matter at hand," I said, resting my elbows on my desk. "As I was saying, Nick… Oh, Cristina, to catch you up, Alex, Nick's partner, who is working with INTERPOL in France found—"

"I know. Two redacted memos connecting Zeke's name with that Russian drug lord, Petro Udo-whatever."

I stared at her for a moment, then continued. "Okayyy. As I was saying, we can't ignore the one piece of evidence that is now clear: Zeke and Udovenko are connected. Armand's inside guy was right."

"You going to call Armand and tell him?" Cristina asked.

I pressed my lips together. "Not yet. We don't know *how* Zeke is connected. In his line of work, he could be working some other angle, trying to find ties to Udovenko himself. But I don't want to wait long to tell Armand." I raised my phone and looked at Cristina. "I'm really struggling with not reaching out to Zahera. She could think I was prying, and maybe even get suspicious of what we're doing. Then she might even relay everything to Zeke. And if he *is* involved in something bad, that might force his hand to…" I couldn't finish the sentence.

"Are you suggesting he'd hurt Zahera?" Cristina said, two hands on the desk.

"I can't imagine it, no. He worships that girl. But it's hard for me to completely trust anyone with the people I care about. For now, I think we need to get more information before we reach out to Z."

She lifted her mane of hair and fanned her neck. "Damn, we've got so much shit to tell Z. I mean, even if Zeke's in the clear, she's going to lose it on us once we have to fess up and let her know what we've been doing."

"I know, I know." I put my head on the desk for a second. "Is there more to this story that I'm not aware of?" Nick shifted his sights from Cristina to me.

"It's, uh, well…" Cristina spread her arms.

I pressed my fingers against the bridge of my nose. "We accidentally snooped while we were at Zahera's yesterday evening."

"Hmmm." He tapped his hairless chin. "*Accidentally snooped.* I recall an investigation from years ago where we had this whistleblower who worked for one of the big New York hedge funds. He said something similar. It actually paid off—for him and for us—and we convicted three executives of insider trading. What did the two of you learn?"

I let my arms drop to the table, but said nothing.

"Look, I'm not Zahera's father. I work for the FBI. If you think it's pertinent to our investigation, we need to know. The friendship stuff will work out, believe me." He flipped his fingers, a sign for me to give up the information. I wasn't used to being pushed—I was more comfortable in his role.

"It's…" Cristina started to say.

"Complicated." I smirked.

A single nod. "Sounds like something Alex would say. Okay, I get it."

"I would ask you to keep this to yourself, but I guess that's the business you're in."

Now he smirked, but refrained from speaking. He was waiting on me. I finally unloaded everything we learned from the private correspondence between Zahera's parents, including my uncertainty as to whether to believe what we'd read in the letters.

When I finished, he was sitting back, his arms folded, his beady eyes staring at the blank wall over my shoulder.

"What are you thinking?" I asked.

He tapped his chin.

"He's shocked, just like we were last night," Cristina said.

I ignored her comment. "Nick?"

He finally sat up, laid both hands on the desk. "This changes things."

"How?" Cristina moved over to my side of the table.

"We're talking about an allegiance to our country. This has national security implications."

"Yeah, but we know, or at least we think he beat the crap out of that Soviet spy," Cristina said, apparently not seeing the greater picture.

I jumped in. "You're wondering if he might have turned over confidential information to the Soviets without telling about it in the letters."

"Exactly. And if so," Nick said, "what type of intel did he give up? Or worse, did it lead to Americans or our allies getting killed? This could blow up to be something that is huge." He paused, took in a breath, and then lowered his volume. "For now, let me work my side and figure out how to proceed."

"We need information fast, Nick. I care about what happened in the past, but I'm a lot more concerned about the present."

"I hear ya."

Twenty-Seven

Gripping the metal cage that separated him from four grizzly bears in the middle of the Toronto Zoo, Zeke watched the alpha of the group stand on its hind legs and let out a roar that he could feel in his chest.

"Mommy, Mommy, the bear's going to eat us up."

He turned to see a toddler barreling into the legs of his mother. She scooped him up, and he buried his head in the nape of her neck. The bond of a mother and child, a nearly unbreakable connection.

Just last year, he'd spent countless days spoon-feeding his own father, Harold, after he'd suffered a massive stroke. Day and night, Zeke stayed by his father's side, shirking his duties both professional and personal to take care of the man who'd raised him and his little sister with an iron fist and ostensibly on his own—his mother had run off with another man when Zeke was just four years old.

Discipline, and the highest form of it, was mandatory in the Moffett house, a symmetrical one-story just outside of Vancouver, with a view of the North Shore Mountains from their backyard. On countless occasions, his father, nicknamed Dirty Harry by his comrades in the Canadian Army, had used the enormity of the mountains to convey analogous messages of perseverance, overcoming adversity, and all sorts of life's lessons. Usually, it was quickly followed by a mandatory jog up and down the surrounding hills while wearing a twenty-pound backpack.

Zeke had always said boot camp was just like a normal day in the Moffett house—when he was only twelve years old.

He cracked a smile, thinking about how many times he'd silently cussed out Dirty Harry. His dad's tough-love approach had helped shape the man he'd become, something he didn't begin to recognize until later in his teens. Giving up, to him, was never an option. And while he'd learned to exercise caution in the face of danger, his well-developed skills of negotiation had proven quite useful in his current line of work—don't offer any deal you can't walk away from, and never let them sense desperation. In his business, one slip-up could impact his health in a very permanent manner.

He checked his digital watch and casually rotated his body, searching through the maze of humanity, both young and old, for a man with a slight limp. The man may or may not be using a cane, from what he'd been told, although he'd done his own research to confirm the same. The man was in his sixties, but his physique was as powerful as his aura—again, he'd found that information through his own channels.

The sun had just dipped below the trees surrounding the bear cage and temperatures had fallen into the fifties. He shifted his arms and raised the collar on his sport coat, giving him the opportunity to feel the weight of his Glock against the inside of his arm. The last thing he wanted to do was use the firearm in a crowded public place, but it did give him an extra sense of security. He couldn't help that feeling, even if it was misguided. The Glock, along with his quick instinctive responses, had saved his ass on more than one occasion. Lives had been lost, but not his, and not anyone he cared about either. Most times, in fact, it had made the world a better place—that much he couldn't deny.

"Brown bear, brown bear, what do you see?"

A cluster of people cleared out of the way, and he saw a girl with curly hair and two missing front teeth standing next to the cage, her hands at her waist. He knew she was quoting the lines of a popular children's book—one he'd read dozens, if not hundreds of times.

"Mommy, how come the brown bear isn't answering me?"

He followed her gaze to the same motherly woman from earlier. She was a bit harried. An open purse swung from a long strap cinched in the crook of her elbow while she tried to corral her son, who was now bucking like a wild horse. The boy arched his back and lunged to the side—for a second Zeke thought the mother wouldn't be quick enough to recover. But just as she grabbed the boy's shirt and regained control, the boy yanked her scarf off her neck. Somehow, like all task-juggling parents, she was still able to respond to her daughter. "I'm not sure, Olivia. Maybe you should ask again and see if he's in a talking mood."

The little girl turned and put her nose up to the cage, uttering the same phrase. Zeke brought a hand to his mouth, covering his smile.

"You must have kids."

The woman had noticed his gaze.

"I'm sorry. I didn't mean to interrupt your family moment." He pulled out his phone, looking for a quick distraction.

"Are you not a father?"

She'd moved closer, so close that the little boy was waving her orange scarf in his face. He kept his focus on the boy and playfully plucked the scarf out of the boy's hand, stuffing it into the palm of his own, then closing his fist.

"Where did the scarf go?" Zeke asked him.

The little boy's eyes got wide. He hesitated for a second, then pointed at Zeke's fist. "That one."

"Good guess," the mom said.

Zeke ran his opposite hand over his curled up fist as if he were casting a spell, and then he moved it off to the side. "Are you sure?"

"Yep," the boy said, biting down on his lower lip.

Zeke popped open his hand. It was empty.

"What?" the boy exclaimed. He jerked his head to the right to look at his mom, then back to the man who'd pulled the most amazing trick in the history of mankind. "Where did it go?"

Zeke moved his opposite fist up next to the boy's ear. "Look what I just found behind your ear." He brought his hand around and opened it to show the orange scarf. The boy's jaw dropped open. "You're a magician. Wow!"

Everyone laughed, and then the mother said, "Are you a professional?"

"Ha. I have more than a few tricks up my sleeve." He began to slowly inch up his coat sleeve.

"Mom, I gotta pee." The little girl tugged at her mom's arm.

"Okay, okay." She held her gaze on Zeke as if she had more questions.

"Mom. I gotta pee bad. Real bad."

"Gotta run," the mom said. "Say thank you to the nice man."

"Thank you," the kids said in unison as the family scampered into the crowd of people in search of a restroom.

The cycle of life. It never ceased to amaze him. He'd cared for his father up until the very end, when the once-resilient man had shriveled into a ninety-pound skeleton. If he hadn't been there for every step of his father's demise, he would have never believed it. He had grown accustomed to it, though: the irreversible process of death.

Painful memories of his father's last days quickly flipped to the opposite end of life's spectrum—his two little rugrats. Images flashed across his mind, happy times filled with Saturday morning pillow fights, soccer games played on a muddy pitch, and countless times reading *Brown Bear, Brown Bear* while rocking in the creaky chair in his kids' bedrooms.

In his son's room he could recall the glow of green planets affixed to the ceiling as he rocked his son while feeding him his bottle at two in the morning. It was really quite surreal. Even with so little sleep, he had treasured those moments to the end. It was a ritual he could never get enough of.

A tinge of emotion crept up to the back of his throat, and with that, a flurry of questions swept through his mind, most of which started with the word *why*.

In Zeke's peripheral vision, something caught his attention. Was that man limping? Zeke narrowed his eyes as he gazed through a sea of people. As the man came into full focus, Zeke quickly realized it was a false alarm. This man was under thirty years of age with a head full of dark curls. He was hopping on one foot while entertaining a little boy.

Zeke turned back to the bear display and immediately sensed his personal space being invaded.

Twenty-Eight

"Good evening, Zeke. Just keep looking at the bears."

The man to his left had an accent, but his English was much better than Zeke had expected. Zeke kept facing forward, but saw the man's hand reaching out to the cage. His arms were oddly short. A dark patch of hair, which looked like burrowing beetles, covered the top of his hand.

"Are you Petro?" Zeke's head still faced a bear who had grabbed a piece of fish with its massive paws. Between his extended side vision and the trajectory of the man's voice, he could determine the man was no more than five-six.

"He couldn't make it. I'm his proxy."

That confirmed what he'd been thinking. Now he turned his thoughts to why this man had shown up instead of Petro Udovenko. Had they decided to dispense of Zeke? Would he soon feel a searing pain in his side as the man pumped him full of lead? At this point, Zeke's patience was thin, and he decided to take the risk. He slowly spun toward the man, taking in a full view, and then continued until his back was against the bear cage.

"Be careful, Zeke. For a moment there, I thought you were going to attack me." The man had a bald spot on top of his head, a surprising contrast to his gorilla hand.

"Come on, man. I don't even know your name. Why would I harm you anyway? I thought we—at least Petro and I—were to do business together. That's not how business associates treat each other."

"My name is Sergey. I am his proxy. I speak for him."

"So, Sergey, why are we meeting at the Toronto Zoo? After all, Petro called this urgent meeting, saying only I could help him meet his goals."

"Your reputation, your experience tells us you can provide transportation and logistical support for special items that have high market value."

He nodded. "I see you've been checking up on me. That is all well and good. At least we don't need to bicker on price."

"Price?"

"My price to help you set up transportation and logistical support. If you've done your homework, then you know how I price my services. Fixed fee up front, then ten percent of the haul payable on the first Monday of each month into a new account, the details of which I send you the night prior."

Sergey lifted his chin. "It is good to do business with a man who has structure. Too many unstable people in our business."

"Indeed." He took another quick glance at Sergey and wondered what special skill he offered Udovenko. Sergey was built like a fireplug, but perhaps it was the fact that he would do anything Petro asked. And from what he'd learned, that could extend into acts that many would consider quite inhumane.

"I want to review your recommendations for entry and exit points for the United States," Sergey said.

No mincing words here, Zeke thought. He had been worried that this would be some pointless encounter, but Sergey's straightforwardness either said something about his personality or the directions given to him by Udovenko. Most likely both.

"That is well and good, but first we must settle on the fixed fee. My offer is seven digits, American currency."

"One million dollars up front?" Sergey asked, although he didn't sound shocked.

"I never told you the first number."

Sergey offered no immediate response, but instead reached into his pants pocket. Zeke quickly slid his hand inside of his coat until his fingertips touched the dimpled grip of his Glock.

Sergey pulled out a bag of peanuts, threw a bunch in his mouth. "Three then?" He chomped on the peanuts.

Zeke moved his hand to his opposite pocket and removed a pair of leather gloves. "Given the risk and the fact that I don't know what I'll be transporting, I'm more inclined for the first number to be five."

Sergey tossed more nuts into his mouth. "I guess that means we've settled on four." He tilted his head toward Zeke, who gave him a single nod.

That had to be the easiest four million he'd ever negotiated, although he knew very well that a simple verbal acknowledgment had a tendency to be altered even twenty-four hours later. But given what he faced in the coming days, he needed that money.

Turning around to face the bears again, he pulled a piece of paper from his pocket and handed it to Sergey. "We can discuss routes and products once I get a down payment on the four million. Five hundred thousand to this account."

Sergey stared at the paper, then reluctantly took it from Zeke. "I don't have a bank account in Toronto. I live in Boston," Sergey said.

"But you can get on the phone and talk to someone who can transfer the money."

Sergey picked peanuts from his teeth. "You have balls."

"So I've been told. But I'm good at what I do. The market says this is my worth. And you know that, which is why you're here."

Sergey took out his phone, tapped his screen three times, then shuffled three steps to his left and spoke in his native Russian. From what Zeke understood, Sergey didn't have to convince anyone to do what Zeke had asked. Sergey gave basic instructions, then said he'd wait until the transaction was completed.

"Hold on," Sergey said, over his shoulder.

A moment later, Sergey stepped back to him. "It is done. Now, your plan."

"I need to know the product we will be transporting."

Sergey's eyes scanned the area for a moment, then he looked back to the bears. "Generally, the size of a cooler. And it needs to be temperature controlled."

"How many of these coolers?"

"It won't be the same every time. Maybe two, sometimes as many as ten. Most importantly, we might only have twelve hours advance notice."

The list of possible smuggled items had just narrowed quite a bit. Zeke could guess, but that would do him no good. He would find out before he left the zoo.

He explained to Sergey the two preferred routes, one up through Seattle and over to Vancouver, using a private mail courier service that delivered packages to corporations on both sides of the border. The second path, one far less known, involved taking small, two-lane roads through the countryside south of Montreal, connecting into Jay, a small, unassuming town in New Hampshire. And the delivery method was ideal—the back of food delivery trucks where products were temperature controlled.

"That route might be our best option," Sergey said, digging his sausage-sized fingers into the peanut bag. "Now, we might have a need to take or receive the product outside the continent."

"Perhaps eastern Europe?"

He nodded. Zeke and the man both knew that would eventually be communicated as a requirement. The fact that Sergey had so quickly gone there again made Zeke take notice. "I've got that covered. A small private airport near Montreal, and on the US side, my drivers can make it down to Boston. Too many eyes on anything in the New York City area. Around Boston, there are a couple of small, indiscriminate ports we can utilize and travel by a small boat, or we can access a small air strip south of the city."

"Putting it in a boat would be much slower, but—"

"Would be virtually impossible to stop. Now, if a small boat could meet up with a much faster boat out in international waters, then that would eliminate the need to use planes. Planes always attract more attention on both sides of the pond, depending on the product being shipped in or out of the country."

"Impressive," Sergey nodded. "You appear to have thought this through quite a bit."

"This isn't my first rodeo."

"Spoken like a true Texan." Sergey showed his first grin, and it was enough to turn Zeke's stomach. Between bits and chunks of peanuts, he could see blackened and chipped teeth. Dental visits were apparently not a priority for Sergey.

"I've spent some time there," Zeke said.

"Considerable time, from what we can see."

Udovenko's proxy or someone from the international organization had been keeping tabs on Zeke, which didn't surprise him entirely. But there were aspects of his life that he didn't want revealed. He'd gone to great lengths to keep those parts hidden. But he knew more than anyone that secrets could only be kept for so long, especially when others were involved. He tried to ignore the pang of unease deep in his gut.

Sergey turned back to the bears, who were now rolling in the muddy water. "Dual citizenship has its benefits, does it not?"

Where was Sergey going with this question? How closely had he been followed in the last twenty-four hours? Was it possible he knew about Zahera? Deflection was usually the most effective tool in situations as these, but he couldn't walk out of the zoo without knowing if Zahera was on their radar. People like Udovenko were always looking for ways to enforce loyalty, and typically they sought the most personal connection and then would exploit that emotional tie. It was part of the playbook for people like Udovenko.

Ideally, Zeke knew it was best to live a life void of any connections to loved ones. To break all ties and not look back. But even with knowledge of how the criminal element operated, his heart seemed to function independently of his best judgment. And there wasn't a day that passed that his decisions didn't scare the shit out of him. The safety of those who owned a piece of his heart—their happiness—was always at the top of his mind, even above his insatiable thirst for walking this dangerous tightrope, where one misstep could alter his life, or even many lives. Despite his strict upbringing and being forced to look at things in a black-and-white manner, he knew his life was a contradiction—the opposite of what he'd advise anyone else to do in this line of work. Guilt was a sidekick that he knew all too well.

This operation, however, would be his last rodeo. He'd made that decision months ago when he'd first made contact with the Ukrainian cartel leader. It had been his main justification for sidling up to such a detestable person. The final play to set up the next chapter of his life. One which would finally allow him to not have to constantly look over his shoulder, wondering if the cordial gentleman on the other side of the ticket counter was secretly taking his picture or if a sawed-off shotgun was pointed at him, ready to fire.

"Dual citizenship allows me to cross the US-Canadian borders almost at will. Serving my clients—many of whom appreciate my discretion and low profile—is my number one priority. I've been known to use what I call field props to help create a persona for how I'm perceived in both countries. I think it's been very effective."

"I would agree. You know how to manipulate the system and all the people who get near you. Even if they have the look of an international model." Sergey arched an eyebrow, a slight smirk at the corners of his lips.

Zeke felt the air leave his lungs. Sergey was describing the exotic look of Zahera. The woman could take the breath away from a blind person. She had done the same to him on countless occasions, when he least expected to feel that jolt of primitive attraction. He saw irony in his current location, the zoo. The lust generated between him and Zahera had often resembled two wild, uncontrollable animals. It, like far too many things in his life, brought about much internal conflict. But all that aside, he couldn't allow Zahera to be sucked into this vortex of danger.

Face it, Zeke, it's already happened. Sergey, in his own way, has identified Zahera as an important person in your life.

The next step would be Sergey making a direct threat. What Zeke called an if/then statement. *If* Udovenko or even Sergey sensed even the slightest hint of betrayal—which could be anything really—*then* something bad would happen to someone close to Zeke. And if that person was deemed to be Zahera, then...

"I told you already, I incorporate many unsuspecting individuals to aid me in servicing my clients. They are—"

"From what I've seen, she's someone I'd like to service." Sergey chuckled so hard that remnants of peanuts flew out of his mouth.

An icy-hot patch formed on the back of Zeke's neck, but he somehow managed a matching chuckle. "Recently, I've become friendly with a former Swedish Miss Universe contestant. She might very well be my next accompanying date."

He'd purposely told a lie. Anything to divert the focus away from Zahera, while also introducing doubt in Sergey's mind—

doubt that he knew as much as he thought he did about Zeke's personal life.

"Is she also the kind that you'd marry?" Sergey's stare was blank now. It was as if he were the big brown bear asserting his alpha position, almost daring Zeke to play dumb or to counter his question with some type of weak denial.

Now wasn't the time to cower. Nor could Zeke afford to be belligerent. He had to strike a balance.

"Do you like fine wine, Sergey?"

Sergey blinked, then looked away for a split second. The question had thrown him off.

"Through all of my world travels, I have had the pleasure of drinking some amazing wines, from France to Argentina, Australia to California. I could, right here and now, recite to you the top ten wines that have passed my lips."

He moved his gloves to his opposite hand, purposely nudging his arm against his coat. The weight of his Glock made the coat sway ever so slightly.

Sergey's eyes shifted. He'd seen the weight in his pocket. He knew it was a gun. He held Zeke's gaze, not blinking, not even moving.

"I love women more than wine, I know," he said, popping Sergey on the shoulder, "but I'm probably not alone in that. After all, weren't women put on this earth to enrich the lives of men?"

"Indeed," Sergey said, his voice flat. "But many are too stubborn to realize their place. And the number is growing every day."

Sergey had answered his question. This was moving in a direction that Zeke could live with. "The only difference here is that while my taste in women is....eclectic, they do require a certain amount of coddling if we have any intention of—"

"Getting our way."

"I wasn't going to use that exact term, but yes, getting our way. As such, I have had the need to appear to make obligations. Women tend to want to repay the favor tenfold, and in many different forms. I feel it's part of the process, part of doing business in our current environment."

Sergey's eyes narrowed, and then a smile cracked his lips. "You are a lucky man, Zeke." He popped Zeke on the arm.

"I will talk to Petro and get back to you. Expect to hear from me in less than twenty-four hours."

Zeke took the first step away, then quickly flipped around. "You never told me the product being shipped."

"Body parts from children."

Sergey hesitated, perhaps wondering if Zeke would instantly back out of his commitment. The thought turned Zeke's stomach, but it had confirmed his suspicion. He slipped on his gloves.

Sergey continued. "There is a huge demand for them, especially if we can narrow our transport time. That will be one of our goals. We do that, and the profit margin could make our heroin business look like a lemonade stand."

Zeke nodded and walked off, quickly blending into the crowd. His phone buzzed. He pulled it from his pocket to see a text from Zahera, asking when he'd be able to break away from his meeting.

Sitting high atop the CN Tower waiting on my fiancé. Join me soon for a drink?

He didn't break stride. In fact, he moved even quicker as he made his way out of the park. He needed to keep Zahera safe, both now and in the future. But first things first. He couldn't resist the tugs at his heart. He'd have to stop by home and visit his two beautiful kids and wife. And to lay down a plan to ensure his family would forever be out of harm's way.

Twenty-Nine

Cristina and I had been working the phones, searching every foxhole on the Internet and brainstorming during the lulls. We'd been going at it for about ten hours. There were enough empty cracker wrappers, half-filled cups of coffee, and opened Coke cans spread across my desk to prove as much. And while we still had more of a theory on the connection between the victims of the fake kidnappings—what amounted to parental terrorism with a side of extortion—rather than cold, hard facts, our intense focus had paid at least some dividends.

Nancy Klein, the moody nurse at Zahera's office, had been caught trying to sell patient data—Kelly had given up that information earlier. While I eagerly looked forward to quizzing Zahera further on why she'd kept her on staff, it had opened a mental window for me: all of the victim families used the same pediatric facility. Extracting data from a medical facility's computer system was probably easy pickings for a seasoned hacker. The SAPD's running assumption had long been that this fake-kidnapping crime spree was nothing more than a group of hackers looking to make fast cash. Whether they worked out of a fraternity house basement in Lincoln, Nebraska, or a shack in Mumbai, India, was anyone's guess at the moment.

Realizing our theories needed multiple pillars of evidence to form even a modest foundation of a case, I put in two phone calls to Kelly to try to extract the name of the facility that had tried to buy the patient data from Nancy. In the first two conversations, she'd said that as much as she didn't trust Nancy, she didn't want to propagate the tension in the office. While I felt uncomfortable sharing the exact nature of our investigation or our theory, I did tell her that the families who had been victims had been torn apart, forced to give up their life's savings. At the end of my second call, I finished it by saying, "Who's to say the next victim might be a close friend, or maybe your sister?" She'd told me she had a sister with three adorable children, all under the age of ten.

Apparently, her conscience could only suffer so much. She finally turned over the name of the place to which Nancy was selling patient information: Stonebrook Pediatric Group. That was our first building block. The second one came a couple of hours later—Cristina found a nurse working at Stonebrook Pediatric Group with the last name of Klein. We stared at each other, shocked at the finding, then debated what it could mean. We volleyed questions and theories back and forth. At one point, Cristina suggested that Klein was a rather common name; the fact that a Nurse Klein worked at each office could just be a coincidence.

That supposition didn't last long. I found a picture of a pediatric nurse, Lisa Klein, on the Stonebrook website. She looked just like Nancy with her toothy smile, her full cheeks, and her straw-colored hair. From there, I put in a call to Stonebrook Pediatric Group, saying a friend had recommended them, offering high praise for one nurse in particular, Lisa Klein. The receptionist said Nurse Klein was off for the day, but she'd be happy to set up my first appointment for my seven-year-old daughter named Kaira on the next day Nurse Klein would be working. It was, of course, a complete fabrication. But I'd already accomplished my goal of ensuring that Lisa Klein was still employed at Stonebrook Pediatric Group. After I hung up the call, more questions came to mind: if Lisa Klein was involved, was she the sole connection point into the hacking group? Or could the level of corruption and maleficence go higher in the medical organization? Maybe she was the sole intermediary with her sister. Were the sisters partnering with a group of hackers? Or was there another arm to this conspiracy we'd yet to uncover?

Then an entirely separate question came to mind: was our ever-expanding theory actually more a product of our imagination? Had our hopes and desires fabricated a false trail of evidence? For now, we stayed true to course—the connection between the Klein nurses and the fact that Nancy had been caught selling patient data being our foundation for moving in this direction. While I had to feel that some progress had been made, we'd quickly become quite frustrated that we hadn't been able to find that one piece of evidence that made it all come together. But unless we could find someone to come forward and expose the entirety of the crime, the only place to focus, for now, was on the data—finding out who each kid's pediatrician was.

Part of me wanted to reach out to Stan with what we had, but I felt like we needed that next big find before I made the call. Maybe the SAPD would then decide to bring in one or both of the Kleins. Boy, how I'd love to conduct that interrogation.

Cristina and I had been pouring over the victim data and not getting anywhere. At a few minutes before five, the frustration finally punched a hole into the pragmatic side of my brain—I had to go straight to the source. I knew Kelly probably wouldn't answer me, and Zahera was essentially off limits for some period of time. Given Megan's off-the-wall behavior and her seemingly constant inebriated state, I wasn't sure I could trust much of what she said. On top of that, I wanted an answer at that moment without waiting for hours or days for a return call. And I was almost certain that my hunch would pay off.

I called up Zahera's office, spoke to a nurse not named Nancy, and was able to disguise my identity as an ER doctor to ask questions about the birth of Annie Espinoza, saying it pertained to the issues she was facing in the ER facility.

We didn't get past the first question. The office had no records of Annie Espinoza being born through Zahera's practice. I wasn't a woman of a thousand voices, so I couldn't use that trick on all of the remaining kids. I'd used my one and only ace card. I'd been thinking that the trail of evidence connecting the families could have originated right in Zahera's office through all of the kids she'd helped bring into this world. I was shot down on victim number one—our client.

Undeterred, I put in a call to Megan, and as I'd expected, it rolled straight to voicemail. She could probably help, but it might take a day to find her, maybe more. I wasn't confident.

For the moment, we were stuck. I felt deflated.

Pushing back from my desk, I rose and stretched my arms toward the ceiling. I could see the intermittent flash of yellow splashing across the white tile—the result of a faulty street light. I glanced over at Cristina, who was intently focused on her laptop screen—as she had been for the last two hours without a break. If someone were to walk in, they'd never suspect that she suffered from dyslexia. But thanks to her ILA teacher, she had figured out ways to reduce its impact on her life, without muting her desire to learn. I still wanted to drop by and visit her teacher, even if she might not be the same woman who'd taught me a decade earlier.

"You want to call it a night?" I asked.

Cristina immediately shut her laptop and rubbed her eyes. "I needed you to tell me to stop. Thanks."

"Sure. No problem. We'll jump on it tomorrow morning. Maybe by then we'll hear from Zahera," I said, walking to the door, looking up and down the street.

"Don't count on it. She and Zeke are like hormonal teenagers. They can't keep their hands off each other."

"Says the teenager who's dating a Hollywood star." I glanced over my shoulder to see her shit-eating grin.

"Leo's not a teenager. And I wouldn't really call it dating."

"What would you call it?" I braced myself for a more vulgar description.

"Good friends who occasionally mug down."

"Ah, friends with benefits."

"We don't go that far. I think he's cool with hanging out with someone who's not trying to get something from him. Know what I mean?"

It was odd to think of Cristina in a mature relationship...or any relationship at all. She was like my little sister. Since she met Leo, though, she'd decided to go back to school and get her diploma, so it was nice to see her motivated by something other than a spontaneous adrenaline rush. "I'm glad you and Leo are happy." Of course, I worried that she wasn't the only one who was making him happy; but then again, I worried too much.

I moved the conversation to our investigation of the fake kidnappers. "Tomorrow morning, maybe we can figure out a way to reach out directly to each family, try to get the name of the pediatrician they use. We'd have to think of a convincing story. People are very protective with anything to do with their kids."

"You know me, I like the direct approach," she said. "Oh geez, Ivy, look." She was pointing at something outside.

"What?" I raced to the window and saw a motorcycle cruising down the street. No big deal there. Then I spotted a pair of legs splayed across the concrete. I quickly opened the door to see

Megan Espinoza sitting against the wall, barely able to hold her head up, paper sack in her hand.

The wall of booze hit me immediately as I leaned down. "Megan, what's going on?" "Fucking Carlos, that's what's going on."

Thirty

She slowly began to tip over, and I grabbed her arm.

Cristina hopped to Megan's other side to keep her upright.

"Let's get her inside." Against Megan's wishes—she'd started out by cursing Carlos, but Cristina and I were soon added to the mix—we somehow dragged her into the office and sat her in Cristina's chair.

"You're not going to puke or anything, are you?" Cristina asked.

"Already did." Megan held up the sack that contained a bottle of something clear. I was guessing it was tequila, judging by the invisible pungent cloud that surrounded her. "I'm going for round two."

Cristina plucked the sack from her hand and tossed it in the trash.

"Hey, that's mine. You can't steal from me. I'm basically your boss. Give it back."

"Fire me, but you don't need any booze," Cristina said.

Slouched in the chair, Megan brought a hand to her face. Her jaw began to quiver. "I'm…I'm not sure I can go on much longer."

I crouched to my knees and touched her arm. "Megan, why are you drinking again? Is Annie okay?"

She rolled her eyes shut for a second, releasing a shaky breath.

"Megan, things can't be that bad. You have your daughter. She's safe, right? Everything else you can work out."

She let her arm drop to the side of her chair, her gaze a blank stare. "My marriage with Carlos has basically disintegrated."

"I'm so sorry, Megan. After everything you've been through, I'm sure it's the last thing you need."

She sniffled. "I woke up this morning with the intent of going to my first AA meeting. I know I have a problem. I don't want Annie thinking she has a lush for a mom."

"That's cool," Cristina said.

"It's never too late to get help, Megan," I said.

"Sure it is." Her nasally voice was monotone, her eyes almost catatonic.

I gripped her arm, hoping to snap some life into her. "Megan, I'm sure Carlos is just trying to figure out how to deal with everything. He was probably just as traumatized as you were by the fake kidnapping. And then there's your drinking. He might be at his limit as well."

She slowly shifted her eyes to me. "He blames it on me."

"The kidnapping?" I shook my head in disbelief.

"How the hell did he go there?" Cristina asked.

"He said that I was such an obnoxious bitch to everyone I interacted with and, as a result, we probably had a list of enemies a mile long."

Cristina and I swapped wide-eyed glances.

"Don't be so surprised. I told him he was right. I actually admitted that my bitchiness to everyone probably led to us being a target."

I didn't have time to remind her that was simply illogical—all signs told us that many others had been terrorized by the same group. She was singled out likely because a group of hackers had access to her personal data and because she had money.

A heaving sob came from deep within. It launched her forward, bringing with it a flood of tears. Cristina ran to the meeting room and grabbed a box of tissues, plucking out a few from the box and handing the fistful to Megan. She simply covered her face, her elbows now leaning on her knees. She wore faded jeans and a faded Trinity University T-shirt. She looked and acted nothing like the pretentious woman whom we'd first met.

It took five minutes, but eventually her uncontrollable gasps subsided. She blew into a new tissue every few seconds, dropping the used ones into a pile under her chair that had grown into a sizable mound. When she finally took in a breath and said, "I'm sorry for breaking down," Cristina handed her a bottled water.

Megan drank some water and paused, her eyes staring at the floor. She needed some space. I got up, gestured with my head to Cristina. Then we busied ourselves with cleaning up, organizing paperwork, reading this or that.

When Cristina walked by with a huge load of trash, she accidentally dropped an empty can of soda near Megan's feet. Megan grabbed the can and handed it to Cristina. "Carlos kicked me out of the house. Said I can't see Annie."

Cristina froze and looked at me. It was obvious she had no idea how to respond.

With a handful of papers, I walked to the other side of the desk, hoping to avoid another emotional eruption. "Megan, this isn't a very good excuse, but it sounds to me like Carlos is hurting too. It's a shame he isn't bonding with you over this."

"He called me earlier, said he was getting a court order to keep me out of the house and away from Annie." She gulped as tears pooled in her eyes. But surprisingly, she didn't break down again. She sniffled, then said, "I know I only have to look in the mirror to figure out why this happened."

"Why are you thinking this way?" Cristina asked, her arms still full of trash.

"Megan," I said, getting her attention back to me, "I know you've still got alcohol in your system, so I hope you can understand this: you had nothing to do with that horrible incident. You, and to a lesser degree, your husband, were victims." Of course, it irked me to no end that the husband was treating Megan like the enemy, like she had somehow caused all this. It wasn't just sad, it was outright mean.

She shrugged, then rubbed the area under her eyes.

It still didn't seem like she believed me. I pressed on. "Stan said there have been thirteen other families victimized in the same manner. You're not alone, and it has nothing to do with your personality. I think Carlos is lashing out, or is just using this as an excuse to be mean to you."

"I hear you, but it's not registering. I just don't know why."

I'm not sure how, but this confident, tough-nosed, accomplished woman had the aura of an abused wife, one who was having a difficult time differentiating fact from fiction—or at least the fiction her husband was spouting. I altered my approach, recalling why we'd wanted to reach out to her earlier.

"Cristina and I are making some headway on this investigation."

She blinked. "Really?"

"But we need some help. We figure there's some connection between all the families—some similar thread that no one has picked up on yet. Our current running theory is that everyone used the same pediatrician or group of pediatricians. We're thinking computer hackers accessed the patient files, retrieved all of the pertinent patient data, then determined the ones who had the most money and targeted them…meaning you."

She licked her lips and seemed to have more energy.

"Can you tell us who Annie's pediatrician is?"

"That's an easy one. It's…" She put a hand to her forehead. "My mind's a little off. It will come to me."

I badly wanted to say, "Stonebrook Pediatric Group, by chance?" Given her state of mind, however, I didn't want to lead her on and have her just agree with whatever I threw out there.

She snapped her fingers, arching her back. "Raintree Pediatrics. That's it."

It wasn't what I was hoping for. I looked at Cristina. "Does that name do anything for you?"

"I can start looking it up. Maybe there's another Nurse Klein working there, who knows?" Cristina dumped the trash into a larger garbage bag and then went to her laptop.

"Hold on," I said, putting my hand on Cristina's arm. "Let's do this tomorrow, or maybe you can tackle it later if you can't sleep tonight."

"I let you down, didn't I?" Megan's head slumped downward. Whether it was the alcohol or her general sense of self-worth—courtesy of Carlos—her life had been shattered. She wasn't the same person.

"Megan, it's nothing more than a factual question. What you told us, that Annie goes to Raintree Pediatrics, is a fact, correct?"

She nodded, but I could still sense her emotions teetering near the edge of another valley. There really wasn't much she could do at this point for our investigation, and I was beginning to wonder if we were simply spinning our wheels. Maybe we should just fold it all in, turn over what we know to Stan and the other detectives, and see if they can figure it out.

I felt Cristina's gaze on me, and I looked in her direction. She wore a quizzical expression. She seemed to sense my uncertainty, about the investigation, our role in the investigation, and certainly Megan's ability to help us out.

I looked at Megan, who was gripping a tissue with both hands. Her hardened face was covered with splotches. Every few seconds, she'd blink and flinch at the same time, as if she'd been hit with an electric jolt.

My heart was torn for Megan, for her personal torment, being ridiculed by her unsupportive husband, and having to worry about being able to see her kids.

And what about the other mothers and fathers who were on the receiving end of the phone calls? Were they in the same condition as Megan?

I knew what we needed to do—and it didn't include giving up on our theory. We needed to follow through with the other thirteen families. That would be our first priority in the morning.

"Megan, do you have a place to stay tonight?"

"The street. That's where I belong. I'm going to find the first guy in a bar and fuck him. How do you like that?" She was still drunk, certainly belligerent.

"You're coming home with me. Tomorrow, we can see if you have a family member you can stay with."

"But—" She reached for me and missed.

"That's how we'll handle this, Megan."

She teared up. "I'll pay you extra. Thank you for being my friend."

I put a hand on her shoulder. "It will be okay."

The door opened. I huffed out a tired breath and turned to see Armand at the threshold.

"We need to talk," he said. "Privately."

More drama. Just what I needed.

Thirty-One

Armand Roussel was a tough man. His presence would never go unnoticed in a room. And not because he always wore some type of army gear. He walked with purpose. He spoke with purpose. Even when he wasn't speaking, his aura drew you in. Tonight was no exception.

He gripped the top of the leather chair in our meeting room, the lines on his face more pronounced than I remembered. He was intense, though he hadn't said a word. He certainly had my attention, even as the sounds of Megan puking in the bathroom filled our space.

I waited for him to say something. But he didn't. He just stood there, glaring at the table.

Cristina popped out of the bathroom. "She's not very good at hitting the target." She looked at Armand, then me. "I've been around a lot of lushes and seen people deal with a nasty hangover, but she is disgusting."

I shrugged, palms up. "I know it's not fun, but can you handle it? Please?"

She glanced at Armand again. "Yeah, I can handle it. Just giving you an update."

"That she's missing the toilet?"

"And she keeps…you know, going on and on about Annie and Carlos. It's—"

"I get it. Just give me a few minutes, okay?"

"No probs."

She disappeared, and I turned back to Armand. I wanted to ask him so many questions, but I could see he had something on his mind. I had to take it at his pace for now.

When his eyes finally shifted in my direction, I expected him to speak, but he just looked at me. Had he hit a wall of some sort? Had something happened? Was he having second thoughts? *Come on, Armand.*

I heard another guttural heave from the bathroom, and then Cristina shouted, "Oh God, is there any way you can…?" Then the toilet flushed.

I grimaced, but Armand's expression didn't change. I was getting antsy and even irritated. If he wasn't going to speak, then I had to decide what, if anything, I should bring up. I recalled Nick saying that he needed some time to check with authorities on possible next steps. He was concerned that he might have stumbled upon a case of espionage. The look in Nick's eyes had been serious. While I wrestled with the urge to confront Armand about what we had found in the letters, I knew Nick would disapprove…vehemently.

And then there was the information we'd learned from Nick's partner, Alex. Zeke's name had been identified, along with Udovenko, in two memos originating from the Ukrainian SBU. Alex was trying to find out why Zeke's name had been included, if or how he was involved in the drug trafficking operation. On the surface, I knew it didn't look good for Zeke. But I still didn't have definitive proof—hopefully that would come from Alex. But when? I'd been so wrapped up for the last several hours researching the fake kidnappings that I hadn't asked Nick for an update. But he hadn't reached out to me either. Surely, if he'd learned that Zeke's involvement with Udovenko was not of a criminal nature, he would have called or texted, or even dropped by.

As for his quest to gather information on Armand's past, I knew that might take longer than a few hours. But once he learned everything he could about Armand, I wondered how much he'd actually share. He might have finally reached the point of trusting me, but he worked for the FBI. And matters of treason, I was certain, were not something to be shared with just any civilian.

Was there any way that Zeke's connection to Udovenko could be related to Armand's interaction with the KGB spy, Anton Kovalchick? Besides their Russian names, was there a connection between Udovenko and Kovalchick? I had no idea. That would be a good question to ask Nick.

"Ivy."

Armand's voice shook me out of my trance. I gave him a quick head nod.

"I can see…hear that you have a great deal going on, so I appreciate you taking a few minutes to hear me out."

I'd already been waiting for him to speak for about ten minutes. But I wasn't going to nitpick. "Sure. What's on your mind?"

He lifted his chin a couple of inches higher and took in a deep breath. "Many years ago, when I was stationed in Italy—"

"Holy shit, Ivy, you won't believe the crap spewing out of this woman's gut. It's not human."

I looked blankly at Cristina as I processed Armand's first few words. His time in Italy. Was he about to share what we'd read about in the letters? Would it be the same story?

"Cristina, I don't know what to say? Is she dying? Is she puking up blood?"

"No, nothing like that. She's just... Well, it's nasty." She paused, caught the expressions on our faces. "But I can deal with it. Just had to share. Later."

She scooted back into the bathroom.

"Sorry. Please continue," I said.

He cleared his throat. "It had been nearly a year since I'd been back home. I missed my family. Zahera was still quite young, four years old, I believe. Maybe once a month I'd be able to speak to Simone or Zahera by phone. We communicated by letters mostly."

He paused a second, and a panicked thought hit me. Did he know that I had taken possession of the mound of letters from Zahera's condo? I held my breath, waiting for his next words.

"Simone was a lovely writer. She sometimes wrote me poems." He tapped his chest. "They were really quite meaningful. She was an amazing woman."

"Your daughter says the same thing."

"Ivy, I was targeted by the KGB, the Soviet Union."

I nodded, then realized I shouldn't know this information. So I put on my astonished face. "Wow. That sounds pretty serious."

"It was. They were very careful in how they tried to draw me in. A local bartender befriended me. I knew he was from Eastern Europe, but we clicked, you know. He knew a lot about football...what you call soccer. And we became friends. Or so I thought."

He walked a few steps toward the window where only a dim light illuminated the water fountain. I saw no birds nearby. It was as if every living thing other than the four of us had vacated the premises.

"What do you mean?"

"His name was Anton Kovalchick. He was a Soviet spy, with the KGB. One night he drugged my drink, and I awoke next to another woman."

I made my eyes go wide. "Did you...?"

"Apparently so. They had pictures. I was devastated." He looked off, as if shame had temporarily gained control of this larger-than-life figure.

"What did you do?"

"At first, I just returned to the base and went about my job. I worked in the communications group. I knew I'd committed a horrible act, even if it was a setup. But it only got worse. On my next time off base, Anton found me and confronted me, saying I could be a great asset for the Soviet cause. He said my family would be taken care of, said I could make a lot of money if I would begin giving him confidential information."

"So he wanted you to be a…"

"A spy. Kind of a double agent."

"So, not to defect."

"No." He paused. "Why would you say defect?"

I almost put a hand to my mouth to stuff the words back in. *Dammit.* He had used the term "defect" in his letter to Simone. Could he read my mind? I hoped not. "I don't know. It just seems like a logical thing. I guess I don't know what exactly you did in your role with the Army."

The toilet flushed again, and he shifted his eyes in that direction for a moment, then back to me. "I oversaw operations on confidential communications between US military leadership in Europe. It was essentially using what we call the Internet today. The type of information in those communications was highly classified, and could have exposed names of key people doing work for us in the Eastern Bloc, as well as divulge military strategies of the US and our allies. Remember, this is before the wall came down and the Soviet Union broke up."

"They didn't think about giving you the type of security protection that they would a general or someone on the receiving end in those communications?"

"Times were different back then. We were IT grunts, at least in their minds."

"So, what happened? I mean, you did continue to serve in the Army."

"At first, Anton tried the softer approach, using enticements to draw me over while subtly bringing up the affair and the photos. He didn't demand anything; he told me to take my time."

"Did you not go to your boss and tell him?"

He pressed his lips together. I could see he didn't enjoy being interrogated, but he didn't tell me it was none of my business either. "I needed time to think it through."

"You considered the offer?" I asked a little too quickly.

"No." He rubbed his hand across his face. "I was trying to figure out what I could do. How to get myself out of that mess. How to keep my wife and family safe, out of any scandal, and yes, to save my reputation within the Army."

"And?"

"I did something I'm not proud of, but it allowed life to continue. And for that I have no regrets." He brought his arms behind his back.

What was *that*? He was going to end his story there? Not if I could help it.

From my standing position, I leaned over and planted my hands on the table. "I'm glad you have no regrets. But if you came here to tell me something that was pertinent to my investigation of Zeke, I haven't heard it, unless I missed something. I need to hear the *complete* story."

He held up a defensive hand. "I…I realize that. I just needed a few more seconds."

I gave him a slight nod.

"I had contacts within the Italian military. People I trusted." He paused another second, swallowed. "I must say, I've never shared this with anyone on the outside."

"Outside of your military contacts?"

"Yes," he said. "And no one has heard the entire story, not the full truth."

"I'm honored." It sounded a bit sarcastic, but I couldn't take it back. He ignored it anyway.

"I got my hands on some cocaine, and I planted it in Anton's apartment when he wasn't there. Then I gave my Italian military friends the tip. They passed it along to the Italian police, who were in the middle of a countrywide crackdown on all types of drug-related crimes. They arrested Anton."

"Wow," I said, standing straight up again. "You took quite a risk. Screwing with a KGB spy; planting drugs. I didn't take you as a thrill seeker."

"You are right. I'm not. I care for my family, my friends, our great country. But I was desperate to not lose all of that. To not lose my life."

I heard water flow from the bathroom sink. I hoped Megan was cleaning up. Then a thought hit me, and I met his gaze. "If Anton was KGB, did the Soviet government get involved to keep him out of prison?"

He nodded. "I knew the Soviet government would step in—if only to keep him from sharing classified information. But I hoped it would send a message. As it turns out, the Italians played hardball. He spent four months in prison as they haggled over what they wanted in the trade deal."

"Trade?"

"In international politics, when one country identifies a spy, usually they will allow that person to return to their homeland, but only if that country offers something in return. It could be releasing prisoners, paying off debt, changing a hardline stance on a particular political topic. There are a million ways spy trades are made."

"So you succeeded?"

He looked down for a moment. "In some ways," he said, his voice pulled back a degree. "In the middle of all this, I had to tell Simone. I did so through a letter. And in her response, I could see she was devastated. And it crushed me."

Tears welled in his eyes.

"But your marriage survived."

"It did. All because of her ability to forgive."

"So why are you telling me all of this?"

"Because of Anton."

I tilted my head.

"I've not heard anything from him in years. Yet, I've always wondered if he was watching me, waiting for the right opportunity to ruin my life."

"How?"

"I have no idea. It's just this sense of pending doom. Perhaps my guilt is still heavy in my heart, even after all the years."

A blue vein snaked down the middle of his forehead. This typically rugged man was anything but rugged right now. He took in a breath and continued. "With the fall of the Soviet Union, everyone was a free agent. People like Petro Udovenko began to create mini empires, and authorities didn't have the resources to stop it. On top of that, the whole system was corrupt. Still is, I think. It's more fractured with the former Soviet countries trying to maintain their own sovereignty. But from what I've read, corruption inside many of those countries, including Russia, is rampant. People trade information for power. That's always been the case, I suppose, and because of greed and paranoia, I wouldn't expect that to change any time soon. I don't know. It just seems like bad people tend to cross paths eventually. It's possible that Udovenko and Kovalchick could be connected. And if they are, I wanted you to be aware of my past."

He did not look away in the ensuing silence. I didn't either. Thankfully, there were no toilet flushes or gagging sounds to interrupt the sinking-in of his words. I could see how difficult it had been on him to relive that time in his life, when he wondered if he or his family would survive.

"Thank you for sharing this, Armand."

"I'll do anything for Zahera. I love her with all of my heart. She's all I have." He wiped his hand across his eyes and released a breath. "I just need to know if Zeke is clean, if Zahera will be safe going forward. I won't be around forever, and I just need to know that she'll be cherished."

Now I was the one tearing up.

He pulled his phone from his pocket. "I've actually tried reaching her a few times today. She's not responding to my text messages."

Probably because she was lost in Zeke's eyes in Toronto. But maybe she didn't want her father to know, so I stayed mum for now.

I heard someone clearing their throat. I turned to see Cristina waving a hand. "She's finished hurling, only because there's nothing left to throw up."

"Good, I guess. Is she feeling better?"

"I think so, but she's uh…" She bit down on her lip, glancing inside the bathroom. "She's kind of nasty right now."

"We need to get her to my place. Did I hear you say you volunteered to help?"

She spread her arms. "Huh?"

"Good. Thanks." I gave her a wink.

Thirty-Two

By the time we made it outside, a dense fog had draped the city. I couldn't see the top of the five-story building next door. The nearest streetlight flashed on and off—mostly off; it was about to fail altogether—and the periods of darkness lasted longer, making visibility extremely poor. There was a stillness in the air, and only an occasional rumble of a pickup with no muffler passing by on a nearby cross street.

Megan was worthless. She'd essentially passed out, waking up every few seconds to mutter some type of derogatory comment. Armand had hung around to offer his assistance in getting her to my car parked on the curb across the street.

Cristina locked up the office as Armand and I each grabbed one of Megan's arms, helping her to walk...actually, more like slide along. I grumbled to Armand, "Ready?"

Before he could respond, Megan came to life. "Hell no. I want to lie down right here and take a nap." Her body went completely limp. She dropped a foot or so before Armand and I recovered and pulled her back up.

"You think it might be easier to get a pole and tie her arms and legs to it?" Cristina had just pulled around in front of us. She was carrying our laptop bags as well as supplies for the road trip to my apartment: paper towels, a barf bag, bottled water, a package of wipes, and a box of tissues.

"You want to treat her like a wild hog?"

She shrugged and accidentally dropped the water. She picked it up before it rolled too far away, and then walked across the street to unlock my two-door Civic. Other cars were also parked along the curb.

"Let's go." Armand and I took two steps, and then the area went dark again. I could barely see Cristina on the other side of the street.

"Hey, Cristina, do you think you could break out your phone and shine some light for us?"

There was nothing extra-large about Megan, but with her offering no assistance, keeping her body upright wasn't easy, even with Armand on the other side.

"Hold on," Cristina said. I heard keys drop to the concrete.

"Come on," I said to Armand. We dragged Megan a few more steps. One of her shoes slipped off. Armand stopped and tried to reach down to pick it up without dropping her.

My whole body broke out in a sweat. "Just leave it. Cristina can get it."

"Right," Armand said.

We scooted a few more steps, then Megan's eyes popped open.

"What's wrong? Please don't tell me you're going to throw up again," I said.

"Keep her away from me," Cristina called out. The streetlight flashed on for a couple of seconds. Cristina was standing next to the open driver's side door. And then it went dark again.

"I want my shoe," Megan said, trying to turn her head around. "Those shoes are all I have from home."

"Cristina can get it," I said, trying to keep the momentum moving toward the car.

She began to whimper. "I've got nothing. No Annie, no Carlos, nothing from home. I only want my shoe, dammit."

"We'll get your shoe, Megan. We just need to get you in the car, okay?"

She didn't respond, just wiped her face and sniffled. We kept moving forward. Ten feet away from the car, I could see Cristina at the door, pushing up the front seat. I said, "No way we'll be able to squeeze Megan into the back seat."

"You should have a four-door car," Cristina said.

"Not happening in the next five minutes."

"You could just push her in."

"Nice. She is our client, remember."

"It seems like we're babysitting a little kid."

"Shh. She could hear you."

Megan's head slumped forward, and she released a loud snore.

"How much did she have to drink?" Armand asked.

"No clue," I said. "Let's take her to the other side of the car and put her in the front passenger seat."

The streetlight flashed on for a second, and then turned off just as I stepped toward the curb. My foot clipped the side, and I began to fall. I caught myself with my other hand, but Megan's weight slammed my knees to the concrete.

"You okay?" Armand asked, lifting her back up as I got to my feet on the sidewalk.

"Bruised, I'm sure, but I'm fine."

A moment later, a cone of light shone on us. I looked to Cristina, who was angling her phone in our direction. "Thanks for coming through after we're already here."

"Sorry." With sweat now dripping off my face, we made it to the car. Cristina helped get Megan's feet inside.

"Where's my shoe?" Megan said, suddenly awake.

"I'll get it." Armand scooted away.

"Thank you." I said, leaning over to try to get the seat belt fastened.

An engine revved so loudly I jerked my head up, hitting it on the ceiling. Tires squealed and a breath caught in my throat. The roar was on top of us in a single heartbeat. I blinked, then the streetlight flashed on; in the middle of the street, Armand had started to stand up. Before he could take a step, a pickup mowed right over him. I could hear his body crumple—a sickening series of muffled thuds, as if he were nothing more than a cardboard box. The truck screeched away, and the street went dark again.

Two screams. It was me and Cristina.

I ran around the car just as the streetlight flashed on again. Armand's body was a mangled mess. He had to be dead.

Thirty-Three

It was dusk, the sky was gunmetal gray, and a thick humidity choked off the oxygen.

This was my first Muslim funeral. There were things about it that were different than what I was used to. In many respects, though, it was similar to most other funerals I'd attended—full of heart-wrenching emotion.

Zahera had decided to only have a ceremony at the gravesite, bypassing a service at the mosque with which her father was associated. Zahera had told me he'd rarely attended services in the last several years since her mother's death. And Zahera herself wasn't exactly on a first-name basis with the Imam, which was why she'd customized the event for what was best for her.

For that, I was thankful.

The mood was somber, but respectful. I heard sniffles throughout the crowd positioned around the gravesite. I was told that not everyone in attendance would have known Armand. Apparently, the death of someone in the Muslim faith was not just a loss to the family, but a loss to the community. From my vantage point, I saw a diverse cross-section of people. A few women wore head scarfs, but many of the women were dressed like I was, a black dress that fell below my knees. There were men and women wearing military fatigues, while others arrived in Wrangler jeans.

The sheer number of people was probably the most shocking aspect. I guessed we were surrounded by at least three to four hundred folks. Maybe more.

Zeke and I flanked Zahera, who stood as still as a statue, staring straight ahead, a pair of large sunglasses covering most of her face. I'd yet to see a tear trickle down her cheek at the funeral, but plenty had been shed since I'd spoken to her the night before. When I first shared the horrific news, I'd heard no response. I wondered if I'd accidentally disconnected the call. Then, Zeke jumped on the line and said she was in shock. Later, she called me back, and we cried together.

When she arrived at the airport early this morning, I hugged her the moment she walked out of the restricted area. We rocked back and forth for five, ten minutes. Maybe longer. Time had become irrelevant. When we let go, cries turned into a quick laugh. We pointed at each other's faces. She looked like an exotic zombie, if there was such a thing. I'm sure I looked far worse. From there, we went straight into planning for the funeral. People of the Muslim faith tried to have their funerals within twenty-four hours of the death. It made sense to me.

Throughout the day, during downtimes, more tears were shed. I even saw Zeke break down after Zahera had told him how much she appreciated his kind heart. I tried to block my mind from opening the door to all the questions I had for Zeke. The only update Nick had provided was a one-sentence text that said: *Sorry about the loss. I'm still working things on my end.* I wanted to ask what he was still working and why, but it could wait until tomorrow.

A wedge formed in the sea of people, and I could make out the top of Armand's coffin being carried by six of his longtime friends. Zahera dug her nails into the palm of my hand.

The men carried the coffin to the large hole in front of us and carefully lowered it inside. A single shovel of dirt was dropped on top. Zahera pressed her nails even harder into my hand, and then the torrent began. A waterfall of tears poured down her face. I quickly gave her a wad of tissues from my purse, but they did little to stop the flow. Through all of the tears and the kind words, she stayed upright, and that was saying something. When the service ended, a number of folks walked by and offered their condolences, not only to her, but to Zeke and me as well. It felt a bit strange, but all funerals have a little awkwardness to them. People didn't know what to say or how to act exactly. They realized that kind words do little to change the feeling of loss and grief. It seemed like many people were forcing themselves to talk to Zahera, as if they needed to feel at least some of the anguish that she was experiencing.

Again, Zahera handled herself with great poise. Well, until she'd had enough.

"Get me out of here," she said into my ear.

I leaned forward and saw a line of folks still waiting to speak to her. "Okay," I said with some hesitation. "We can do that."

"Ivy, I don't know any of these people. I know they're just trying to be nice, but I—" She brought a hand to her face.

I whispered, "I get it." Then I took a step forward and spoke in the general direction of the people still in line. "Thank you for coming to the service. Zahera greatly appreciates your support. She needs some time to herself right now."

Zeke gave me a nod, and the three of us turned around. Stan, his wife Bev, and Nick were standing right there.

"Zahera, we're so sorry about what happened," Stan said. "We just wanted to offer our condolences."

Zahera took a step forward and wrapped her arms around Stan's neck. He reciprocated with his one good arm. I looked at Nick, trying to read his face. It seemed like he was avoiding my gaze. Had he told Stan about Armand's past? I had a million questions for him, but now certainly wasn't the appropriate time or place. Later, hopefully. No, definitely.

Zahera stepped back and said, "Tell me you know who did this, Stan."

Stan licked his lips, shifted his eyes to me for a quick moment.

"Zahera, dear," Zeke said, touching her arm. "Are you sure this is the best time? We know Stan and the SAPD are working on finding the person who did this. Why don't we go back to your place so you can rest, and then maybe Stan can talk to us tomorrow?"

She turned to him, removing her sunglasses. "Zeke, I know you think you're helping me, but I don't need to be coddled. I'm a grown woman whose father was just run over like he was roadkill."

Out of the corner of my eye, I saw Bev wince at Zahera's use of the word "roadkill."

"I didn't mean to upset you," Zeke said.

Zahera took his hand in hers. "I'm being a bitch, I know. I'm just glad to have you by my side through all of this." She kissed his hand, and he put his arm around her and kissed the top of her head. For a moment, he snagged my gaze. I wasn't sure what I saw. Stress for certain. But part of him seemed distant, as if his thoughts were somewhere else.

Zahera turned back to Stan. "Do you have anything you can share?"

"Actually, we do."

She reached out and grabbed his arm. But it was his prosthetic, and she quickly pulled back. "Sorry, Stan."

"No problem." He lowered his prosthetic arm. "If I tell you this, I'd appreciate it if you didn't draw any conclusions. Investigations have many lows and highs. And I feel confident—"

"Just tell me, please."

"A street camera three blocks away captured a picture of the vehicle Ivy described, a silver, older model pickup with a cattle guard on the front."

"Did you get a plate?" I asked.

"We did." He paused. "But it doesn't exist."

"How can that be?" Zahera said.

"We've had occasions where stolen license plates are basically torn in two, then welded back together to make it look like a regular plate. So when you look it up in the DMV database, it doesn't exist."

Zahera shook her head slowly. "Who would do something like that?"

I'd been wondering the same thing since the horrific incident happened. I looked to Nick, but he was staring at the ground. No doubt in my mind—he was avoiding me…or the topic of Armand and his past.

Stan wiped a line of sweat off his face. "Professionals."

"Professional what?" she asked.

"Professional criminals. People get up every day knowing they're going to break the law. Look, this investigation might take weeks, or even longer. I know you want closure and all, but the justice system works on its own schedule. So, please let Zeke and Ivy and all of your friends take care of you. Take care of yourself."

A slow nod, then she put her forehead against Zeke's shoulder. I was about to lead the entourage over to the parking lot when she suddenly turned back to Stan.

"If you're saying the person who killed my father is a professional and not just some asshole who had a beef against a guy in a military uniform, then that tells me he must have interacted with someone dangerous."

"It's very possible. We still have a lot of interviews to conduct to try to understand everything about your father, his past, people he'd spoken to in the last few days, two weeks…as far back as we can go."

Zahera turned to me, grabbing my wrist. "Ivy, I don't think I knew my real dad. He must have been involved with some bad people, and I didn't even know it." She planted her face on my shoulder and cried. And I cried with her, but for a very different reason.

Guilt.

Thirty-Four

Leaning against the island in Zahera's kitchen, I downed an appetizer with crabmeat and something else I couldn't distinguish. But it was damn good. I paused mid-chew—the doorbell had chimed for the fifth time in the last minute. Apparently, none of the twenty or so folks in the condo could open a door. Zahera was sitting at the kitchen table, her legs crossed, talking to a woman and her husband who lived on the floor above her condo. I'd actually seen her crack a smile in the last thirty minutes when they were trading dog stories. Her dog, Clint, a faithful Doberman, had made a brief appearance earlier, then parked himself back in his crate.

The influx of friends and their homemade food, while unexpected, had been a healthy dose of medicine for the good doctor. I scooted out of the kitchen, passed a few people clustered together in conversation, and went to the front door. I opened it to see Cristina and Saul standing there.

"We were beginning to wonder if she'd moved," Cristina said.

"You were just here a couple of nights ago."

"With her kind of money, anything is possible." Cristina walked into the foyer, her backpack over her shoulder. She'd skipped Armand's burial service, saying, at age seventeen, it just wasn't her kind of scene—and that was one thing we agreed on.

She'd texted me earlier saying she wanted to stop by the condo and pay her respects, as well as share some new information she'd learned.

Saul took me in his arms, and we hugged. "Sorry I couldn't make it to the service earlier. Ross cracked the whip and—"

"I know," I said, holding up a hand. "You told me he threatened your job if you didn't stick around for some deposition."

"It was ridiculous, but I'm here now."

I patted his chest and shut the door. "Did you check to see if you received your bar exam results today?"

"Early this morning. Nothing. I'll check again later. Trying not to get my hopes up."

"Your hopes of leaving that asshat, Ross, right?" Cristina said.

Saul tilted his head, keeping his eyes on me. "Can't she tell when someone doesn't want to dwell on something because it makes them feel uncomfortable?"

"Hello, I'm right here." She waved her hand in front of Saul's face.

"McFly, we couldn't help but notice," Saul said, with a wink to me.

"My fly's not open," she said, looking down at her jeans.

Saul and I shared a quiet chuckle, then I led them into the kitchen. Zahera came over and received a double hug from Cristina and Saul. As they chatted for a couple of minutes, I scanned the area for Zeke. No sign of him. I wasn't sure why, but I had this urge to keep him close by.

Saul recognized the couple Zahera had been speaking with as clients of the firm for which he worked—Wilson, Mendoza, and Ross. He grabbed a plate of appetizers and walked over to talk to them. Cristina, with a twitch of her head, gave me the signal that we needed to talk.

We walked back through the dining and living rooms, then reached the carpeted hallway that took us to the main guestroom. The door was shut, but I paid it no attention and walked right in.

I stopped so fast Cristina ran into my back. Zeke was sitting on the edge of the bed, a phone against his ear.

"Oh, sorry. Didn't know you were in here." *Did I just see tears in his eyes?*

He quickly stood, held up a finger toward me, and then turned his back and walked to the far side of the room. I turned and traded a glance with Cristina. "Is he crying?" she whispered a little too loudly.

I shook my head to get her to be quiet and turned back to Zeke. He was nodding, talking quietly. He scratched the back of his head and then ended his call.

"Hey, sorry about that. It was one of my needy clients. He rambles a lot. I think he pays me just to listen to him." He gently tossed his phone in the air and caught it after a complete flip. He smiled as if we should be impressed.

Actually, I was—he hadn't even looked at the phone during his little trick—but it seemed forced, as if he were trying to lead us away from what we'd seen in his eyes. Of course, it could have just been that he was sharing the news of Armand's death, but his follow-up move was out of place.

"We've all had to work for clients who've had their issues, I suppose." His eyes moved from me to Cristina, and then back to me. He was reading our expressions. I walked over to the desk. "We can set up right here, Cristina, where we were last time."

"I'll let you ladies have your privacy." He pocketed his phone and walked past us.

Cristina began to pull her laptop out of her bag. I noticed he'd stopped at the doorway. He glanced at us, then his eyes dropped to the floor.

I said, "We'll be out in few minutes. You've got Z for now?"

"Yes. I won't let anything happen to her."

He left.

And I stood there questioning everything I'd just seen and heard.

Thirty-Five

Cristina snapped her fingers in front of my face. I swatted at them and missed.

"You were in one of your trances."

"I know that."

"You saw that he was visibly upset when we walked in, right?"

"That's not all I saw."

She lifted the lid on her laptop and logged in, then looked up at me.

I held out my hand and began tapping my fingers with the opposite hand. "First, if he was talking to his client, then I'm the fricking Pope."

She crossed herself, just to be sassy. I ignored her and continued. "Whoever was on the phone, he knew well. Real well."

"I'm following you, but unless we ask him, we'll have no idea."

"We can't ask him. Although, if Nick ever hears back from Alex—"

"Who's Alex again?"

"His partner. She's at INTERPOL in France, remember?"

A nod. "She's a chick. Got it."

"So, back to Zeke's little act. Second, he was trying to read us. It's like he suspects that we're on to him."

"You think? But we're not really on to him, not yet. We just have our suspicions."

"Maybe. And third, did you see his eyes when he left the room?"

She was starting to type on the computer. "Pretty dreamy, huh?" She stopped and looked up at me. "Don't tell Z I said that, okay?"

I propped a hand against my hip.

"What? I wasn't really watching closely. What did I miss?"

"He looked under the desk…where the satchel full of letters used to be."

"Crap," she said. "We should have brought it back here today."

"Too late now."

She put her hands on the computer keys but didn't type a thing. "So you're thinking he knows about the letters?"

"It's possible."

She shook her head. "What if he knows we took them?"

"Even worse." I paced behind Cristina and ended up over at the windows. I peeked through the blinds to see the sparse San Antonio skyline, then twirled around. "You said those letters were organized, stacked neatly."

"They were. So, I guess that means he probably didn't read the letters."

"Or he's just real good at covering his tracks."

"More James Bond shit."

"This is real life, Cristina."

She smirked. "I know. I just like screwing with you."

"Not sure what to make of Zeke right now. I really need Nick to get back to me. And I'm kind of freaking out about Zahera. She hasn't asked what her dad was doing at our ECHO office, but she will."

"What are you going to tell her?"

I rubbed the back of my neck. As usual, it didn't help. "I don't want to add another lie on top of everything else she's dealing with. She's been through so much, yet if some of this stuff is true, it seems like it could just be the beginning."

"You're talking about if we get word that Zeke is part of this international drug cartel?"

"And with Stan saying that a professional ran down Armand, I'm wondering if somehow that connects back to Zeke's other life. *If* he has another life, I have to remind myself."

"Wait. What did Stan say?"

I remembered she hadn't been at the service, and so I filled her in. When I was done, neither of us said a word. She raked her fingers through her mane of hair, while I tapped my foot against the floor. Then we both sighed at the same time.

"My stomach is in knots," she said. "I don't have a good feeling about all of this. We're waiting to hear the worst news from this Alex person, Nick, even Stan."

I tried to clear my head for a moment and let the information we knew marinate a bit. Through the muddled mess of all the facts and suppositions, a very clear warning zipped to the front of my mind. "Stan said that Armand's death was a professional job. While Zahera is worried that her father was connected to some bad people, we have no reason to suspect that, right?"

She nodded.

"But we do have all of this mounting…" I couldn't think of the right word.

"Bullshit?"

"No, no. I guess you could call it evidence, but it's also our intuition based upon Zeke's behavior. Whatever we call it, Zeke is in our crosshairs."

"I like the term."

I walked toward her. "What I'm trying to say is, what if Armand was killed because of Zeke's connections?"

"To that Russian." She paused, looked off for a second. "Well, the Russian drug dealer."

"Stay on point. We have no knowledge of Armand being associated with criminals, but Zeke very well could be."

"Armand did frame a KGB spy though—that Anton guy. And he was concerned Anton might somehow be involved in this."

"True, to a degree. The KGB thing with Anton happened umpteen years ago. How it all unfolded…it's disturbing and, even after Armand shared the details, hard to fathom. But, dammit, Zeke's association—possible association—with this drug leader is present day. It could have gotten Armand killed. If so, then Zahera could be in danger."

Cristina didn't respond. She didn't have to. The tension in our space was unnerving, but it didn't come close to the stress I felt inside. It all started the moment Armand had walked through the ECHO office door and asked me to secretly dig up dirt on Zahera's fiancé. Well, he didn't say that exactly, but that was how I had taken his request. My instinct initially told me not to take the case. And every minute since then, I'd felt like I'd betrayed my best friend. The myriad of lies and cover-ups had only made the trench that much deeper.

Thirty-Six

Before this all started, I would have done anything to keep Zahera as a friend. I still would. Our friendship now, though, seemed like it was on a collision course with fate. And it was hard to imagine anything except an abrupt and painful end. And what about her marriage? I could be responsible for breaking up her relationship with Zeke before she walked down the aisle.

Dammit, Ivy, just think if you hadn't taken the case? What if you'd told Armand to leave without even hearing the name Petro Udovenko? Just because you don't see it, doesn't make it all go away. Zahera might be in grave danger, and no one would know a damn thing. Nick and Alex wouldn't be on the hunt for more details. So cut yourself a break.

Cristina snapped her fingers at me. "Are you still with us?"

"I'm here. Just thinking through how we got here—not that it matters at this point. Look, we can't undo everything that has happened. If I don't hear from Nick by morning, I'll track him down. One step at a time, right?" I took a seat on the edge of the bed. "Now, didn't you say you had something to share on the fake-kidnapping investigation? Wait, what happened to Megan? I left her on the couch, still sleeping it off."

"She's cool. I stopped by your place, and she's actually sober. A little depressed, but watching TV, eating cold pizza."

"I forgot I had any left over. She could have heated it up."

"Said it reminded her of the good old days, when she was in college."

"The excessive drinking or the cold pizza?"

"Probably both. By the way, Zorro was stuck to her like Velcro. I think his feline ways are helping her to relax and chill out; she didn't seem like she had the same doom-and-gloom attitude."

I emptied my lungs, allowing my shoulders to slump just a tad. "We all need some of that." I pointed at her laptop screen, then said, "You've got good news?"

She clicked the laptop mouse three times, then waited.

"What's going on?"

"I think my laptop froze."

"I don't want the detail. Give me the headline."

She flipped around to look at me. "I have verbal confirmation that eight of the thirteen families have kids who are patients at Stonebrook Pediatric."

"Wow. That can't be a coincidence."

"Do you think Stan and the SAPD have this information yet?"

"Who knows? We need to share it with him. Maybe he'll have something to toss our way." My sights drifted to a brass lamp sitting on the desk. I guessed it was worth more than my entire bedroom set.

"Do you want to bring that lamp home?" she asked.

"What?" I asked, not able to connect the dots.

"The lamp. You were staring at it as if you'd fallen in love with it. I could try to stuff it in my backpack."

"I know you're kidding; probably not the right day to get a rise out of Z."

"True dat."

A single shake of my head.

"What?"

"You're such a teenager, that's what."

She patted the top of her laptop. "But I'm pretty resourceful, huh?"

I got to my feet and motioned to the door. "Look, I need to go spend some more time with Zahera. I'll try to set something up with Stan for the morning. Hoping I can get Nick to join in and just lay everything out."

"Wait, you want to discuss Armand's past, the whole spy-seduction thing?"

"Every bit of it."

"But now that national security is part of the case, Nick is taking his FBI role seriously. At least that's what you told me." She began to pack up her computer.

"He'll get over it. I'm tired of keeping everything in the shadows. I know we can't put it on the evening news."

"Evening news? When does that come on?"

I arched an eyebrow. "Am I really that old?"

"You're really that old."

I had nothing to add to that, so I started to open the door. But something in the back of my mind rushed to the forefront, and I turned back around. "By the way, how did you get all of the confidential information from those eight families?"

She smiled.

"Do I want to know?"

"Well, at first I was having a tough time. Two families caught on to my story of being a life insurance agent."

"Life insurance? That was the best you could come up with?"

"But I changed my story after that."

"To?"

She smiled.

I tilted my head.

"I said I worked for Stonebrook Pediatrics."

"You did what?"

"I said I was confirming their emergency contacts, as a matter of routine. They gave up their information in a heartbeat." She giggled. "Is that what they call a pun?"

I ignored her attempt to get out of it. "What if one of the families starts to ask questions, calls up the doctor's office? That could alert this Lisa Klein person or whoever is involved in this conspiracy."

She twisted her lips. "I didn't think that far ahead. Damn."

I had to remember she was only a kid trying to do an adult's job. "It's okay. You meant well." I put my arm on her shoulder. "You're not the only one exercising questionable judgment."

"I guess that helps."

I opened the door and yelped. "Damn, Z, you scared me."

Zahera had raised her fist, as if she were about to knock. Her lips were pursed. "Ivy, something has been gnawing at me all day. But every time it pops into my mind, it's gone a second later when I'm overcome with grief and my thoughts go back to Dad and how he died."

I reached out and touched her arm. It was stiff, unbending. "That's understandable." Then, I looked into her eyes and saw a determination I hadn't seen recently. "What's on your mind?"

"Why was Dad at your ECHO office?"

I quickly felt my throat starting to shut.

Thirty-Seven

Reading a facial expression isn't as easy as it seems. Take Nick, for example. He was on the phone, pacing outside the front door of the ECHO office. I couldn't read his mood—he'd perfected the poker face, likely a requirement for working as an FBI agent.

"You think it's good news or bad news?" Cristina asked, a hand near her mouth to muffle her volume.

"It's impossible to know, based on what I'm seeing."

Cristina's voice blended in with the hum of the overhead light. My eyes drifted back to my laptop. The browser was open to the adoption registry web page that showed my real parents had yet to signal they wanted to meet me. While a positive response would have been a nice surprise, I wasn't harping on that. Not now. Maybe later with Saul.

My mind was spiraling with a myriad of thoughts about Zahera, her all-too-visible pain from the loss of her father, and, in particular, my role in accentuating that suffering. Last night at her place, she'd confronted me with the question I'd been dreading to hear. Time seemed to freeze as I replayed the previous twenty-four hours.

After debating whether I should come clean and just share everything I knew, I'd decided that, for her best interest, I had to find a way to defer that discussion to a later date...when I had a better idea of whether a true threat existed from Zeke. I'd conducted several internal brainstorming sessions yesterday, in anticipation of her question, trying to find that balance between offering information that would allow her some moments of peace and trying not to dig my trench of deception any deeper.

But after hours of toiling over what to say and how to say it, I'd realized I'd given myself an impossible task.

So, when Zahera confronted me at the guest bedroom door with the question of why her father was at the ECHO office, my mind went blank—because it was blank. I had nothing packaged and ready to deliver, and I couldn't just unload everything. All I could muster was, "Your dad was a wonderful man. Even on a night when he'd planned to meet some old military friends for a beer, he offered to help us out."

I'd somehow pieced together a sentence that made sense, but it only bought me a few extra seconds. Zahera looked at me and then Cristina, who didn't move. After a couple of beats, her eye twitched. The ball was back in my court. "My car, remember?" I touched Cristina's shoulder.

"Yeah, right," she said in a tone that seemed forced, at best.

"She thinks everyone should just handle things on their own." I smirked, leaning closer to Zahera, pretending that Cristina couldn't hear me.

Zahera maintained her stoic expression. "Kind of like you."

Okay, that went nowhere. And she has a point. "Anyway, Black Beauty had been sputtering on the ride to work. When your dad called wondering why you weren't responding to his text messages, I mentioned that my car wasn't running well. He insisted on coming to take a look at it before I tried driving home."

The stress marks at the edges of her eyes relaxed as she released a heavy breath. "He really had a soft side to him." She began to turn and walk away, but I could see something, a thought or memory, sweep across her face. She stopped her movement. "If

Stan said Dad was killed by a professional, then how did this hit man know that Dad would be at ECHO?"

"If you ask me, whoever did this had been tracking your dad. For how long, who knows?"

A slow nod, then she walked off. She had believed me. Then again, I actually believed me—if a professional was behind this deed, then Armand must have been followed.

Still, though, the rest of my story was all vapor, a desperate, pitiful attempt to give Zahera a positive thought about her father, while allowing us extra time to figure out what was really going on. I then spent the entire night battling my inner-guilt demons while unable to drown out Megan's snoring from the couch.

Unlike my previous periods of falling into a trance, this time I wasn't awakened by the snap of Cristina's fingers. It felt like someone had turned up the volume on my invisible pair of earbuds. She was still talking, which meant my lack of attentiveness hadn't been noticed.

"Can you believe this? It's like we're looking at a toddler." Cristina snorted out a laugh. "Nick's so involved in his conversation that he's swatting at the sunrise shining in his face like it's a gnat."

I caught just enough of a glimpse of Nick's act to smile before he finally turned away from the eastern sun, pocketed his phone, and walked back into the office. "It's already a hundred degrees out there. Damn," he said, rubbing his forehead with the back of his hand. "I think I'm going to wash off my face, cool down a bit."

As if on cue, we heard the flush of the toilet. Nick pointed toward the back. "That's got to be Stan?"

Cristina and I nodded. "I guess I'll pass on going to the restroom."

"By the way," Cristina said, holding up her phone, "it's only eighty-four degrees."

"I'm sure he needed that clarification, Cristina. Can you get him some water?"

Another flush of the toilet.

"Wow," Nick said, glancing toward the back.

"I got you covered, Nick," Cristina said, jumping out of her seat.

"Much appreciated. Thanks."

She zipped around Nick and nearly ran into Stan at the threshold to the meeting room. "Whoa, there." He was cleaning his sunglasses with a piece of toilet paper.

Cristina covered her mouth but couldn't hide her laughter.

"What? Can't a man have five minutes of peace?"

I jumped in. "Are you feeling okay, Stan?"

"Sure." He pocketed his glasses, then cinched up his trousers.

How many times had I seen him do that? Too many to count.

"Your metabolism. It's a lot faster now, isn't it?" Nick asked, hands at his waist.

"How'd you guess?"

He saw three blank stares.

"Oh, right, the toilet." He offered a single chuckle. "Bev found this awesome recipe for a vegetable smoothie."

I stood up. "Shut up. You had a drink full of vegetables?"

"Kale and a whole bunch of other shit that's good for you. Gotta admit, it does feel like it's cleaning out my system."

A snort from Cristina.

Stan glanced at her with a look of annoyance, then back to me and Nick. "Ever since you guys were at the house and gave me the pep talk, cleaned out our fridge, Bev has been on a mission. She's really into this get-healthy craze. If you happened to notice, I didn't need either one of you this morning to push me to do my morning cardio workout."

Nick and I traded a quick glance, as Stan pulled up a chair near the desk. "We're proud of you, Stan," I said.

"Thanks." He pulled a notepad from his pocket. "Not sure Bev and I will be able to work out together like that very often. Seems like every time we leave Ethan at the house, even if for just a few minutes, he gets upset. And then it takes a while to calm him down."

Damn, that had to be tough, not only on the child, but his parents. I lightly bumped his shoulder with my fist. "We can help out on that front too, you know. I have experience with all types of kids."

"We'll see." He sat down.

Thirty-Eight

With Stan and Nick both finally in my grasp, I wasn't going to waste another minute. "Who wants to go first?" I asked, looking at the Radowski cousins.

They both exhaled, but Nick's was more prolonged, so I started with him. "What have you learned from Alex?"

He cleared his throat as if he were biding time.

"I figured you told Stan about Zeke and Armand and all of this crazy—"

"James Bond shit," Cristina finished for me.

"Yeah, that."

"I told him," Nick said.

Stan was chugging from his bottle of water so fast it dribbled off his chin. He used his sleeve to wipe his mouth. "Yeah, he told me. Why does it seem like I'm the last one to find out, when I should be the first to find out?"

I opened my mouth, but he held up his water. "Don't answer that. I don't want to hear it. But I'll tell you something I just learned on the investigation into Armand's death."

"Are we saying that his death is definitely linked to Zeke somehow?" I asked.

"Too early to tell," Nick said, looking at his cousin.

"Cops found what we believe to be the vehicle that killed Armand, and—"

"Did you lift the prints? Have you picked them up?" Cristina said faster than I could comprehend Stan's words.

"Uh, no. They found it in a junkyard. It had been torched on the inside and was in the process of being crushed into a tin can."

"Any record of someone dropping it off?" I asked.

He shook his head. "Just left there overnight. And no cameras either. Whoever committed this crime has done this kind of thing before."

I strummed my fingers. Before I could process my next question, Stan chimed back in. "So when Nick said he filled me in, that means he told me everything." His beady eyes went to Cristina and then to me. "Well, at least everything that you told him. There might be more, right?"

"What the hell does that mean?" My defenses were quick and stabbing. A night of no sleep and watching your best friend's soul get crushed will do that to you.

"Look, I know Armand put you in a tough spot," Stan said.

I could feel my pulse peppering my neck. "You think?"

"But you could have come to me."

"How were you going to help me find a connection between Zeke and an international drug dealer?"

"I couldn't, but I know people. Dammit, Ivy, I thought you trusted me."

"I thought you trusted me." Each retort increased in volume and intensity.

Cristina put her hand on my arm. She's lucky I didn't bite it.

"Hey, guys." Nick scooted to the edge of his chair, holding up both hands like a boxing referee. "Is it really a trust issue here? Stan, Ivy was just trying to do what was right for her friend. She was in a no-win situation."

"Thank you," I said, smacking my hand off the desk for a little extra emphasis.

Nick turned to me. "Ivy, Stan's got a point."

I gave Stan a tight smile. Emotion moved up the back of my throat. I swallowed and said, "I never really thought there was inherent danger, at least not immediate danger, and not here on the streets of San Antonio." I put my hand to my cheek. "Does that make me responsible for—?"

"Don't blame yourself for what happened to Armand," Nick quickly interjected. "You had nothing to do with it, okay? You'd already told me about Armand and his past transgressions. If anyone could do anything about this Zeke connection, it was me."

"That's what we've been waiting to hear." Cristina set her water bottle on the desk. "So, what do you have for us? Because we're pretty much at that place where the rubber meets the road, the shit is about to blow into the fan…whatever cliché you want to use. Our friend is suffering. We're hiding all of this from her, and every minute that goes by makes us feel like Winston Arnold."

We all turned our heads to Cristina.

"What? I'm tired of dancing around."

"Did you mean Benedict Arnold?"

"Yeah, whatever. I'm not so good at history."

I tapped the top of her knee and looked over at Nick. In fact, we were all looking at Nick. He scratched the back of his head, then let out an exasperated sigh.

"Ball's in your court, cuz," Stan said, leaning back in his chair.

Nick pulled a small package from his pocket, then unwrapped a stick of gum and folded it into his mouth. "Oh, does anyone else want one?"

"Don't mind if I do." Stan plucked one from the package.

I found myself strumming my fingernails on the desk again. Nick's eyes went there. "Enough delays," he said, clearing his throat. "I have to remind everyone how confidential this information is. If it gets out that I shared this with you, then I'll be fired and possibly brought up on charges."

"Nick, you can trust us," I said, turning to my right. "Right, Cristina?"

Cristina stood up, raised her hand, saying "I swear to tell the truth. The whole truth, so help me—"

"She's being sassy, Nick, but she won't say anything. She's got more secrets than most of us."

Everyone laughed, including Cristina, who sat back down. The tension had been cut in half.

Thirty-Nine

"**O**kay," Nick said. "I had a long conversation with Jerry, my SSA."

"SS what?" Cristina asked.

"Just another federal acronym. He's my boss back in the Boston FBI office. Anyway, he asked for a day so he could work his sources."

"And?" I said.

"Jerry has an old…uh, I think he called him the 'sonofabitch from Southie.'" Nick paused, saw three confused looks. "Oh, that's a small town just next to Boston. Kind of a rough place. So, he and his contact go way back, when both of them weren't exactly living by all the rules, if you know what I'm sayin'."

Part of me wanted to mock his suddenly extra-thick Yankee accent, but I refrained, staying focused on the content of what he'd said instead. "His contact. What agency does he work for?"

"Yeah," Stan said, shifting in his chair. "I always wondered how something like this went down, possible treason by an Army soldier."

"It's actually pretty simple. Army Counterintelligence is a group within the US Army. They're mandated to assess and/or neutralize any type of US internal threat, foreign threat, or international threat to the US Army or Department of Defense."

"And I thought it was either FBI or CIA that swam in those waters," Cristina said. "Learn something new every day, I guess."

Nick nodded, then quickly licked his thin lips. "So, Jerry's contact currently works in the US Army Intelligence and Security Command."

"He moved up the food chain," Stan said. "That's what you're saying, right?"

"But he used to work in the 66th Military Intelligence Brigade." Nick let his teeth show—it wasn't pretty. He should have kept his mouth closed.

"And that's supposed to mean what to us, Nick? You act like we're all working for the Feds," Stan said.

Nick gave me a quizzical glance. I turned my palms to the ceiling. Boy, it was nice having Stan on my side.

"Okay, sorry. Army Counterintelligence Special Agents—"

"There you go with the 'special' tag again," Stan said, more animated. "When are you Feds going to get over yourselves?"

Nick stared at him for a few seconds. "Are you done yet?"

Stan huffed out a breath. "Go ahead."

"Okay, so the Counterintelligence Special Agents operate in units all over the globe. The 66th is the brigade that operates out of Europe."

I turned both hands to the desk. "Are you saying Jerry's contact investigated Armand?"

He nodded slowly. "Apparently, he recalled some parts of the investigation. He went off and did some research and got back to Jerry."

A pause, which I found a bit too dramatic, considering the circumstances. Our space was absent of all noise and movement.

Nick said, "Armand's story checks out. He—"

"Which one?"

"Which one what?" Stan asked, a look of confusion on his face.

"Did Anton Kovalchick, the KGB agent, try to get him to defect or become a spy for the Soviets?" I interjected.

Nick pursed his lips. "It's complicated, Ivy."

I arched my eyebrows.

"I'm going to put it all out there, but I'm just saying that it's messy."

Another *just sayin'* comment. Must be a Brooklyn thing. Thankfully, he kept going. Because if he didn't, I was about to jump across my desk and strangle the guy.

"Armand's official statement to the CI agents was that Kovalchick tried to get him to defect."

"There's an official statement?" Stan asked.

"Not from Armand. But CI agents were able to find the woman and interrogate her."

The so-called other woman. She was the last person I'd thought about. "What did she share?"

"A lot. She basically turned over everything she knew about KGB espionage activities against the US and its allies. How they identified and worked a target; how much time and money they were willing to invest, depending on what level of information they thought they could get from their target; as well as how they made decisions on whether to use other methods of enticement. It could be setting up a target with a girl, or kidnapping a loved one, killing a loved one. Everything was on the table."

"Damn," Stan said.

"I know it's seedy, but this shit goes on in the world."

We all exhaled. "So, how does this impact Armand's case?" I asked.

"She also admitted that even after Kovalchick was arrested by the Italians, she was ordered, and paid, to continue the seduction."

"It happened more than once?" Blood flooded my brain so fast I felt lightheaded.

Nick nodded. "And during that continued seduction, she tried to turn him into a Soviet spy."

My stomach did a flip-flop.

"A fucking spy," Cristina whispered.

Nick held up a finger. "Key point is, Armand was able to fight off the temptation. He didn't agree to give her any classified information."

"That was the conclusion of the investigation?"

"Yep."

Stan shifted in his seat again, his brow furrowed. "What happened to Armand, since he didn't tell the truth and all?"

Nick eyed each one of us. "Nothing."

"How's that?"

"According to Jerry's source—"

"He wouldn't tell you his name?" I asked.

"Nope. And I didn't push him on it either. Anyway, Armand was too valuable. So, they made it go away."

A stunned silence shut down everyone for a moment.

"Is that how it works in the adult government world? Because you're so 'valuable,' they just pretend something didn't happen?" Cristina asked.

I shrugged. "Apparently, it's like professional sports."

"And politics," Stan said. "But please don't get me started."

I put my hand up. "I won't. Guys, this isn't la-la land. This is the real world, and—"

"The real fucked-up world," Cristina said over me.

The Radowski cousins couldn't help but crack up at Cristina's timely comment. She acted like it was no big deal. Good for her to play it down, unlike Mr. and Mr. Mature.

Forty

As the boys released some nervous tension, my mind went back to Armand, how he'd portrayed himself all of these years, to his wife, to Zahera, to me, and I would imagine, to just about anyone he met.

When he'd shared his story about being set up by the KGB agent, he had shown a side of himself I'd never seen. He was vulnerable, aware of the pain he'd caused his wife, even though she'd died years ago—or maybe it was because she was no longer around. It was hard to tell. But to see him open up and share those painful memories showed me how much he cared for his daughter.

Now, though, after hearing the actual investigative facts from Nick, I was nothing less than stunned.

Armand's ethical code was who he was. It was the compass by which he made every decision. But in reality, he was no different than every other politician roaming our land—ethics were to be used selectively, in a manner that only made you look the best, or even just the "least worst," if that was even a term.

I tried to swallow, but my throat was dry, so I sipped more from my bottle of water. "Now that I feel like I need to take another shower, let's get this out of the smut bubble and talk about the fun world of international drug trafficking." Clasping my hands in front of me, I gestured at Nick. Then, another connecting thought zipped to the front of my mind. "Actually, before I go there, did Jerry's source say anything about Anton Kovalchick? Remember, Armand only opened up and told me the truth—well, the half-truth—about him being set up by a KGB agent because he thought there might be a chance that Kovalchick could be connected to Zeke."

"The only thing Jerry said about Kovalchick was that he dropped out of sight shortly after the Soviet Union was no more. After that, according to his source, they have nothing on him."

"So, he died, or maybe moved to New Zealand to become a graphic artist?"

Nick shrugged. "Sure. Who knows?"

"I bet he was killed," Stan said. "During the transition from the Soviet Union to Russia, it was mass chaos."

"How would you know?" Cristina asked with a tone that bordered on mocking. I tried to give her the signal to turn down the snapping sarcasm, but I don't think she saw me.

"I read countless stories about the mass chaos in the government, especially within the intelligence community."

"He's right," Nick said.

Stan continued. "No one knew who was in control. Little fiefdoms were being created, some driven by intimidation, others by who paid the most. People were killed randomly without question, and there wasn't a law enforcement presence that anyone trusted. A lot of people wondered if the country would implode."

"Impressive."

Stan rubbed his forehead with his prosthesis. "Thank you, Ms. Nash."

"So we take Kovalchick out of the equation for now." I motioned again toward Nick. "What did Alex tell you about Zeke?"

A labored sigh.

"Should I read into that?"

He pressed his lips together. "Alex has pushed and prodded the Ukrainian officials to explain why Zeke's name is in those memos, but they won't do it."

"Oh come on. I mean, I know it isn't easy, but you gotta know how to push for information."

He chuckled. "You wouldn't be saying that if you knew Alex. That being said, she can't create an international incident. If this were another US agency, or internal FBI, she'd put the guy in a headlock."

Now I released a quick giggle.

His eyes met mine. "You think I'm kidding?"

"I guess not."

"Look, Alex is fully vested in this."

"Then why aren't we seeing results?" My temperament went south in a heartbeat, and I pushed my chair away from my desk and stood up. Turning toward the front bank of windows, I could hear the crinkle of crushed plastic and realized I was squeezing my half-empty bottle of water.

"Ivy, there is a thread of hope," Nick said.

Nick isn't the enemy, I told myself. I found a distraction—two old guys smoking outside the building across the street. They seemed to be tolerating each other. Without turning around, I said, "What could that be?"

"Alex has gotten to know one of the interpreters, a junior official with the Ukrainian SBU."

"She's banging a spy? Now this shit is real crazy," Cristina said.

"Did she really go there?" Stan looked at me.

"Sorry. Just calling it like I see it…or hear it," she said.

"Alex is happily…well, she's got a serious boyfriend, a colleague of ours named Brad. He's a good guy, even if he is eleven years younger."

"What the fuck? She's a cougar." Cristina smacked the table and released an ear-bursting cackle.

I flipped around to my ECHO partner. "Can you put a muzzle on it for just a few minutes?"

She looked like a tortoise as her shoulders came up around her neck.

Then over to Nick. "So Alex has befriended this SBU official. What does she hope that will accomplish?"

He rubbed his face, taking a gander around the office while mumbling under his breath. I looked at Stan, who gave me a *who knows* shrug. Another few seconds passed, then Nick finally said, "Alex's new SBU contact said the Ukrainian SBU has someone on the inside of Udovenko's drug trafficking operation."

"You mean, like a mole?" Stan asked.

"Yes, that's the term I would use."

"So, this guy is going to catch Udovenko with his hand in the baggie of cocaine and then put a pair of handcuffs on him? Then, it ends just like that?" I asked.

"Won't be that easy, I'm sure. Never is. These drug traffickers typically have several layers of people between them and the real world; it insulates them from possible insider assassination attempts. But the way Alex framed it, I get the feeling this person has access to Udovenko, although she didn't say that explicitly." He scratched the peach fuzz on his chin. "By the way, I never said it was a guy. In fact, Alex made a point in describing the mole as a person, not specifically male or female. But that could just be Alex."

"A chick?" Cristina said almost to herself.

"Moles can be chicks too," I said.

I found myself over at the window, trying to piece together what all of this meant. It didn't take long for me to draw a conclusion, and I twirled around to the group. "Here's how I'd sum everything up. After hearing that Armand lied for no reason other than to protect his image, we find out that Alex, through working her global sources, discovers the Ukraine drug sniffers have a guy or girl on the inside of Udovenko's business. On this side of the pond, Armand is killed by a pro, who covers his tracks by torching the vehicle. Meanwhile, we've got Zeke jet-setting all over the continent, and even when he's in town supporting Zahera, he's acting strangely—distant one moment, overly emotional another."

"Hadn't heard your thoughts about Zeke's current behavior," Nick said, trading glances with Stan. "Interesting."

"But what does it give us?" I asked, my arms swinging out to my side. "We don't know if Zeke is part of some drug-trafficking operation. We don't know if his mere presence to Zahera could bring her harm or for that matter, could have caused Armand to be killed." I exhaled, now crossing my arms against my chest. Then, like a meteor hurling across the sky, a thought penetrated my mind. "What if Zeke found out that his father-in-law was snooping around, about to create major problems for him? What if *he* had Armand killed?"

The office erupted. And I just stood there and looked out the window, as the meteor exploded into a million pieces in my gut.

Forty-One

Our meeting suddenly sounded like something I'd seen during a news cut of English Parliament members yelling and screaming at each other. Not that Stan, Nick, and Cristina were arguing, per se. Voices were at elevated levels. There was lots of finger-pointing and plenty of opinions and accusations.

All because I opened my mouth and dropped a one-liner on them that could stop the presses of the *National Enquirer*. But as much as I wished my question was baseless and nothing more than a shock statement, I couldn't dismiss the awful notion from my mind.

We'd taken a ten-minute break, allowing everyone to cool off and, in the case of Stan, use the restroom. Cristina and Nick had just walked into the front area without uttering a word, their faces void of expression. We were, again, waiting on Stan to join us.

The toilet flushed, and the three of us cracked smiles, dialing back some of the tension. Stan joined us a moment later, walking in with some spirit in his step.

"You're moving like a thin man, I'll give you that much," Nick said.

"Just wait, cuz. I've got you in my sights." Stan shifted his two fingers from his eyes to Nick, who chuckled. "Okay, the fake kidnappings…" Stan said, pulling out his notebook.

"Hold on," Nick said. "We can't just leave Ivy's shock-jock comment lingering. While it borders on outrageous, it's a theory that shouldn't be ignored."

"Thank you," I said, relieved that someone was truly hearing my concerns. "But what can you do with it?"

"Well, Stan and I discussed the possibility, or even the likelihood, of sharing this with our leadership and getting approval to formally create a joint task force."

A bureaucratic response if I'd ever heard one. I grabbed a pen and started clicking it to keep myself occupied and not firing off a zinger.

"You rolled your eyes," Stan said.

"No, that was me," Cristina said, raising a hand.

"I was looking at Ivy."

"Okay, I might have rolled my eyes slightly. I'm just tired of road block after road block."

Stan grabbed the arms of the chair to pull himself forward, but his prosthesis slipped, and he dropped a foot before regaining his balance. We all stayed mute, and he ignored it. "A joint task force will put eyes on this, Ivy. We'll get more resources. It won't just be me investigating Armand's death."

Nick raised a hand. "It's not like Zeke isn't on our radar, but we haven't formally put plans into place. On top of that, we won't have to conduct conversations in a whisper; we can get everything out in the open. We can start to map out Zeke's digital footprint. You said he was in Canada twice, and then Mexico. We can verify that to hopefully figure out where he went, and whom he might have met with. You get the picture."

It sounded intriguing, but it also sounded agonizingly slow. A couple of thoughts came to mind on how I might want to supplement their effort, but I knew I couldn't just blurt it out. They'd shoot me down in a nanosecond. "How long until your big machine is up and moving?"

"I hear sarcasm in there, but I get it. The government isn't exactly agile. Still, though, Stan and I are here, brainstorming with you guys, which has been our best source of information and possible theories. He and I will continue working this even as we wait for the additional resources to show up."

"*If* you get approval for this joint task force."

Both cousins tilted their heads, their palms facing upward. Well, three palms and a prosthesis.

"Okay, I don't mean to be a doubter, but something tells me we don't have four or five days to ramp this up."

"We'll do the best we can," Nick said with a bit of extra zeal.

I blew out a breath, then rubbed my temples for a moment. "I know you and Stan are invested in this. I appreciate everything you've done. Honestly." I sat back in my chair, folded my arms across my chest. "I think my nerves are on edge, worried about Zahera, upset about seeing her father killed in front of my eyes. And knowing Zeke could be part of some larger drug-trafficking cartel, wondering about his role in all of this. I'm about to blow."

"Isn't that part of Saul's job?"

I slowly turned my head toward Cristina.

Nick's eyebrows popped up. "Wow, did she just say that?"

"Oh yeah she did," Stan said.

"That's not something you should be thinking about," I said to her, then turned back to the fellas.

"I do have a boyfriend...well, more or less."

"Has anyone ever given you the talk about the birds and the bees?"

She exploded with laughter. "Do you not recall my background? Birds and the bees? I've been exposed to fucking snakes."

"I know, I know."

"Not that this is the time or place, but my new teacher, Mrs. Foster, she's given me a solid."

We all just stared at her.

"Oh, that means she's talked to me a couple of times about…you know, men stuff."

Men? I didn't even want to go there. Yet, something about her going elsewhere for advice on such an important topic gave me pause. Maybe I felt a little underappreciated. Or jilted. Something like that. It just added a new layer of frustration on top of the other crap.

Forty-Two

I looked at Stan, hoping he could rescue me from Cristina's shock talk. "So, the fake kidnappings..."

"Right." He cleared his throat, flipped a few pages in his notebook.

I noticed that his dexterity with his prosthesis had improved. He seemed more confident in using it. Or maybe he'd just come to terms with his situation and was making the best of it. That was one bright spot to cling to.

"So, just to show how a good law-enforcement partnership works..." Stan said, momentarily glancing at Nick. "Working with the IT guys at the local FBI office, they've been able to narrow the scope of possible locations of the phone calls to fifteen."

"Just fifteen?"

"Yeah." He thumbed through a couple of pages in his notepad, apparently not noticing my sarcasm. "That's an improvement of ninety-four percent." He raised his eyes, a look of accomplishment on his face. I went with it.

"Okay, so we're down to fifteen. Seems to be a workable number. Where are the locations?"

"Let's see, one is in San Mateo, California—"

"Near Silicon Valley," Cristina said. "Could be a couple of young punks who are computer geeks and can hack into any system they want."

I heard a buzz, pulled my phone from my purse, and then set it face down on the desk. One drama at a time.

"Well, that's the basic profile we've compiled. But realize that when I say San Mateo, I mean anywhere within that general area. They're still working to try to narrow it down further, possibly to a specific neighborhood."

"They could be on the move," I said. "They could be in San Mateo one day, Vegas the next."

His mustache twitched. "It's possible."

I could feel my neck getting stiff. I forced myself not to rub it. "The other locations?"

"One in Idaho, one in Northern Virginia, one in—"

"Isn't the FBI headquartered in Quantico?" Cristina asked, looking at Nick.

"Well, we have the FBI Academy there, as well as other operational functions."

"Maybe it's someone there who's turned to the dark side."

"Can't rule anything out," Nick said.

"The next one is in..." I motioned my hand for Stan to continue with his list. My phone buzzed again. Now I was beginning to think I was being spammed.

Stan turned a page in his notepad and continued. "One was in Austin, or they think more than likely in Round Rock, and then eleven more across the globe. I can read them all if you want, but it's kind of a waste of time."

It seemed like this entire arm of the investigation was a waste of time, or just taking too damn long. Emptying my lungs, I set that notion aside. "Cristina, do you want to share with Stan what you learned about the victims?"

I saw Stan's eyes shift between Cristina and me at least four times.

"Something wrong?" I asked.

"You tell me."

"We're all good," Cristina said. "Don't look so worried, Stan. It's not like we're felons or anything."

I took note of her including me in that statement, as well as using the term "felons."

Stan carefully lifted his fake arm and rubbed his nose. The way he concentrated on making that small move was as though he were disarming a bomb.

To keep us focused on what really mattered, I went ahead and communicated the information Cristina had learned. I also shared the details on the Klein sisters—they appeared to be sisters—how Nancy was accused of giving patient information to Stonebrook Pediatrics, and how we found out that Lisa worked at that same medical group.

Stan nodded when we finished, while Nick seemed to be in another world, texting on his phone.

"What?" I asked Stan.

He motioned to me and Cristina. "Have you asked Zahera the details of why she let Nancy stay on as an employee, or if she had actual evidence of data being given to this other company?"

"She was out of town, and then her father died. Now that she's back, I didn't want to put anything else on her, especially if we're not sure about the details. She might have a perfectly good reason for why she kept Nancy."

"Although, Kelly couldn't think of one, right?" Cristina added.

"Who's Kelly?" he asked.

I told him, then said, "You're right about Kelly, Cristina. She couldn't. She thinks Nancy should have been fired. But Zahera takes her business very seriously. I can't imagine her blowing this off and giving her a second chance."

"Yeah," Cristina said. "She's acting as if Nancy might have just taken a pen from the office supply cabinet."

My phone buzzed three times, all in short stabs. I began to lift the edge of the phone when Stan said, "Maybe this Nancy person has something on Zahera."

I dropped the phone. "Do what?"

"You've got my mind thinking about every possible conspiracy theory out there with Zeke and this Udovenko creature. I'm just sayin' there has to be a logical reason, even if it's a little seedy."

Again with the *I'm just sayin'*.

Stan went on to say that a crime could have likely been committed, and he wanted to know more. We agreed to give Zahera one more day to grieve, and then we'd have no other choice but to have a discussion with her.

"Now," he said, his fake arm swaying back and forth between me and Cristina. "How did you get this information?"

"Don't answer that." I pointed at Cristina, then turned back to Stan. "Do you really want to go there?" Stan growled. He knew me. He knew he could trust me. But he also knew I would do anything to protect my friends and my clients. I then said, "The point is, a majority of the victims intersect at Stonebrook. I think we need to take a deeper look at this Nancy Klein, for starters."

Stan said he would do just that and get back to us. I waited to hear more, but that was it. I'd hoped he would say that the SAPD would raid the Stonebrook offices, confiscate all data and communications, and arrest Nancy Klein on suspicion of conspiracy. But that wasn't going to happen. Another lesson learned for me, even at age twenty-eight.

He pulled his stuff together while having a quiet conversation with Nick in the corner. I finally turned my phone over and looked at the screen. There were a dozen text messages, all from Megan.

The last two said: *I'm devastated*, and then, *I'm going to kill that SOB*.

I grabbed Cristina and ran out of the office.

Forty-Three

As we sprinted for the Civic, Megan texted her location, followed by a string of curse words. She wasn't making a lot of sense. When I turned the ignition key, my phone dinged again. Cristina plucked it out of the cup holder and read the message out loud: *"If something happens to me, then take care of my kids."*

"What the hell?" I felt a jolt at the base of my skull at the exact time I hit the gas. Tires screeched off the hot, dry pavement.

"I don't know, Ivy. What should we do?"

"Text her back. Keep her talking. While you're doing that, tell me where to go. Never heard of Flying Arrow Drive."

She pulled out her phone and punched in the address. "Go north on 281 for now." She then used her left hand to type something on my phone as I rolled down the windows. The damn AC seemed to be blowing out warm air.

"What are you saying to her?" I quickly asked.

"Asking her if she knows of a good swimming pool to go to."

With one eye on the road, I turned in her direction. "What the—"

She gave me a forced giggle. "Too much pressure. It's all I could think of. I figured it might be so strange that it would take her mind off whatever was stressing her out."

"I like the strategy. Hope it works."

Cristina took another look at the address. "It's in Stone Oak, that ritzy area. I think it might be her home, or her former home."

We zipped up Highway 281 north of San Antonio, where all of the rich folks lived. As the wind rippled through the open window, I worried about what might be going on with Megan. Even though it was only midmorning, Megan could have already downed a bottle of vodka, returned to her home, and…what? I couldn't take my fears to that next step. I'd seen heartbreak from Megan that was tough to stomach. Frankly, I felt like she had the capability of doing anything in a drunken state.

I increased my speed above seventy, and we crossed Loop 1604 in no time. I exited at Evans and headed west. We entered a gated community where there were numerous signs warning us to slow down to twenty miles per hour.

"Where's Flying Arrow?" I asked, increasing my speed up to twenty-five. Then, I saw a mom pulling her two kids in a wagon, and I lifted my foot off the gas.

"Left, then right at the corner, then another left. Oh, then one final right."

"It seems like they're purposely trying to get us lost in the maze. But it's all just one big box of streets with houses packed in here like it's an inner city. Do these master planners think people have forgotten they live in one of the largest states in the country?"

For once, Cristina held off on her response, so I replied to my own question. "Apparently."

I executed the final right-hand turn, then dodged about a dozen cars parked along the curb. "That's dangerous as hell. I'd think the Homeowner's Association would take away the first-born child with an infraction like that."

"You sound like me," Cristina said.

"Just calling it like I see it." I nudged her arm to get her attention. "Sound familiar?"

She gave me a mocking smile. "Ha." Then she looked up. "Stop here."

I pressed hard on the brake, and we rocked to a stop. I jumped out of the car and took a quick gander around us. The neighborhood oozed money. The landscaping alone on any one of these two-story brick McMansions was worth more than ECHO. Even the gas light hanging near the front door was probably worth a thousand bucks.

"Should we ring the bell?" Cristina asked.

"Text her," I said, realizing she still had my phone.

"No response," she said after about ten seconds.

"Give her a minute."

"A lot can happen in a minute."

"Technically, she's not supposed to be here." I pressed the door handle. It was locked. I tried looking through a vertical window next to the door. A sheer curtain reduced my visibility, but I didn't see any movement. "We can't be sure who is here with her. Let's take a quick run around the house. We might find an unlocked door or possibly see her inside." I led the way around the house, pausing every few feet to look into windows. An empty bedroom. An empty office. Another room with closed shutters.

We made it to the back and entered the gate to the backyard. Once inside, I felt like I was being held captive. The fence, which looked like it had been handcrafted and stained by a world-famous Italian designer, was about ten feet high. I spotted at least twelve landscape lights on the fence. At nighttime, I was sure this gave homeowners a feeling of security, but the way I was seeing the scene, they seemed more like prison lights. Was it all set up to keep bad people out...or to keep good people in?

I wondered the same thing about all of these types of gated communities.

A glint of light from inside the house drew my attention.

"It's Megan," Cristina said, pointing.

I ran up to the window to get a clear view, and my flats crunched over broken glass. I looked up to see Megan disappear down a hallway before I could call out her name. "I think I saw a knife in her hand."

"What? Are you sure?" Cristina leaned closer to the window. "Yell for her, dammit."

"Hold on. Not sure who else is here." We spotted a broken pane in the window. "Wonder if that's how Megan got in."

"Doesn't she have a key?"

"I'm guessing Carlos had a locksmith change out the locks."

"On top of the court order. Dickwad," she said. "He really knows how to kick a person when they're down."

"Yeah, I know. Even though Megan's a client, I guess we have to look at it from his perspective too. I mean, she's kind of gone off the rails. He might be afraid for the kids. Or maybe just sick of her alcoholic episodes."

"Wow, who's the cold-hearted one?"

I ignored her and walked around about thirty potted plants— most filled with plants so vivid with color they looked fake, somewhat like the neighborhood. I got to the back door. It was locked.

Cristina pulled up next to me. "How the hell does she expect us to get to her when she's locked herself inside?"

We locked eyes as realization hit us.

"You don't think she brought us here to find her dead—"

I put my hand up to her mouth. "Don't say it." I flipped around and banged on the door. "Megan, please open the door. It's Ivy and Cristina." I paused, cupped my hands to the window in the door. Cristina did the same. "See anything?"

"No," she said, shifting down the long bank of windows. "Still nothing. Where did she go?"

She couldn't kill herself. We couldn't let it happen. "Follow me." Fear ignited an extra burst of energy, and I sprinted across the porch and into the yard. Around the far side of the house, I ran into another gate. I pushed down on the lever, but it didn't move.

"It's locked," Cristina said, putting an eye to the crack. "Looks like Carlos has a padlock on it. Combination padlock."

I retreated five steps to look over the great wall. I could see the top of a framed window on the other side. "I think she's in that room. Come on." We had to run all the way around the house to travel about ten feet in real distance. Once there, we only saw the lining of a curtain. We both used open palms to bang on the window, yelling and screaming her name. That went on for a good minute. But no one came to the window.

"Ivy, what if—"

"Hush." I panted like I'd run a mile. "Crap. I think we're going to need to break the window."

"Let me find a rock."

"My gun. It's in the glove compartment."

"I'll get it," she said.

"No, you won't. Stay here." I ran to the car, unlocked the glove box, and pulled out the gun. I didn't bother loading it with bullets. I stuck it inside my jeans and covered it with my shirt. I was sure that if any unsuspecting soccer mom saw me racing across the lawn with a gun—having pulled it from my beat-up car—she would call in some private SWAT team. So far so good, from what I could tell.

I made it back to the window on the side of the house, huffing a bit. "Any movement?"

"Nope. Nothing. Ivy, I'm really worried." Cristina bit down on her fist. I could see tears welling.

"You can go to the car. In fact, get ready to call nine-one-one. I'll give you the signal."

"No. Just go ahead, bust out the window."

"Get back," I said, moving in front of her. Facing the grip of the gun toward the window, I brought up my arm to cover my face. I reared my arm back and...

"Stop!" Cristina screamed.

I lowered my arm to see two ominous eyes staring me down through the window.

Forty-Four

With her face dripping with tears, Megan opened the back door and ushered us inside. My eyes, however, were stuck on the butcher knife in her hand.

"What are you doing, Megan? You know you shouldn't be here."

Her chin quivered, her gaze drifting until it landed on a family picture on the sofa table. She picked it up and ran her finger across the images of her son and daughter. "My darling, sweet kids. Annie and David," she said, in a soft but raspy voice.

I wondered if she'd screamed half of her voice away.

"A mom couldn't ask for two more perfect children. They are the light of my life. The only things that make me want to live." She raised the knife, but then only scratched her chin with her finger.

I glanced around, listening closely for any other noises. "Megan, I'm assuming no one else is home?"

She shook her head, but her eyes never left the picture. I spotted an open bottle of what looked like vodka or gin sitting on the mantle.

"Hey, let's get out of here. We can take you to a diner, get some food, and you can share everything you're feeling."

"I don't want to go. I want to stay here…until Carlos gets home."

Cristina and I exchanged a quick look.

"Megan, I know you're upset. It sucks to not be allowed in your own home."

Her lips moved, but no words were spoken. Was she having some type of nervous breakdown?

I took a step closer. "Megan, can you hear me?"

"That piece of shit! He's not going to get away with this." She hurled the framed picture across the room, smashing it against the fireplace mantle. Glass sprayed everywhere. She began to pound her feet like a little girl throwing a tantrum. I had my eyes on her knife. Her arm was flailing. She was going to cut herself, or worse, if she wasn't careful.

"Megan, you need to calm down. We can talk through this, come up with a strategy. If we get out of here and stop this before anything bad happens, I'll make sure you're able to see your kids. Carlos can't keep you from seeing Annie and David."

She was in full-on freak-out mode. She didn't register a word I'd said. I moved closer, as did Cristina, but I motioned for her to stand back.

"Hey, Megan, you want to hear a good joke?" Cristina said.

I just shook my head. That certainly wasn't going to help.

Just as Megan raised the knife, I jumped in and grabbed the arm that held it. She screamed as if I were Freddy Krueger. Then, she dropped her arm downward, ripping it out of my grip. The knife swiped my hand, cutting the webbing between my thumb and fingers.

"Shit!" I jumped backward, holding my hand. Blood guzzled out of the cut.

"Are you okay?" Cristina said, running to my side.

My hand felt like it was on fire.

"Oh…no. Did I do that?" a sniffling Megan asked.

She dropped the knife then, and it clanged off the Travertine floor.

"Do you have a towel or something to stop the bleeding?" Cristina asked.

"My bedroom. Follow me." Megan darted away faster than I expected in her whacked-out mood.

"Do I need to call for paramedics?" Cristina had a thumb on the screen of her phone.

I looked at the cut. No severed tendons or ligaments that I could detect. I could move my thumb, even if it felt like I'd been stung by a thousand wasps. "No. If we call them, cops will show up and ask too many questions. Megan will get arrested. She might go to jail. I'm fine."

"Right, says the woman with a fountain of blood cascading off her hand."

Cristina's face was contorted into such a grimace I could barely see her eyes.

"You're not helping," I said as blood dripped to the floor. I looked to the bedroom. "Want to see what's taking Megan so long?"

Cristina shuffled away, then kicked the knife by accident. "Crap!"

"Get that out of sight." She bent down to pick it up, but another thought hit me. "Wait. Don't touch it. Your prints will be on it."

"You planning on pressing charges against her or something?"

"Cristina, we still don't know what the hell has gone on here. Find something to pick it up and put it someplace." She ran toward the kitchen, grabbed a handful of paper towels. She gave a bunch to me, which I used to wrap my hand. She used a couple of spare paper towels to grab the knife.

"Just don't let her find it," I said, holding my hand up to minimize the blood flow.

"Right." She moved two feet in every direction, then found a closet. She opened the door and placed the knife on the floor. "Good for now."

"Let's go find Megan." The mound of paper towels was almost completely crimson already. I needed a regular bath towel, or maybe two, to get the blood flow in check.

Two steps into the master bedroom, I stopped.

"What kind of fucking tornado hit this place?" Cristina said.

The bedroom was in shambles. Clothes were thrown everywhere. Pictures and cologne and other knickknacks that had probably been on the dresser or side tables had been knocked to the floor; some of the framed pictures were shattered.

I took a few more steps into the room; it was hard not to step on something. Then my eyes went to the bed. The mattress had giant slashes in it. But it was the red against the white sheets that made my pulse skip a beat.

"What the...?" Cristina said. "Wait. Do you smell something?"

I ignored her. "Megan. Where are you?"

I walked toward what I assumed was the bathroom. Megan shuffled out before I got there. "I'm sorry..." She was holding a towel in one hand, but her eyes were on the item in her opposite hand. A sheer, black bra. It was rather obvious it wasn't hers.

Forty-Five

Cristina ran over, gently plucked the towel from her hand, and gave it to me. I handed her the soaked paper towels.

"Thanks," she said, holding the wad as if it were the tail of a rat. She moved past Megan, looking for a trash can in the bathroom.

I wrapped my hand while approaching Megan. "I'm so sorry, Megan."

She blinked a few times, but said nothing. I glanced at the bed. "Megan, where is Carlos?"

"At work, I guess. Or maybe he and his slutty whore are at some hotel room."

I released a deep breath. "So why are the sheets red?"

She lifted her chin. "It's ketchup."

Cristina walked out of the bathroom. She was wiping her bloody fingers on her shirt. "Told you I smelled something."

We ignored her. I had no idea why she'd used ketchup, but now wasn't the time to ask her questions about her methods of displaying her anger and pain. I was just thankful she had calmed down. She looked at my hand.

"Ivy, I don't know what to say. I think I just…lost it."

"You been drinking again?"

"Yes, I had a few drinks, but I stopped before I went overboard. Three shots of vodka to an old pro like me…that's like peeing into the ocean." She cackled so loudly I put a hand to my ear, but I smiled along with her. Anything to lighten the mood.

"Do you think we need to clean up before we get out of here?" I asked, but she had already fallen back into a trance. She walked across clothes and torn sheets and a busted radio clock. Then she dropped to her knees. She pulled a card from a pile of trash.

"I only came home so I could try to feel close to my family, mostly to Annie and David. But this note…this is what I found on the table next to the bed.

I walked over as she read it aloud.

My dearest Carlos,

Not only are you the kindest man I've ever met, but you are the rock of my life – in more ways than one. ☺ I love you with all of my heart – and every other body part. I can't wait to have you between my legs again. Even if I have to share you, I will always be there for you.

Yours forever,

xoxo

Megan dropped her chin to her chest, her arms falling to her side. I could feel her pain ripple through the air, as if an aftershock had pummeled my chest. "I'm so sorry, Megan." I put my good hand on her back. "We'll help you clean up, and then we can leave. He's going to know you were here when he sees the mattress, but I'll help you find a lawyer. Just know that you'll be able to see your kids. Cling to that thought for now, and it will get better."

Cristina began to place items back on the tables, and after a few minutes, Megan even helped with the effort. The purple towel wrapped around my hand was a darker color on one part, but it felt like the bleeding had stopped. I held it upward and did what I could to help.

Megan stopped and looked at me, the one-armed bandit. "I have some bandages in the cabinet above the toilet. Let me get those for you."

"That's okay. I can do it. You can tell Cristina where everything should go."

I walked into the bathroom, opened the cabinet above the toilet. I grabbed a basket of bandages, resting it on the toilet seat. I removed the towel, washed off my hand—nearly biting through my lip as the water poured into my open cut—then dried it off, applied bacitracin, and put on three bandages. I could hear some banter from the other room. It seemed low-key, which allowed me to relax a little, even though my hand was still hurting like hell. My webbing was now held together with adhesive and bandages. I couldn't move it without reopening the cut.

As I placed the basket in the cabinet, I spotted the edge of a photograph sticking out from under a folded hand towel. This wasn't my house, and I didn't want to be nosey, but given the note that Megan had just read, I pulled out the picture.

I stopped breathing. It was a picture of a man and woman…naked, intertwined. It was Carlos…more of him than I wanted to see. As for the woman, I could only see her from the rear, so to speak. She had shorter brown hair and a full figure. I looked in the cabinet and lifted the towel all the way and found five more pictures. I thumbed through them, then stopped on the last one. "What the hell?" I whispered. This photo was different. It was Carlos with a woman, but not the same one in the other pictures. She had a similar body type and hair color, but a few more curls. The pair was in the same basic position. She had a small tattoo of a heart with an arrow through it on her lower back. "A tramp stamp." I stuffed two of the photos in my jeans.

My sixth sense told me there was more to this than just a guy going through some type of crisis, or reacting to Megan's crisis. And I had to find out what it all meant.

Forty-Six

Zeke locked his apartment door, then peered through the peephole for a few seconds. A middle-aged mom sauntered by in a bikini that likely hadn't fit ten years earlier, much less now. A little girl wearing sunglasses that covered half her face bumped against her mom's hip every few steps. Neither seemed to notice or care as they both giggled intermittently while staring at their phones.

He felt a prick at the base of his skull. For a brief moment, he wondered if there was any way that the clueless mom could be one of *them*. Normally, he would roll his eyes and move on. But he couldn't take any chances, not after Armand's murder. He quietly pulled the door open a couple of inches and watched the mom and daughter until they got on the elevator at the far end of the hall.

He exhaled heavily as he locked the door again. He tossed his Texas Rangers cap and sunglasses on the bed—he'd used a Toronto Blue Jays cap when north of the border. He had little time to pull everything together. And even then, he knew that the odds that someone would be killed—someone very dear to his heart—was all too real.

As he grabbed his duffel bag from the closet, he felt a pang deep in his gut. Thoughts of his two kids filled his mind. His little boy's first birthday, when he'd tossed birthday cake around like he was playing in a sandbox. His sweet baby-teeth smile and infectious giggle were etched in Zeke's soul.

As for his daughter, he always went back to that time when she had played a game of cat-and-mouse with a squirrel in the backyard. He had stood on the back porch and watched as she gave instructions to the attentive little animal. It went on for a good couple of minutes, and then the squirrel darted out of its stance and started chasing her. She screamed at a pitch that would rival any opera singer as she scrambled around the yard. Zeke had waited to see if her true personality would show itself. A moment later, she came upon a stick. She grabbed it off the grass, quickly turned around, and demanded the squirrel start to behave. The squirrel wanted no part of her and took off for the nearest tree. She then proceeded to stand under the tree and give the squirrel a nice long speech.

Zeke whispered to himself at the memory, "Oh, Mandy, just like your mother."

Eva. Their attraction had been instantaneous and full of fire. What he didn't know early on was that her red-hot passion wasn't reserved just for their love life. She wanted things done a certain way…all of the time. She was very particular about how the kids were raised, what they were exposed to. At first, he admired his wife for these traits. But after a while, the two of them began to butt heads, and neither had the propensity to back down. Instead of uniting and bonding over the kids' various milestones, they tended to experience those events individually. He knew that over time it would create a chasm in their relationship. And it had.

Theirs was what one would call a loveless marriage. And it didn't help that he spent a majority of his time on the road, away from home. She resented him for it. He'd told her early on that his career, his calling, required him to be on the move. While it pained him every day to not see those little changes in his kids—the first tooth to fall out, the first hit in baseball, the first starring role in a school play—the wedge in his relationship with his wife grew wider.

But that didn't mean that Eva deserved to die.

He walked into the kitchen, poured a glass of water, and chugged until it was empty. Over the years, his line of work had involved a certain level of risk. At times, those risks came to fruition, whether it was on behalf of one of his clients, or when he'd had to take matters into his own hands. Yes, he'd been forced to perform certain acts that most would call reprehensible. But in his mind, the end result was far better than living with the status quo. Society as a whole was better for it.

Or so he'd convinced himself.

While he had no death wish, he also never truly concerned himself with being killed. His skills, both physical and mental, were advanced. He'd accepted this way of life long ago, knowing peril could be right around the corner. He did so because that was the way his father had taught him. In some respects, he believed he was only carrying on the family mission. But he knew his genetic makeup was slightly different. His propensity to take on assignments that brought him face to face with the most vicious and repugnant humans on the planet had, at times, even made his stomach queasy. But it never made him flinch. And it never led to him walking away.

He filled his glass once again, his eyes glaring out the window into the endless blue San Antonio sky. There was nothing serene or calming about it. Not today. Not with what lay before him.

He'd done everything in his power to shield his family from his way of life. Dual citizenship, changing names...essentially living a hidden life. All for Mandy and Ryan, and yes, even Eva.

And then there was Zahera. An exotic beauty who, at times, had taken his breath away. But the relationship, he hated to admit, had been born out of necessity. One that gave him the appearance of a life in San Antonio and, when necessary, a new woman on his arm when traveling, whether that be to his beloved Toronto or to other locales.

And Zahera certainly knew how to fill out a bikini in the perfect way.

He slammed his glass to the counter and thought more about the brutal death of Zahera's father. He had miscalculated the breadth and depth of Udovenko's organization. He'd been told that they had just begun penetrating the fertile US market. But it was apparent that Udovenko—even if it was through his proxy, Sergey—had developed a foundational structure in this country that allowed him to attain information and then quickly carry out certain tasks in a bold and definitive manner.

Thinking about the grief and despair he'd seen from Zahera since they both had learned Armand had been run over, he shuddered. Her pain had been one of the most difficult things he'd ever witnessed. It had chipped away a piece of his heart to know that Udovenko had killed Armand to simply make a point.

He had incorrectly assumed that San Antonio, the smallest big city in the US, would be so far off the grid that neither Udovenko nor his right-hand man, Sergey, would have any knowledge of his existence in the southwest. He had been wrong, in the worst way. The drug traffickers apparently had contacts that were far-reaching, their tentacles in every agency. He knew how they thought. Because they deemed him untrustworthy, they had sacrificed a life. A way to drive home a cautionary point: if you fuck with us, we will not hesitate to kill those who are close to you.

But was it a one-time warning, or would the killing continue? That was what Zeke did not know. He'd not predicted this last move by Udovenko's demented team. The real question came down to this: did they still view Zeke as a necessary asset in propelling their trafficking operation—drugs and now child body parts—to the next level? If so, then it was likely that they would halt their retribution. For now.

That was what Zeke was counting on. Just a few hours. That was all he needed. It would still require a certain amount of luck. And he might have to kill…again. But if he could save his family, it would be worth it. And he wasn't about to let Zahera perish just because he'd simply used her.

He would use the half-million dollars Sergey had already given him to set up his family in a location no one would find. He had hoped to get the full four million before executing this plan, but he had to settle for the lower sum for now. Most importantly, if he could get the required help, his family would be safe forever. He would likely remain on the run. But he'd worry about that later.

For now, he had two calls to make. The first was to a man he would trust with his life even on the darkest of days—this would solidify the plans for his family. The other call would set his strategy in motion. He knew that could be one of his final tasks on this earth, if it didn't go off without a hitch. And recently, nothing seemed to go according to plan. But he saw no other way. He grabbed his phone and punched in the first number.

Forty-Seven

I dropped off Megan and Cristina at my apartment. As the pair got out of the car, I signaled for Cristina to drop her head into the passenger-side window. I told her she had one primary task: make sure Megan stayed sober and didn't leave her sight.

"I think I can handle that. She slept most of the way over here. She'll probably just conk out on your couch."

I put a hand to my chin. "Hey, I think I have a bottle of wine in the cabinet next to the fridge. When she isn't looking, hide it. Or better yet, just dump it down the sink or the toilet."

"Sure thing." She stepped away from the car, and I put my hand on the gearshift.

"Hey," she said, suddenly back at the window. "What if the cops show up to arrest her for breaking into her old home and slicing up the mattress?"

We'd been able to clean up most of the mess, but we didn't have time to purchase a new mattress. And I couldn't be certain there weren't drops of blood—my blood— somewhere on the floor or in a sink. The towel and paper towels were in a trash bag in the trunk of my car.

"I'm a little nervous for Megan," Cristina said, with a quick check of our client over her shoulder. "I mean she broke a court order. She could get arrested, taken to jail. It might send her over the top again."

I looked around Cristina and saw Megan leaning against a Jeep, her eyes staring at the crumpled note in her hands.

"I thought you told her to leave the note there," Cristina said.

"She didn't listen. Are you surprised?"

"I guess not. But damn, she listens less than I do. And that's saying something."

"You got that right."

"Ha. I guess I set myself up on that one." She tapped the top of the door and began to turn around.

"Hey, Cristina. The cops might also want to arrest the two of us for assisting Megan in this crime."

"We didn't do shit. We probably kept her from hurting herself, then we helped her clean up the best we could."

"I was there, I know. But officers don't care about details. The HOA or a nosy neighbor might have pictures of us. So, I'm just saying, it's a possibility."

"You're 'just sayin'?" She used air quotes, grinning.

"You think I sound like the Brooklyn cousins?"

"Not as obnoxious, thank God."

"Anyway, if you see cops roaming around, just call me. If I don't answer, then call Saul."

"Why? He's not a lawyer. Wouldn't I have better luck calling the donut shop to try to get a delivery?"

I tilted my head and cocked an eyebrow. She'd lost me on that one.

"You know, cops love donuts. It might distract them."

"Ah. Good one. But please cut Saul a break. He's not a lawyer just yet, but he could be any day."

"And you're still going to want to hang out with him?"

"Hard to believe, I know. Later."

She walked off, and I drove to SAPD headquarters to talk to Stan in person. Midday traffic was light and moving at a good clip. Even the pedestrians seemed to be moving at a faster pace. Probably had something to do with the fact that temperatures had actually dipped into the eighties. And I could see a dark bank of clouds off in the distance. Everyone usually viewed imminent rain as hope for even more temperature relief.

Once inside the station, the desk officer called up to Stan. A moment later, he called my cell phone.

"What's up with the official visit? I'm busy working on...well, you know what I'm working on."

"That's why I'm here."

"I'm sorry. You just confused me."

"I need to see you in person."

"I'm flattered you want to see me again after seeing me just a few hours ago. But, Ivy, I really don't have the time. I'm trying to write up a warrant that shows probable cause so we can get our hands on the computer system, emails, any form of data at Stonebrook Pediatrics."

"Wow, you guys are moving fast."

"I've got the full support and partnership of the FBI. Nick's presence has helped smooth over any hard feelings with the local office."

"About?"

"Just another case where we were pointing fingers at each other. Anyway, they're going to help us sift through all the data, try to find any communications about buying or selling data, and what, if any, kind of connection there could be to this group pulling off the fake kidnappings."

"I'm glad you're going down this path, Stan. I think it's more efficient than knocking on every door in fifteen different cities, looking for hackers."

"Thanks for the endorsement."

"You know I didn't mean it like that."

"Just yanking your chain. But obviously I'm swamped. And I'm not real good working with one arm, if you know what I mean."

"Then come downstairs, please."

"Still?"

"It will be worth it. Trust me."

He said he'd be down after he finished typing up his warrant. I opened a magazine and read smut headlines for a couple of minutes. I found myself gravitating to the stories about kids, most of whom were the children of famous stars. They were either involved with drugs, running with a crowd involved in drive-by shootings, or suffering from mental disorders that led to eating disorders and cutting themselves. It was beyond sad.

I was reminded of a time a number of months ago when I thought I wanted to bypass the boyfriend-husband path and just move straight into having kids. Zahera and I had joked about me going to a sperm bank and sifting through the prospects. Since then, the desire to have kids of my own hadn't lessened, although my life had been filled with too many horrors to bring a baby girl or boy into it.

And then there was Saul. We'd kept our relationship simple thus far—no labels or pressure. But we'd have to address the future eventually. He may not have a clock ticking on his baby-maker, but he wasn't a woman.

I watched two kids walk in with their mom. She asked if she could see her husband who'd been picked up for drug possession. After that, I couldn't hear anything else she said. The kids, who had matching blond curls and blue eyes that could melt butter, had dirt and grime all over their faces and hands. One was in diapers, but he looked to be at least three years old. The other, a little girl, wore a T-shirt that hung below her knees. Did the mom consider that a dress?

I sighed, realizing there were countless kids in the world—in my very city—who were being neglected, yet no one did a damn thing about it. Just because two people could procreate, that somehow gave them the license to raise kids? It wasn't right, not for the kids.

"What's up?"

Stan caught me by surprise. I stood up. "Over here," I said, waving him toward the wall away from the flow of traffic.

"Why are you being so secretive?" he asked, scratching his forehead with his fake hand.

"I need to show you two pictures."

"This is pertaining to what exactly?"

"Stonebrook Pediatrics, and this conspiracy to get patient data, and as a result, the fake kidnappings."

"Now I'm really interested."

I held the first picture in front of his face. He quickly pulled my arm downward, while glancing over his shoulder. "What are you doing?" he said under his breath. "That's two people doing the nasty."

"I agree with the nasty part. But do you know who they are?"

"Not a clue. I only saw the picture for a second."

"You want another look?"

"No," he shot back. "Follow me." Moving hurriedly, he dodged the two kids I'd seen earlier and walked into a room off the lobby. He shut the door behind me. "We use this room for lawyers to meet with people whose family members are in jail. Now, I can take a closer look at your porn."

"Funny."

I handed him the same picture from earlier. He looked at it for a few seconds, then handed it back. "Is there someone famous in that picture I'm supposed to know?"

"Nope."

He flipped his wrist and checked his watch. "I don't have time to play guessing games. Who is it?"

"Well, even though we don't see the front side of her, I'm almost certain it's Nancy Klein."

He went still. "The nurse from Zahera's office who was supposedly accused of trying to sell patient data to Stonebrook?"

"That's her."

"I never got around to telling you, but she's on our list. I'm going to bring her in for questioning."

"Does Z know?"

"Not yet. I wasn't sure how to handle it. You want to volunteer to talk to her?"

I told Stan I was headed to her place after our discussion and that I'd relay the message. I knew it would lead to more questions. I'd have to figure out how to handle it later.

"So who's the stallion?" he asked.

"Are you sitting down?"

"No, I'm standing right next to you."

That was what I got for using a figure of speech. I let it ride. "It's Carlos Espinoza."

He raised a single eyebrow.

"The husband of Megan."

"Oh," he said, cocking his head. "Wait. Ohhh nooo."

"I know, right? He's a pig, but he might be a bigger pig than you think."

He lifted his fake arm, stopping me before I could continue. "Hold on. What's he doing with Nancy Klein…well, besides the obvious?"

"There's more." I reached into my pocket.

"I don't want to see any more naked pictures. They do nothing for me. And why didn't you answer my question?"

"Because I don't know the answer. I have an idea, or maybe a few ideas. But I need to show you one more picture."

He motioned for me to show it to him. And I did.

His brow furrowed. "It's the same damn picture. You trying to play a trick on me?"

"Look closer."

"I don't want to look, Ivy. I might see something I really don't want to—"

"Here." I put my finger on the lower back.

"Is that a tramp stamp?"

I couldn't keep from smiling. "Ever served a warrant to look at a tattoo?"

"Whose is it?"

I explained my theory on who the second person might be.

"Damn, that's good. I need to keep this as evidence."

I told him where I'd found the pictures, and he promptly returned them to me. "Evidence won't hold up. Does me no good, thank you very little."

I then explained the fiasco at Megan's house. "If you can verify that cops haven't shown up yet, then I can go put them back and they can find them…legally."

"I didn't hear you say that."

"Do you have a copy machine?"

I made two copies and hurried out of the SAPD.

Forty-Eight

I once heard a basketball coach quoted as saying, "It's better to be lucky than good."

Not exactly a great message for the younger generation, but it matched my thoughts after successfully breaking into the Espinoza house and putting the two missing pictures back in the bathroom cabinet where I'd originally found them.

Once I finished the task, I literally jumped through the open window into the front seat of my Civic, smacking my forehead against the frame of the car in the process. I looked in the rearview and could already see a rectangular bruise forming just above my eyes. "Sonofabitch!" I said, spewing out anything that came to mind to counter the throbbing pain. As was the case every time anyone did something boneheaded, the cussing didn't help. Well, not as much as I'd hoped.

I pulled away from the curb, taking a cursory glance around the immediate vicinity. No sign of neighbors holding up their phones. Then again, if they happened to catch that smooth move on video, it might go viral, and then I'd... I'd what? I'd be the laughingstock of the Internet for at least twenty-four hours.

I motored my way out of the neighborhood, pausing at a stop sign. Just as I hit the gas again, I heard a scream. My heart jumped, and I slammed on the brake. I spotted a woman standing on the sidewalk at the corner. She was purple Spandex and boobs—that was where my eyes went first. Next to her was a boy sitting in a wagon.

Why the hell had she screamed? I slowly eased by and waved at her. She just stared me down. I was certain she'd spread the word now, maybe posting something to their HOA Facebook page, and then she'd revel in watching all of the other cookie-cutter women pile on.

Oh brother.

On my way back into the city, I put in a call to Stan. It rolled to voicemail and I left a message: "Hey, just finished my *mission impossible*. I survived, more or less. Just checking to see if the cops were called out to the house yet. I'm sure it's only a matter of time, either by a neighbor or once Carlos gets home. Let me know."

I ended the call and coasted into the parking garage at Zahera's condo building just as a few large raindrops hit my windshield. I waved to the doorman downstairs and took the elevator up to the eleventh floor. Just as I was about to knock on the door, I heard shouting from inside the condo. My body tensed. I put my ear against the door. It was Zahera. I could feel my flight instinct shouting at me to turn around and come back later.

But I couldn't keep avoiding a confrontation with my friend. Why I thought there would be a clash, I wasn't sure. I just knew there were too many secrets between us, and something would come along and knock over that first domino. After that, I'd have no choice but to let everything out. The timing might be off, and someone could witness our clash who shouldn't—mainly Zeke.

For now, I tried to focus on my initial purpose for coming to the condo: to inform Zahera that Stan would be bringing in Nurse Klein for questioning. The waterfall of questions that would soon follow might drown me. But in the process I hoped to have one big question answered for me: why had Zahera let Nancy continue to work at her practice?

I knocked, and a few seconds later, Zeke opened the door. He didn't say a word.

I didn't see Zahera, but I could hear her. "I just don't understand why hired help feel like they have to take advantage of those who've had a little success!"

Zeke extended a hand for me to come in. I nodded, scanning the area for Zahera, all the time feeling Zeke's eyes on me. Most women would be flattered. I felt awkward at best, and slightly intimidated.

Then I realized he was staring at my bruised forehead. I touched it, then asked, "Where is she?"

He pointed toward the back bedrooms. I nodded and walked in that direction. I reached the entry to the guest bedroom, but stopped before walking in. The room looked like it had been taken over by a fifteen-year-old girl. "Hey there," I said as casually as I could muster. "What's going on?"

She mumbled something under her breath as she threw an empty bag behind her, continuing her search for something under one of the two queen-size beds. Mattresses were askew, covers and pillows were piled up in the middle of the room. Dozens of pairs of shoes and shoeboxes were thrown everywhere. I followed the trail to an open closet. She was tearing the room apart.

"Z, are you looking for something? Can I help you?"

Just then, I felt a hand on my shoulder. I turned to see Zeke give me a slight, but definitive shake of the head. I started to turn back around, to leave his gaze, but I found myself rapt by the look in his eyes. Was he ordering me not to offer any help to Zahera because of some signal I'd yet to pick up, or was he simply concerned about agitating Zahera's emotional state?

"Mother..." Zahera began to say before sticking her head under the bed. A second later, she popped up, her hair covering her face—a very atypical look for my best friend. She swatted the hair out of her face. "You going to help me or what?"

A quick glance at Zeke, then I set my purse on the desk and moved to the other side of the bed and looked beneath it. Zeke stayed at the doorway.

"What am I looking for?"

"A satchel. It's brown with tan on the sides, made of leather."

I lifted my head and banged it on the bed frame. *The satchel.*

"You okay?"

I was shocked she noticed, given her level of anxiety.

"No harm, no foul." I lifted up from the bed, rubbing the back of my head. A bump on the back to match the gruesome bump on the front of my head.

Zeke was still standing in the doorway, watching me intently. That was when I knew something was different. Prior to all of this mess, he'd been friendly, chatting away about topics that had no teeth—the weather, the stock market, the traffic. Ho-hum stuff. But something was up. He thought I knew something—I just couldn't tell if his deathly stare had to do with our search for his possible connection to Udovenko, or if it was just a feeling he had about me.

Forty-Nine

I heard a loud huff, which brought my attention back into the room.

"I'm sick of people ruining my life," Zahera put her elbows on the bed, her hands covering her face.

"Z, I'm sure it's around here somewhere." *Of course you do, Ivy. It's in your own damn closet at your apartment.*

"There's no way." She shook her pointer finger. "I don't even know why I'm tearing this room apart—maybe because I don't trust my own instincts right now. Dammit!"

I walked around the bed, steering my sight away from Zeke, and put my hand on her back. "You want to go into the other room and we can talk about it?"

"No, I don't want to go to the other room. Stop treating me like a child, Ivy."

She had venom in her voice. I removed my hand from her back. "Sorry."

Tears bubbled in her eyes. I found tissues on the desk and handed her one. "I'm sorry I'm being such a bitch," she said.

"It's okay, Z. You've been through a lot. More than…" A rush of emotion ran up the back of my throat.

"Don't tell me you're having a sympathy cry." She giggled through her tears as she stood, then embraced me. After a few seconds, I realized I was holding her tighter than she was holding me.

Taking a step back, I flipped my head toward the door. "You still have some of that homemade lemonade?"

"I want to know why the cleaning people took my satchel of letters." She put a hand on her hip, pointing toward the desk. "It was sitting right under there."

She looked at me, then Zeke, who said, "I don't recall the satchel, baby. I'm sorry. You sure you didn't put it in another place, maybe the hall closet or—"

"I told you before, Zeke. I put it right there."

Her eyes went back to me. "I never told you about the letters, did I?"

"Letters?" I asked unconvincingly. Dammit, I hated lying. My face felt flush, and I broke out in a sweat that was normally reserved for July days on the sizzling concrete in front of the Alamo.

She ran her fingers through her hair. "Dad..." She paused, took a swallow. "He dropped off the bag a couple of weeks ago and said he wanted me to have them. They were notes that he and Mom sent back and forth while he served overseas."

Armand must have thought that the damning letters weren't included in the bunch. "And?"

"And the damn cleaning people took them, that's what! I want their number. Zeke. Can you get me their number?"

He patted his pockets. "I'm not sure I have that contact in my phone. Do you want me to get your phone?"

She ignored him, turning to me again. "Yeah, I only read a couple, and they were the sweetest things I've ever read."

I felt my shoulders drop just a tad. "That's really cool."

"Yeah, I know, right? No one wants to think of their mom and dad getting it on or anything, but once they're both…gone, it's nice to read how much they loved each other."

She'd only read the good parts, thankfully. I reached over and touched her arm. "It's great to have those memories."

"But I don't have them, dammit."

Wrong move by me.

"I just know the cleaning people must have taken them." She put a hand to her chin, her eyes drifting off. "Wait a second. We had that party over here. The girls from the office. Do you think it's possible one of my own employees stole the satchel?"

I shrugged, and then I looked at Zeke, who did the same thing without saying a word. He was quiet. Too quiet.

"Do you really think one of your own employees would steal something from you?" I asked, grasping the opportunity: she'd opened the door to lead us toward Nancy Klein.

Zahera looked off in the distance. She seemed to ponder that question, or perhaps her mind was back to thinking about her mom and dad and those letters—which, to her, were full of positive memories. I thought about how much the truth might destroy her impression of her father. I was afraid, in her current fragile condition, the truth about her dad's transgressions might shatter her.

The doorbell chimed, and we all jumped a little, but no one moved toward the door.

"Oh, Zeke, that might be Liu." Zahera had some excitement in her voice.

Zeke's eyes went to me, then back to her. "Yeah, let me get that. He can set up in the living room." He paused, as if he were waiting to hear something more.

Zahera's gaze turned to the floor under the desk. "I wonder who could have done it."

"Perhaps Nancy Klein?" In some respects, I felt guilty associating Nancy with an offense I knew she didn't commit. But it was the only way to move the conversation where it needed to go.

Her big brown eyes got wider. "Why would you say Nancy?"

"I know she stole patient data and tried to sell it to a pediatric group."

"How…? Wait, you probably talked to Kelly, am I right?"

"She mentioned it when the drinks were flowing at the party."

Zeke was still at the door. It felt like he was eavesdropping, albeit in plain sight. I looked at him, hoping to draw Zahera's gaze in that direction.

"Baby, aren't you going to get the door?" she asked with a little bite.

"Oh, sure." He gripped the door frame, his eyes on me until he disappeared.

My concern, which might be shifting into the fear department, was that Zeke had something against me. I wasn't sure how, but he must have learned that we'd been looking into his connection to Udovenko. Was there some type of leak at INTERPOL, perhaps the person Nick's partner, Alex, had befriended?

Too much cloak-and-dagger shit for me to deal with right then. But I had to deal with it, dammit. For Zahera.

"I just don't think Nancy would steal my personal letters. It's not in her nature."

Zeke called out for Zahera, and she trudged out of the room, stopping in the hallway. "Let me change into my robe." She disappeared into her bedroom as I walked into the living room.

"I'm Yao. Do you also want a massage?"

Zeke looked at me. "I thought it would be good for Zahera to relax. She mentioned Liu is her favorite, but it turned out he was busy. So, Yao, his partner, came in his place."

"Cool." I turned back to Yao. "I'm good. Just take care of Zahera."

"She will get white-glove treatment." The man, who spoke in monotone, had some type of Asian accent. He looked like a bodybuilder. He had bumps all over his body, including his head. I touched the bruise above my eyes. I could tell it was a dandy.

My thoughts shifted to Zahera's response to my comment about Nancy stealing the patient data. It seemed like she'd just glossed over it, not addressing it one way or the other—almost like she was covering for Nancy. But why?

I just knew I couldn't leave her condo until I'd told her about Stan bringing Nancy in for questioning.

Fifty

Zahera swooped into the room, stopping as she noticed Yao. She looked at Zeke.

"Liu was caught up with another client, so his partner, Yao, came over. He's just as good as Liu. That's what he said. Right, Yao?"

"Yes sir." He popped his hand on the top of the chair next to the table he'd set up. "It's nice to meet you, Zahera. Liu has told me so much about you."

He sounded like a robot, or the dumbest form of artificial intelligence I'd ever heard.

She walked over and shook his hand. The big beast was surprisingly gentle with her. I probably shouldn't have been surprised. That was his profession. He uncorked a bottle of champagne and poured her a glass. He then held up the bottle to Zeke.

"May I pour you a glass?"

"No thanks. I actually have an urgent meeting and I'm already late," he said, looking at his watch. From what I could see, it looked like one of those digital numbers.

The bodybuilder then looked at me. I shook my head no.

"Oh, baby, have I kept you from your work?" Zahera held out a hand. Zeke leaned over and kissed it, then started walking toward the door. "You know my job; clients and potential clients are very demanding in my world. But you'll always be my number one priority."

"Thank you for setting this up, baby," she said. "I think it will be just what I need to relax, get my mind off things."

He winked as he walked to the door. He seemed to be trying to avoid looking at me, but our eyes met. Again. My gut swirled with anxiety, uncertain what to make of him. And where the hell was he going when his fiancé needed him the most? I knew Zahera. She was putting on a good front, just to allow him to go about his business without carrying any guilt.

I had to follow him. I had to figure out, once and for all, what the hell he was up to. He closed the door behind him, and I turned to Zahera. In between Zahera taking sips of her champagne, Yao was massaging her neck and shoulders.

"Z, I need to tell you something."

"What is it?" she asked with her eyes closed. Her tension had already been reduced.

My throat became dry, and I wished I'd taken Yao up on his offer. I couldn't delay this any longer, not if I hoped to catch up to Zeke. "Zahera, Stan believes Nancy could be involved—and let me emphasize *could be*—involved in this string of fake kidnappings going on."

"That's insane," she said, her eyes still closed. "Look, I know she's not perfect. She's annoying, if nothing else. But she's got a good heart. I'm sure once Stan looks into everything, she'll be exonerated."

Her calm demeanor caught me off guard. Again, it seemed like she was covering for her.

"Z, why didn't you fire Nancy after you found out she tried to sell the patient data to Stonebrook Pediatric?"

"Is it safe to assume that all of your questions relate to your client...what's her name?"

"Megan."

"Right. Well, it's actually pretty simple." She paused, sipped her champagne, releasing an audible "aah" before continuing. "I don't think she actually followed through with it, for one. She said she didn't, and I believe her."

Talk about gullible. Was this the same Zahera? I kept my caustic comments to myself. Instead, I just said, "Okay. And…?"

She opened her eyes for a moment. "She's had a hard life, Ivy. Well, her family has, taking care of her brother. He has a lot of health problems. It's put a lot of pressure on everyone in their family."

She'd at least piqued my interest, so I played along. "What kind of problems?"

"He has autism. Do you know what it's like to raise a kid who has autism? Severe autism. It has taxed her entire family, emotionally drained her, her sister, her parents. She basically broke down in my office. She only wanted to sell that patient data to make more money, to try to pay for an operation he needs."

"Operation? For autism?"

"Well, she did mention some sort of advanced research going on, something like that. It was hard to get much out of her after she broke down."

Was she for real?

"I can see you're questioning my judgment."

"No, I…" My voice trailed off as I glanced at the door. I knew time was of the essence. I couldn't let the opportunity to follow Zeke slip away.

"Ivy, her brother needs a kidney transplant, and he keeps getting turned down. All because he has autism. It's simply not fair. And it's tearing her apart."

I internally replayed what she'd just said. She'd given me new information, alarming information. Had I just connected a couple of dots? Maybe only in theory; more evidence was needed. The only way to get there was to ask questions. For starters—and maybe my most sarcastic question in response to hearing this news—if Nancy was so distraught over her brother's condition and not being approved for his transplant, then why was she jumping into the sack with Carlos Espinoza? When Zahera made her ruling on Nancy, was she even aware that her sister worked at the place where she was accused of passing along the patient data? Did she inquire as to which patients' data Nancy had pulled together, and why those patients were selected? I stayed mum on that arm of the story. "Thanks for the additional insight, Z."

"I know it doesn't look good on her part. By the way, how did Stan make the connection from her to these fake kidnappings?"

I didn't have the time to go down that rabbit hole, especially when it would lead to the seedy pictures I'd found and my theories that had yet to be proven. "I'm not sure exactly. You know him though. He's a solid detective. He knows his stuff."

She waved an unconcerned hand, then sipped more champagne. "Keep going, Yao," she said to the masseur, then looked at me. "I'm sure it will all be worked out. Nancy just needs to explain everything to Stan. She'll be fine."

Nancy, in my mind, might want to be fitted for prison garb, but I stayed mute and simply nodded. "Okay. Speaking of Megan, she's in a bit of a pickle. I need to go catch up with her."

"You sure you don't want Yao here to do his magic on you?"

I was already at the door. "Maybe once things are normal again. Not sure when that will be." I grabbed the door handle.

"Hey, Ivy. Any other thoughts on who might have taken my satchel?"

"Not a clue. Enjoy your massage."

I was out the door before my guilt forced me to unload everything I knew.

Fifty-One

Thanks to the doorman, and the fifty dollars I gave him, he shared with me that Zeke had stopped in the lobby as he talked on his cell phone. He said he couldn't quite hear the exact conversation, but that it was animated. He then said something that surprised me. "I think he was crying when he got off the call."

"What? Are you making this whole thing up? Did he already pay you off?"

"I swear on my momma's grave." He paused, swallowed. "And I don't take bribes. I'm only telling you all of this because you're a good friend of Miss Z. There's something…" He leaned in closer, looking around to make sure no one heard him. "There's something about her fiancé that doesn't seem right."

I wanted to quiz him further, but time wasn't on my side. I asked which way he went. He pointed south. "He's on foot."

"Thanks." I pushed through the revolving door and immediately broke into a jog. Zeke, per his usual outfit in the summer, was wearing a distinctive blue Lycra shirt that accentuated his sculpted physique. Between that and his gelled and cropped blond hair, I knew I could spot him in a crowd rather easily. Weaving around numerous pedestrians, I covered a city block in no time.

Light rain fell from the sky. The drops were nickel-sized, but so intermittent it made you wonder if someone upstairs was merely teasing everyone. I noticed a couple of kids crane their necks upward to try to catch the drops in their mouths. They looked disappointed.

I reached the corner of Broadway and 8th and paused, wondering which way he would have gone. On foot, he had to be close. Unless he knew I was following him, and so he hopped into a taxi. But how would he know?

I cringed, hoping like hell I wasn't searching for someone who was ten miles away. *Stay the course. That's all you can do.* I crossed the intersection, now moving at a fast-paced walk, my eyes scanning everyone in front of me, as well as glancing across the street in case he'd decided to backtrack.

Four more blocks and I saw signs for the Tobin Center for the Performing Arts. Dark clouds roiled overhead. The temperature had dropped, but the humidity and the tension had me sweating. I wiped my brow and kept moving, now back in a jog.

I finally spotted him up ahead. And his walk told me he was not out for a casual stroll. I stayed back, keeping enough people in between us to give me cover. He turned right on Pecan, and I followed, trailing him by about fifty feet. We came upon Travis Park, a square "green space" with trees and grass that was supposed to be green. It was all brown from lack of rain.

Zeke crossed the Navarro intersection. I took a step into the street. He stopped cold. He lifted his foot up on a fire hydrant and tied his shoe. He had on sunglasses, but he turned in my direction. On pure instinct, I pivoted right and began crossing Pecan, blending in with a crowd of about twenty people. Once on the other side, I fought the urge to turn around, and continued moving north. I made it past cars parked on the side of the road, then quickly dipped below the last one.

I heard myself panting. I counted to four, then slowly peeked through the window to see the fire hydrant on the far corner.

No Zeke. I lifted higher to get a wider view. He hadn't followed me—that was the good news. The bad news? I'd lost him. I quickly cut across Navarro as someone yelled out, "Jaywalkers go to jail in San Antonio."

At the corner of Pecan and Navarro, I looked east. No sign of him. I huffed out a frustrated breath and moved cautiously down Pecan, now on the north side of the street. I felt a few more drops of rain on my head. The skies looked like they might explode, but I continued my trek.

"Oh, nasty!" a voice said from a crowd that had halted pedestrian traffic.

I tried wedging my body between the hordes of people. "Excuse me." I made it to the center and found a dog—some type of German shepherd—peeing on the base of a lamp post. Had to be a stray dog, given he had no leash or visible collar.

I spotted Zeke again. He was crossing over to the north side of Pecan, just east of St. Mary's. He glanced in my direction, but there was no way he saw me in the sea of people. I eased my way toward the cross street, St. Mary's, and made it to the other side at the same time he scooted inside a building. I walked closer and saw it was a barbecue place. He had to be meeting someone there for an early dinner in plain sight.

Leaning against the adjacent brick building, I pondered my next move. If I went inside the barbecue joint, he could spot me. And then he would... What did I expect him to do? Sure, he'd know I was following him. He might give me the death stare, but he wouldn't harm me, not in a public restaurant. In fact, the crowd might give me enough cover to where I could finally confront him. Maybe under the pressure of me pelting him with questions, he'd finally share with me the nature of his connection with Udovenko.

Or not.

I rode the wave of my desire to take control and marched inside. A quick scan of the place. I didn't see him. I walked up to the host and asked if he'd seen a man matching Zeke's features.

"Oh, Mr. Ryan. He's a frequent guest. He asked to—"

"Ryan?"

"Yes, Jack Ryan, the man in the blue shirt and short, spiky hair."

The name was familiar—not associated with Zeke, of course—but my adrenaline was pumping so hard I couldn't recall why. I was still stuck on why he'd used a different name. "Where is he?"

"As I was saying, he offered to do a security check for us, since he's in that business." He paused, looking at one of his colleagues, then back to me. "Are you a friend of Mr. Ryan's?"

"Definitely. Tight," I said, crossing my fingers. "Where did you say he was?"

"I think I last saw him in the kitchen." He pointed behind him.

I walked past him and said, "Thanks."

"You're not allowed in the—"

His voice dissipated as I walked into the kitchen, a symphony of grease-popping sounds. I glanced behind me and saw the host heading in my direction. I asked one of the men wearing white hats if they'd seen Zeke. He gave me a quizzical look. "I mean Jack Ryan."

The man with a tattoo of the Alamo on his arm wiped sweat from his brow and said, "He went through the kitchen door in the back there, and down the back steps."

"Steps to where?"

He smirked. "The River Walk, of course."

Had Zeke seen me and now was trying to elude me? I thanked the man, found the back door, and flung it open. Two flights of stairs led to a parking lot adjacent to the River Walk, the barren section. I'd forgotten there were no access points at this northeastern spot. Basically, at the river level, there was nothing. Just a narrow sidewalk on either side of a dirty, green pool of river water. No restaurants. No shops. No people.

In other words, the perfect place to meet someone without being seen.

I scooted down the stairs, all the while scanning the narrow sidewalks looking for Zeke, or Jack Ryan, as the case may be. I saw no one. Part of my vision of the sidewalks was blocked by the streets that crossed overhead. As I reached the bottom of the staircase and walked toward the River Walk, I saw a sign affixed to the street overhead. Convent Street.

In just the next few steps, the scattered raindrops quickly became a thunderous downpour. My hair became matted to my scalp before I had time to start jogging, making my way toward the overpass at Convent.

I jumped over the small curb, landing on the sidewalk, and turned into the overpass.

I didn't see the man until his hand was inches from my face. I gasped as he covered my mouth, his body pressed against my backside. I was locked in his grip, unable to move my arms or head. I raised my leg, taking aim for his kneecap.

"I wouldn't do that if I were you."

Zeke's voice made me shudder.

Fifty-Two

The pounding rain made it difficult for me to process my options, that and the fact that my skull felt like it might crack like a walnut. Only one thought pierced through the roar: fear. What could I do to escape from a man who was cut like an Olympic decathlete and had combat skills that could end my life in seconds?

For now, I twisted my head just enough to find a gap to take in oxygen.

"I don't like being followed." The spit from his breath peppered my neck.

I braced myself for an aggressive action, the twist of my neck until it snapped like a twig, a knife in my back, some type of body blow that would cripple me. But there was nothing.

"I'm going to slowly remove my hand from your mouth. If you scream or try to fight me, I'll have no choice but to silence you."

Silence me. I wasn't sure what that meant exactly, but I wasn't going to ask for an interpretation.

"Nod if you agree."

He loosened his grip slightly, and I nodded.

He removed his hand and stepped back a foot as I gulped in air.

"I didn't mean to hurt you, or even scare you, Ivy. But you left me no choice."

"What are you involved—"

He brought a finger to his mouth, jerking his head to his left to look down the sidewalk that bent to the right. Did he see someone?

"I must go. Please do not move. I will explain everything I can once I'm done with my meeting."

I nodded, then followed his gaze down the sidewalk. The rain was coming down in sheets, greatly reducing visibility. He turned back to me. I noticed his wet sunglasses resting on the top of his head.

"You can't call Stan or any law enforcement. You can't run away, not until we talk. Do you understand?"

Again, I nodded.

"You are afraid. I…I'm sorry, Ivy. I do not want to harm you. But there is great risk with you being here. Right now, we are all at risk. Please let me do what I need to do, and I will try to keep everyone alive."

My eyes didn't leave his. The thud of my heart felt like it was rocking my weight back and forth. "Okay. I won't call anyone. I'll stay right here."

He took a quick glance down the sidewalk, then checked his watch. "I must go. I'll explain everything when I return in a few minutes. Trust me."

He turned and walked into the drenching rain, moving north along the River Walk.

Fifty-Three

Ivy Nash. Another complication that Zeke simply didn't have time for. But he'd have to make time. For her sake and his.

Soaked like he'd jumped into a swimming pool, he picked up his pace as he rounded the bend in the river. He jogged past a cluster of vibrant live oaks, which had obviously benefitted from growing next to the river, and spotted the next overpass, Augusta Street. Under that overpass was the agreed-upon meeting spot.

Just a few more steps...and there—an outline of a man about eight inches shorter than Zeke. It was Sergey, he was almost certain. He moved closer and was able to detect the man's hands stuffed in a windbreaker. He knew Sergey might have a gun aimed at him; he could shoot Zeke dead the moment he got close enough.

But his gut told him that Sergey wasn't going to kill him, not initially.

He reached the overpass and slowed to a walk. He wiped his face, his eyes fixated on Sergey, whose hands remained stuffed in his coat, his face without expression. The two men eyed each other as Zeke stepped closer, nary a word between them. Finally, Sergey said, "You must not look at the weather forecast. That was the headline earlier—heavy thunderstorms this evening. I thought you were proactive, always planning a couple of steps ahead."

Zeke had accomplished his first goal—to get within a few feet of Sergey without being shot. But he wasn't going to stand around and chat about the weather or other nonsense. Who knew if Sergey had called in an accomplice? Who knew if Ivy had ignored his request to hold off on calling law enforcement? The next sixty seconds would define his quality of life—if he were to have any life at all—for his remaining days on earth.

"I'm not going to melt. Then again, I think that's reserved for those who are wicked."

Sergey's right eye twitched, but Zeke was more concerned about the movement of his forefinger stuffed in his pocket. Zeke removed his glasses from his head, then pretended to fumble them into the air. As he'd hoped, Sergey removed a hand and caught them before they crashed against the concrete. "These are expensive," Sergey said, handing them back. "You haven't collected your upfront bonus yet. You might want to—"

Zeke heard a chirp coming from somewhere on Sergey's person. With his gaze staying on Zeke, the squatty Russian pulled a phone from his pocket. He shifted his eyes to the phone screen for a second, then pressed a button on the side of the phone and put it back in his coat pocket.

"Was that the missus asking you to pick up some milk on the way home?"

"You Americans—"

"Don't forget, I'm actually half Canadian."

"Who gives a fuck? All of you westerners think you're so witty. I have to put up with that crap everyday back in Boston." Sergey's eyes moved to the river water, which appeared to be rising higher, near the edge of the stone banks.

Enough chatter. "Do you have the rest of my bonus money lined up?"

"How much do we owe you?"

An odd question. "We settled on four million. After the five hundred K down payment, that leaves you at three point five."

"Right." He nodded, looking off into the distance for a moment. But Zeke could tell Sergey's focus had not left him for one second. Sergey had his guard up.

"So," Sergey continued, "three point five million dollars for someone who is—"

Sergey didn't see the right cross coming until it was too late. Zeke had connected perfectly with the bridge of his nose. Sergey stumbled but didn't fall as blood splattered the concrete around him. Zeke thought he had him on the ropes, but was surprised when the Russian—still trying to equalize his balance—pulled a pistol from his coat pocket. He recognized it immediately, one of those Russian Makarovs.

He quickly calculated the speed at which Sergey's arm was moving, his eyes focused on the motion, even as the opening of the barrel became larger. With all of his momentum, he swung his back leg around and smacked the gun and Sergey's wrist. The pistol flew out of his hand, landing in the river.

Sergey, with blood seeping down his face, pulled a knife from his sleeve. It was a T knife, the kind that one held like an old-fashioned corkscrew. The Russian mobster was circling him, only four feet away. Zeke had a knife strapped to one ankle, his Sig Sauer P938 strapped to the other. But if he reached down, Sergey might be able to stab him, and if the man got lucky, it could be lights out.

"Is this your way of renegotiating the three point five million?"

Still moving to his right, Sergey tried to sneer, but he flinched—Zeke was almost certain he had a broken nose. Sergey threw a right hook, but Zeke hopped back. The knife filleted his shirt, but missed his skin.

Sergey smiled, blood covering his teeth. "You should have never betrayed Petro."

The text. Sergey must have received a message on his phone that cemented his thoughts about Zeke.

Something caught Zeke's eye—movement from over Sergey's shoulder. Before he could identify it, Sergey lunged at his chest. Zeke sidestepped the knife, grabbing Sergey's thick wrist with both hands.

They struggled for dominance, their faces only inches apart.

"Your future father-in-law...he was only supposed to be an example of what we could do to anyone you care about. But now, you will die. And so will everyone else."

Anger-fueled adrenaline flooded Zeke's veins, actually causing him to freeze for a moment. It was a moment too long. Sergey head-butted him, then threw an elbow into his ribs. Zeke dropped his arms, leaving just enough of an opening for Sergey to ram his knife into Zeke's shoulder. The puncture went an inch deep before Zeke regained his senses and push-kicked his adversary away.

Sergey bounced back a couple of steps, his blood-filled smile in stark contrast to the gray haze of rain. Zeke tried lifting his shoulder. It was functional at best.

"I don't have to make a single call. The orders are in, Zeke. Your wife and kids—dead. Your hot fiancée—dead. And we have others on the list. They will get what's deserved, all in due time." He smiled again. "You were going to try to steal four million dollars from Petro Udovenko? You are an arrogant, stupid shit."

They must have learned about my plans to extradite my family. But how?

Now Sergey began to chuckle. "And working with the authorities? We'll make sure that your loved ones die slowly...cutting off one limb at a time. Can you picture that? Your son with one arm, your daughter minus—"

Seething to the point of almost losing his vision, Zeke roared and threw himself at Sergey. The torrent of emotions had nullified all of his training and self-discipline. The violent, animal-like response shocked Sergey, causing him to stumble. Ignoring the white-hot pain in his shoulder, Zeke plowed through his Russian counterpart, whose head bounced off the concrete wall. Sergey's eyes went crazy.

Zeke wasn't going to waste this opportunity. Suddenly back in control of his emotions, he grabbed Sergey's hand—the one still holding the T knife—and rammed it into his thigh. Sergey howled. Then Zeke threw two quick punches into Sergey's nose. His shrill could have shattered glass. Zeke quickly slipped his hand down by his ankle and grabbed his compact Sig. He jabbed it into Sergey's chin.

"Tell me how to call off the hit on my family and Zahera."

"My fucking leg," Sergey grunted.

"Tell me, dammit!" He pressed the gun even harder.

"Aah!"

"Tell me now!"

"Not possible," Sergey whimpered.

"What do you mean?"

"I mean I'm not calling anyone. I'm going to die anyway. But I won't be in hell alone. You'll join me soon. Just think though—your family will die before you."

Zeke moved the pistol down to Sergey's knee and pressed the trigger before another word was uttered.

Sergey yelled, but Zeke covered his mouth and said, "Who's the person giving you the child body parts?"

He closed his eyes, didn't respond.

"Who?"

Still no response.

"You have three seconds until I blow your other knee away. One, two, three." He fired a bullet into Sergey's other knee. "Who?"

Sergey moved his lips, but Zeke couldn't hear him. He moved closer. "Tell me again."

With his eyes flickering, Sergey whispered, "Fuck you," into his ear, then shuddered, gasping a couple of times.

"This one is for Brianna." Zeke then put a bullet in his chest. Sergey's body crumbled, but Zeke caught him before he hit the ground. He dragged him about ten feet and dropped his body into the river.

Two deep breaths. His chin quivered as he stared at the murky water, trying to think rationally for a second.

Did you forget about the movement you saw earlier?

He jerked his head left. It was Ivy, standing in the pouring rain, glaring at him. Then she started to run.

Fifty-Four

If my chest wall hadn't been so thick, I would have seen my beating heart on the sidewalk.

He was coming after me. I twirled around and started running, pumping my arms with everything I had. With the rain beating down on me, I realized I had my phone gripped in my hand—I'd forgotten it was there.

Zeke killed a man. It was a struggle, but he shot him three times. He didn't have to kill him, right?

A quick glance over my shoulder. Crap. He was closing fast—every stride I took, he took two. I cried out; the sound was muffled in the roaring storm.

Call Stan. That thought pierced through my fear. I tried tapping the screen as I was running, but it wasn't working. Was it the rain? My jittery hands?

I was sobbing, but the tears mixed with the rain. I needed to stop moving to allow my finger to tap the right button, but I couldn't risk stopping. Zeke had just killed a man. I was a witness. If he caught me, he'd have no other choice but to put a bullet in my head, dump me in the river too.

Another look over my shoulder. Fuck! Twenty feet and counting. What could I do? I had one chance. I stopped on a dime, wiped the phone screen, and tapped my contacts, found Stan's name and—

Zeke grabbed me, swooping me off my feet. I kicked, flailed my arms, but he carried me like a loaf of bread. The rain had suddenly ceased. I looked around; we were under the Convent Street overpass. I stopped kicking. He set me down, wiped his face.

"You're not going to kill me?"

"What? I'm not a killer, Ivy." He looked back up the river, then to me, probably contemplating his use of words. "I did what I had to do."

I held up my phone. "Give me one reason why I shouldn't call Stan and have you arrested right now."

"People are still in danger. Zahera is one of them. And there are others."

"Why? Who is he?"

"Okay, dammit, I'll tell you. Quickly." He ran his fingers through his hair. "Sergey works for Udovenko."

"That's what I thought. You're associated with that drug trafficking maggot. And that's why Zahera is in danger." I paused, blinked a couple of times as my brain began to process information. "That's why Z's dad was killed, wasn't it?"

He nodded, squeezing his eyes shut for a moment. "Yes, but I—"

Without thinking about the implications, I slapped him with every ounce of energy I had left in me. He touched his hand to his cheek, then glared at me.

"I'm…" I couldn't say it. I didn't know what to say.

His jaw twitched. "I deserve it." He wiped his face again.

Were those tears in his eyes?

"Look, we don't have time to talk right now. I have to make a call, then we need to ensure that Zahera is safe."

"You might have a soft spot for Zahera, but you let her father get killed. And now you murder a man?" I was trembling, screaming at the top of my lungs. My fear had been overtaken by my love for Zahera. "You are the lowest form of scum I've ever come across."

My phone buzzed. But I didn't look at it. I glared into Zeke's eyes for what seemed like an eternity. My phone buzzed again.

I glanced at it. "What?" I said out loud, glancing at Zeke then back to the screen.

"Who is it? Has someone gotten to Zahera?" He moved up next to me as I read the text from Nick out loud.

"Just got word from Alex's source. Zeke is working with Ukraine SBU. He's their mole inside Udovenko's operation."

I looked at him. "Is this true?"

"Yes, it's true. There's more you should probably know...need to know. I will try to tell you, Ivy. But for now, I need to make a call."

He turned to the river and did just that.

Fifty-Five

Zeke had lied. He actually made two phone calls. The first one lasted no more than thirty seconds. It was quick, to the point. The only phrase I heard was, "I owe you my life, Tank."

Tank. Was that a name or some type of code word? Zeke, after all, was much more than just a security guard. Was he working with the CIA? Another intelligence agency? Or was he simply a hired contractor, someone with the right skill set?

And I had a very good idea of his deadly skill set.

His second call lasted a tad longer. It was animated. He rubbed his eyes more than once, rocked up and down, tugging on his short hair. When he hung up, it looked like he'd been skewered.

"Should I even ask who that was?"

His glassy, blue eyes shifted to me. "I can't tell you."

"You can't or won't? I think after all this shit you put me through, everything you put Z through, you'd tell me what's going on. People were killed because of you being in their lives."

He swallowed hard. "I know. I—" He stopped short. "It's complicated. And I don't want to risk any more lives. But there is something I need to tell you. For now, we need to head back to Zahera's. I only have a couple of hours before I need to leave."

He started running.

"Leave for where?"

He didn't answer. He stopped, came back, and grabbed my wrist, started pulling me along. We were in the rain, but the intensity had dialed back. I broke free of his hold, but followed him as he hurdled the curb, running into the adjacent parking lot, his head on a swivel.

"What are you looking for?"

He acted like I didn't exist. He moved quickly, as if he were searching for something in particular.

"I might be able to help, you know."

Ignoring me, he ran up to a rusted blue pickup. I guessed it was north of twenty years old. He pulled something out of his pocket and waved it across the side of the car door. The lock popped up. "Get inside," he said.

I slid into the passenger seat as he searched under the front seat and then the back of the visor. He then sifted through a console that was filled with coins, pens, gum wrappers, a pack of cigarettes, and a screwdriver.

He picked it up, saying, "I guess I'll have to do it the old-fashioned way." He cracked open the casing for the steering wheel, and in less than two minutes, the engine roared to life.

"We're actually stealing this car?"

"Borrowing it. It's not like I plan to sell it for parts. But we can't get another person involved, so Uber or a taxi are out."

He pulled out of the parking lot.

"You said you'd tell me more, although you won't tell me who was on the phone."

"Can't."

"Neither call?"

He tapped the brakes, and we stopped at a light. He looked at me. "I want to, Ivy. Part of me just wants to let it all out, to share everything with everyone. But if I do, you could be on someone's hit list."

"Udovenko?"

He arched both eyebrows. "His network is a lot vaster than I ever knew. If he or anyone in his organization thinks you have pertinent information, then you could be next."

He held my gaze, which I imagined was to drive home the seriousness of his statement. It worked.

"Then tell me the part you can share."

"You know I've been working for the Ukrainian SBU. But I also have another client, another reason why I was trying to embed myself into Udovenko's operation."

Was he some type of double agent? Wait, that was more about governments spying on other governments, similar to what Armand had been suspected of doing. "What other entity would hire you? INTERPOL, another country? What?"

"It's a who."

He looked ahead; the light was now flashing red, obviously malfunctioning. He tried to change lanes, but we were blocked in on both sides.

"So, who?" I asked.

"Richard and Edna Watson."

I gave him a *who-is-that* shrug and a shake of my head.

"Their names aren't important, but their daughter, Brianna, was kidnapped two months ago. Literally stolen right from her own bedroom. Local police, FBI all got involved. They found no clues. None. No prints, no hair, no enemies in their past. Therefore, all the attention turned to—"

"The parents."

"Weeks went by and the pressure built. Then, out of nowhere, they got a call from someone who lives in Poland."

"Poland?"

He nodded. "Apparently, their daughter wore something like a dog tag, which had key information written on it, including her home phone number."

I found myself gripping the cloth seat. "They found her?"

"No, unfortunately. They'd actually just reached out to me. So I looked into it and found out this person had found the dog tag in what we would call a pawn shop. Through a lot of digging and some payoffs to the right people, I found out a person with known ties to Udovenko had sold it."

"Why would Udovenko be involved in some random kidnapping in the US?

"I wondered the same. Now this couple, Richard and Edna Watson, live in Andover, just outside of Boston. That's where Udovenko has developed—"

"I heard. His drugs are on the streets in that city."

"Nick told you."

I nodded, then I began to piece it all together. "Don't tell me, the Watsons were one of Udovenko's drug runners in Boston, and they stole from him or something, and then he got his revenge."

"The Watsons didn't know it, but I checked them out, looking for ties to Udovenko or the drug operation. Nothing there. And no evidence of them being involved in their daughter's kidnapping. They were clean."

"How did you get all of that?"

"A lot of methods. What helped speed it up was wiretapping."

"Seriously? You're just blatantly telling me this?"

"Who are you going to call, the NSA? Please." His voice was filled with sarcasm.

A cop was in the intersection, directing traffic. We began to inch ahead.

"So, whatever happened to Brianna?"

"While there isn't a body, I learned from a person lower in Udovenko's operation that she was a proof of concept."

"A what?"

"They were trying to see if they could kidnap her, get her to some lab where they were supposed to do some type of testing on her, and then, once she died, ship what was left of her overseas to people who would pay for the body parts."

I rolled down the window and let the wind and light rain slap my face. Once I contained my gag reflex, I turned back to Zeke, "This can't be. It's the most heinous thing I've ever heard of."

He pounded a fist against the steering wheel. "I just wish I'd been able to find out who was running this lab, doing the testing that would essentially kill these kids."

"What the hell were—"

"Are. I believe they've procured—through kidnappings or some other means—a bunch of kids with the same condition, using them as test monkeys."

The pickup lunged forward as Zeke hit the gas.

"What condition?" I asked.

My phone rang as he opened his mouth. It was Stan. "Hold on," I said to Zeke before answering the call. "Hey, Stan."

"They got him, Ivy. They fucking got him."

I scooted higher in my seat. "Who, Stan?"

The sound was muffled, as if he'd dropped the phone. "Stan. What's going on?

"Ivy, it's Nick. I'm in the car with Stan. Ethan has been kidnapped."

Blood rushed to my head so fast I began to see spots in my vision. "What?"

"It's true. We're trying to track him, heading west on Highway 90."

I smacked the seat and looked to Zeke. "Change of plans. Call Z. Stan's son has been kidnapped."

Fifty-Six

Zeke hopped the median, then sped down a one-way street—heading *into* the flow of traffic. I cussed nonstop until he screeched around a corner, nearly fishtailing our hunk of junk into a taco stand. But at least we were on a road heading in the same direction as the rest of traffic. I saw a street sign flash by: Old Highway 90.

"This connects with 90 just before you hit the loop."

"Yep." He swung his whole body left, which led to me smacking my head against the door window. We were blowing by car after car like they were standing still.

Zeke used his knee to steer the truck as he patted his pockets.

"What the hell are you doing?" I yelled, reaching my hand toward the wheel.

"I got it. I can drive with my knee."

"Yeah, right."

He pulled out his phone, just as I heard Nick yelling for me from the phone in my hand.

"Where are you guys, Nick?"

"Just outside the 410 loop, still on 90. Stan wanted me to ask you if you ever dropped off those naked photos at the Espinoza house."

"Yes. Didn't he get my voicemail?"

He repeated the question to Stan as I saw Zeke put his phone to his ear. "You calling Z?" I asked him.

"Not enough time to get into it with her. I'm calling Yao."

"Yao? What's he going to do?"

He shot me a knowing look.

"You know him?"

He nodded.

"How well?"

"To trust him. We go back."

"So, Liu wasn't ill, was he?"

"Nope. I needed to know that Zahera was safe."

"So, she's okay."

"I hope so." He adjusted the phone at his ear. "Hey, Yao, this is Zeke."

"Ivy, you there?" Nick said into my phone.

"Sorry, what?"

"Stan never listened to his voicemail."

"Put him on speaker."

"Okay, you're on."

"Stan, why are you asking?"

"I'm trying to figure out in my head how this happened. What triggered it?"

"Don't worry about that now, just keep tracking him. How are you tracking him?"

"Don't tell me not to worry. Help me think, dammit."

"Okay, right."

I could hear Zeke muttering something about Yao taking Zahera to a safe house. I smacked his shoulder. He winced, nearly dropping the phone. I'd forgotten about his stab wound. "Sorry." He brushed me off, kept talking as he dodged other vehicles like it was some type of video game. I refocused on my phone call. Something had occurred to me. But I needed to ask two questions.

"Stan, did you ever bring in Nancy Klein for questioning?"

"Wanted to, but never got out there, and then Bev got the call about Ethan."

"And no break-in reports at the Espinoza house?"

"Nope."

"Stan, I think Carlos Espinoza might be behind this."

"Kidnapping Ethan?"

I'd never heard Stan's voice reach that octave.

"Maybe. I don't know. It sounds crazy. But remember the photos? What the hell was he doing in bed with the Klein sisters?"

"That's the second woman? Nancy's sister—"

"Lisa, the nurse from Stonebrook. I don't know for certain, not until someone checks to see if she has a tramp stamp."

The truck went airborne for a second as it zoomed up the entrance ramp and onto Highway 90. I bounced off the roof and watched Zeke do the same, but somehow he kept one hand on the wheel and another on his phone.

"You guys okay?" Nick yelled.

"All good. So, Carlos knows two of the key people involved in allegedly passing the data along. And we know that at least eight of the thirteen victims had kids that went to Stonebrook."

"Make it thirteen out of thirteen. Bryant, my junior detective, confirmed that earlier."

"Well, then, there you go."

"It gets worse. All thirteen had at least one kid with autism."

"Autism," I repeated.

"What?" Zeke had just hung up the phone.

I smacked the seat so hard he flinched.

"This lab where you said kids were being tested like monkeys. You said they had a condition. What—"

"Autism."

"Did you guys hear that?"

"What lab?" Stan growled.

"Zeke wasn't just working for the Ukrainian SBU."

Zeke looked at me, but he didn't try to shut me up. He knew it would do no good. Not with Ethan's life on the line.

Stan and Nick both asked me about a dozen questions in the next sixty seconds. I did my best to give them enough information in the briefest timeframe possible.

Stan then directed Nick to call his detective colleague, Omar Moreno, and have him pick up Carlos and the Klein sisters. Nick made the call.

"Where are you guys? We're moving at almost ninety, so we might be catching up to you."

"I'm following him on my GPS tracker," Nick said. "Wait. It stopped moving."

"Where, dammit. Tell me where."

Nick said, "Fifteen miles ahead on Highway 90. Just north, it appears near a town called Hondo. Want me to call the local cops?"

"They'll screw it up," Stan said, shaking his head emphatically. "Don't trust them. Don't trust anyone. I'll get us there in nine minutes."

"I think we're about five minutes behind you. Hey, how are you tracking Ethan?" I asked.

"He went through a stage where he'd run away from home," Stan said. "We couldn't risk him getting out and not being able to find him, so we put a GPS tracker in his favorite pair of shoes, just inside the tongue. He doesn't even know it's there."

"Damn, you and Beverly are smart."

No response. I held the phone away from my ear, wondering if I'd lost the line.

"You still there?"

"Yep, we're here," Nick said. "Stan's upset."

"Sorry, Stan. Didn't mean to—"

"He's pissed at how this went down."

"What happened?"

A pause with nothing more than the whir of tires rippling against the grooved concrete. I glanced at Zeke. He shook his head, as if telling me not to press it. I conceded.

"We can talk about it later, Stan. Let's just get Ethan home."

"She thought it was a fake kidnapping, Ivy."

"Beverly?"

"Who else?"

"Right. Why would she think that?"

"Because I told her about these crazy cases. How people were losing their life savings, how gullible they were. I never expected it to happen to us, to Ethan." His voice began to break up.

"Stan, it's not her fault."

"It's my fault, dammit. I'm the one that gave her this information. I should have just kept my mouth shut."

"But Stan," Nick interjected, "you told me it sounded just like one of those fake kidnapping calls. They asked for money, right?"

"A hundred grand. Which we don't have."

"And then you said Bev hung up on them and called you."

"She did. She was upset."

"And then they called her back."

"It was like an out-of-body experience," Stan said. "She hung up with me, then called me back not even thirty seconds later. They told her she'd fucked up and that Ethan would pay for her mistake."

I could feel my stomach tear into a hundred pieces, but I kept it together for Stan. "I'm sure he'll be okay."

"They called back a third time. The first two times, it was a female. The third time, it was a guy. He said we could have Ethan back if we gave them fifty grand. He said they'd give us four hours to round up the money and they'd call Bev with a drop-off location. But as I started watching the GPS sensor leaving the city, I thought they were lying. Now, hearing about this Autism lab where they pick apart kids and then sell their parts to someone overseas, I'm just—"

"Stan Radowski," Nick said firmly. "We will find Ethan. He will be okay."

"You can't say that." Stan was crying now. It tore at my heart. "One mile up ahead, take a right," Nick said.

Zeke flicked his hand against my leg. "We're less than five minutes behind them. Just tell me where to get off of Highway 90."

A few seconds passed, then Nick said, "Turn north here."

I heard tires screech and Nick yelling, "Whoa!" Then he said, "Keep moving. Now turn into this abandoned parking lot."

"Where are you, Nick?" I asked.

"Castro Avenue."

I pointed at a sign for Castro, and Zeke nodded.

We slowed and turned right. I realized I hadn't seen rain or any sign that it had rained since we'd hit 90. The landscape around us was dry, with dust swirling from the wind.

Stan said, "Oh shit, tell me that isn't—"

I heard a car door slam. And then nothing.

Fifty-Seven

We pulled into the parking lot, and I saw Stan on his knees, clothing scattered all around him on the asphalt. His torso was rocking up and down as he held something in his hand. Zeke slammed on the brakes, and I jumped out before the truck stopped.

"Stan," I said, running over to him. Nick was on the phone a few feet away. I looked at what Stan had in his hands—a black and white jogging shoe. "Is that Ethan's?"

He brought a fist to his mouth. His entire head was red. He nodded. I bit my lip to hold back the tears, glancing at Nick, who'd just hung up his call and was talking to Zeke.

"FBI has commissioned a copter. It should make it out here in less than an hour."

"They knew he had a chip on him, Nick," Stan wailed. "That's why they threw out all of his clothes. We'll never be able to track him. Who knows where they went? Hell, they could be so pissed they've been tracked that they could—"

"Don't say it, Stan," I said.

"Why? Will that help him? He's screwed now. We can't help him. We may never hear from him again, unless we find his body. If they kill him out here in the middle of nowhere, the vultures might get to him."

"Wait," Nick said, rushing in front of us, his phone in front of his eyes. "Stan, look inside the tongue of the shoe. Is the GPS chip there?"

Stan peeled apart Velcro and stuck his finger inside. "It's not here."

"The signal, it just came alive again. They're back on 90 heading west."

We all raced back to our cars and screamed out of the parking lot. Once we were at sixty miles per hour and gaining speed, I reconnected with Nick on the phone. "How far ahead are they?"

"Five, six miles tops."

I opened up a map app and changed the view to where I could see the actual road and surrounding land. It was flat and brown. Desolate. "What kind of vehicle are we looking for?"

"The only witness report was a vice principal at Ethan's school. Said she saw a white, box-like van across the street from the school."

Zeke gave me a nod, pushing the speed of the old truck up to ninety. Stan's city-issued Impala was still in front of us. He had a flashing cherry light on top of his car, but with no sirens running. Cars were moving to the slow lane as we zoomed by them.

Five minutes went by without a word spoken. I looked at Zeke. His temples were stressed. The crimson stain on his shirt had dried. I assumed the bleeding had stopped.

"I've been in worse shape," he said.

He'd seen me staring. I went back to looking straight ahead, hoping I'd see a white van pulled over to the side of the road.

"By the way, don't take this the wrong way because you're an attractive woman, but you've seen better days."

I began to pull down the visor, but I was overruled by the part of me that didn't care right then.

"I'm hoping I didn't somehow give you that bruise on your forehead."

I touched it and immediately envisioned Frankenstein. "No, I got it when I was trying to act cool and stealthy when I left the Espinoza house."

"When you put the pictures back where you found them?"

"Yep."

"Sounds like the kind of work I find myself in." He glanced my way, then back to the road. "Sometimes justice needs a little nudge, doesn't it?"

Before I could respond, Nick called out through the phone, "The signal stopped."

"Where?" Stan asked.

"Just on the other side of Sabinal. Two miles tops."

I saw Nick reach on top of the car and pull down the flashing light. We slowed our speeds to a normal level as we reached Sabinal.

"How are we going to play this?" Zeke yelled out so Nick and Stan could hear.

"I don't want to get my hopes up. They could be playing another trick on us," Stan said.

"Stan, how can they actually know we're right on their tail?" I asked.

Nick spoke. "True. They may not have any idea."

"Have to assume they are aware," Zeke said. "Do you guys have a plan?"

"Depends on what we find. But whatever it is, I'm going to get my son back—alive."

Voices went silent for a solid minute. Now wasn't the time to preach to Stan about following protocol or playing it safe. He was desperate and willing to die or kill for his son. We had to do everything possible to keep anyone from dying.

Nick led us off Highway 90. We took Ranch Road 2730 north, a little two-lane road that had no shoulder. I saw a few oil derricks sprinkled across the distant landscape. Two or three miles later, just beyond a cluster of trees, we followed the Impala as it turned left onto a dirt road. We went no more than a hundred yards and were stopped by a closed metal gate. Nick hopped out and found the gate only closed by a simple hook. He unhooked it, pushed the gate open.

We drove cautiously forward. The dirt road was narrow, with countless potholes and tree stumps along the snake-like path. At the top of ridge, I saw the Impala brake lights flash. Stan and Nick got out of the car, and we pulled up next to them. In a small, dusty valley, there was a white van parked just outside of an old mobile home. No way that could be the medical facility Zeke had mentioned.

"What's the plan?" Zeke asked, pulling out his small pistol as he stepped out of the truck.

Stan and Nick glanced in his direction, but neither told him to put the gun away. In fact, neither had said a word about his bloody shoulder or asked what had happened back at the River Walk. I knew why. Right now, the only thing that mattered was getting to Ethan. "I'm not waiting on umpteen cars of cops and FBI agents," Stan said.

Nick, who was chomping on a wad of gum, looked at each of us, then sighed. "But we want him out safe, Stan. Negotiating our way out of this is the best path."

"I'm not going to play their game for the next forty-eight hours." He pushed up and started walking straight for the mobile home.

"Stan," Nick said in a loud, irritated whisper.

Stan kept walking. We had no choice but to catch up.

Zeke began to peel off to the right, but stopped when he saw me moving in Stan's direction. That stare again. "Ivy, you shouldn't be here. Get back to the car." He looked to Stan and Nick for support, but they had all eyes focused on the mobile home. I shrugged and kept moving, falling in behind Nick, the person I deemed the most stable at this point.

All three had their guns drawn as we moved to within about twenty feet of the mobile home, all of us walking like we were crossing a mine field. Zeke disappeared off to the right of us. I noticed an oil derrick in the background.

Stan moved forward and peeked through a window, then turned to us and held up three fingers. I guessed that meant there were three perpetrators inside. Or was it two plus Ethan? I didn't ask.

Nick moved against the side of the mobile home on the opposite side of the door from Stan. I was next to Nick. There were three stairs leading up to the door. Stan peeked through the window one more time. Again, he held up three fingers—amazing how he could hold a gun in his prosthesis. He switched it back to his left hand after he held up his fingers. He scooted closer to the front door, his gun raised.

Was he going to just crash the door in and take them by surprise?

This didn't seem right. Shots would be fired. Someone would get hurt. The bad guys? Maybe. But what about Ethan, or even Stan? I wanted to reach out, tell him to stop, to hold off and wait. But he inched closer to the door. Nick now followed suit from his side of the door, and I was a mere two feet behind him. I could feel my heart at the back of my throat.

Stan nodded, and then Nick began to count down with his hand. Five, then four, then three…

The door swung open, and a thin guy with a little scruff on his chin appeared at the threshold, looking out straight ahead.

He hadn't seen us.

Just as he began to turn his head in our direction, Nick reached up and grabbed his arm and yanked him down the stairs onto the dirt. Stan raced inside.

I jumped on top of the guy on the dirt. I didn't see a weapon. I said to Nick. "I got him."

He turned and ran into the mobile home. The guy tried to push me off of him, but I kneed his kidney and he grunted, falling back to the dirt.

A gunshot pierced the air. I flinched. Was Stan okay? What about Ethan? "Stay here or I'll shoot you," I said to the guy on the ground. I jumped up, ran to the stairs. Before I got to the door, Stan walked out. He was holding Ethan, who was wrapped in a blanket.

"Is he okay?"

Stan nodded. Just behind him, Nick held the arm of another man. He was young, probably not legal to drink. "Who got shot?" I asked Nick as he walked the guy down the steps and ordered him to lie face down on the ground. He turned to me. "No one."

Stan walked up. "Nick saved Ethan's life. A figure came at me with the blanket curled around him. I thought it was one of the kidnappers. I almost shot my own son until Nick pulled my arm down." He began to cry.

I put my hand on his back. Ethan had his arms wrapped tightly around his dad's neck.

"We've got one more here." I turned to see Zeke walking a woman around the corner. "She tried to escape through the bottom escape hatch."

He put her next to the other two guys. I flipped around and asked Nick, "Did you ever figure out where the GPS chip was?"

"No clue," he said.

"It's here." Ethan opened his mouth. I saw something silver on the end of his tongue.

Stan gasped. "How did you know…?"

"I heard you and Mom talking; you were getting worried. I know all about GPS signals. I knew it was in my shoe all along."

Stan let Ethan stand on his own, still wrapped in a blanket. Stan took the chip in his hand. "When did you hide the chip?"

"I heard them talking about technology. Some of it I understood. They had all of this equipment and I thought they might find the chip, so I took it out of my shoe when they weren't watching. Later, they made me take off all my clothes and throw them out of the van."

"They didn't touch you?"

"No sir," Ethan said. "They only talked about how to get more money—from you, Dad, and from other people. They kept talking about kids with autism. It was kind of scary."

While Stan and Nick hugged Ethan, Zeke held a gun on the three kidnappers.

"I can't breathe, Uncle Nick."

They let go, then Nick said. "Where did you get the idea of putting the chip in your mouth?"

"I heard Mom and Dad talking about playing tonsil hockey."

The three of us just stood there, expressionless.

Ethan continued, looking directly at his father. "That gave me the idea. Is that how you play tonsil hockey with Mom?"

We all cracked up as Stan brought his son in close and kissed the top of his head.

Zeke pulled up next to me, his gun still pointing at the three people on the ground. His other hand was tapping his phone screen. "Yao isn't answering his phone."

"Have you tried Z?" I asked.

"She's not answering either. But they could have left so abruptly that she didn't have time to grab her phone."

Zeke asked Nick to take over watching the three kidnappers. "I have to get to the safe house and make sure she's okay." He started walking away.

"I can get a unit there in ten minutes, Zeke. Just tell me where it is," Stan said.

Zeke turned around, looked at Stan, then the kidnappers. "Sorry. I can't share that information. I'll let you know once we're all safe."

He jogged off, and I was just a couple of paces behind him.

Fifty-Eight

On the ride back into San Antonio, as Zeke drove like a bat out of hell, Nick called to tell me that the kidnappers were terrified at what had gone down. The two males had actually started crying, asking if they could call their parents. They had eagerly shared everything they knew.

They were the group of hackers who were responsible for the fake kidnappings. I asked why, then, had they kidnapped Ethan.

The answer was they got their orders from Carlos Espinoza.

"He's the mastermind behind this entire thing? But why would he care about trying to do research for autism?"

"According to them, he doesn't," Nick said. "They said Carlos only knows about them because of his connection to the Klein sisters."

"How did he come across them?"

"Nancy Klein told this woman here that Carlos had delivered a package to her apartment and it was love at first sight. Eventually, she shared with him what she was involved in, this group of hackers extorting money from unsuspecting parents."

A quick thought pinged my aching head. Carlos must have gone home before I'd arrived there, seen evidence that someone had been there with the sliced mattress and stolen note, and then found that his precious porn photos weren't there. He had to have known that Megan was my client. Maybe he found out the cops were looking for Nancy and got pissed. Stan's son might have been on Nancy's radar because of his autism.

I said, "So Carlos ordered them to kidnap Stan's son because he believed someone was getting close to catching him."

"Yep. Said he'd give them fifty grand on top of the money they got in the ransom. But they admitted they didn't really know what they were doing. They're hackers, not kidnappers."

"And by kidnapping Stan's son, what would that buy Carlos?" I asked.

"The girl here thinks it was nothing more than a power trip. She called him a Scarface-wannabe. He didn't really think it through."

"But these people fake-kidnapped Carlos's own daughter, terrorized his wife. Why would he—"

"Apparently, Carlos despised his wife so much he wanted her to suffer. Through his connection with the Klein sisters, he got that hacking group to target his wife."

I knew Megan had issues, but it was hard to fathom how vicious and callous Carlos had been to his own wife, the mother of his children. "So what about this medical lab, where someone is running some type of test on kids with autism?"

"They claim they know nothing about it. They communicate with an email address that they say is untraceable. They share part of their proceeds from the ransoms they get from the fake kidnappings with the person on the other end of that email address."

"That's it? We don't know who's behind this damn thing?"

"Nope. But at least we saved Ethan and stopped these fake kidnappings. And with the FBI fully focused on his case, I'm sure we'll able to find the ringleader. Maybe Zeke has additional information he can share as well."

I looked at Zeke as we turned into an upscale neighborhood of older model homes. His mind was on Zahera. At least I assumed it was.

I hung up with Nick as Zeke slowed to a regular speed. Our pickup didn't fit in with this neighborhood. Old money. The homes were all unique, different sizes and shapes and colors; the lawns were green, glistening from the rain that had ended. We passed a number of walkers, a few older folks, some families using baby joggers. The neighborhood was as close to Utopia as you could find in San Antonio.

Zeke didn't utter a word until he pulled into a long driveway. I could see a small sports car near the back of the house by a detached garage. "That's Yao's car." Zeke made another attempt to call his old buddy. It rolled to voicemail.

I followed him as he walked up on the covered porch. It was a smaller home, blue and gray siding with navy blue shutters. It was quaint, but maybe the most unassuming home in the neighborhood. I wanted to ask Zeke who owned the home and all the other details about how he operated in this other life of his. That could wait until later, once we knew Zahera was safe.

He put his hand on the door and slowly turned the knob. It wasn't locked. "Not good," Zeke whispered as he pulled out his gun.

Three steps into the house and we could see it had been tossed. Lamps shattered on the floor, furniture tumbled over. Zeke ran through a living room and dining room, then stopped at the kitchen. I was right behind him. We saw the body on the floor. I closed my eyes for a second.

It was Yao. He had what looked like a gunshot wound to his forehead.

"Dammit all to hell." Zeke leaned over, checked his pulse. He looked up and shook his head. "It's me, dammit. I'm the reason

Yao was killed. I'm a magnet to those maggots." He stood up, still staring at Yao.

"Who did this? Udovenko? Someone who works for him?"

Zeke's eyes had that thousand-yard stare. He was someplace else.

My heart began to race. "Where is Zahera? Did the person who killed Yao take her?"

"I doubt it. I think Yao probably saved her life." He ran out of the kitchen and into the living room, stopping at the fireplace. It had one of those fancy iron gates covering the opening. He began to unscrew a bolt in the upper left-hand corner. I stepped forward and quickly did the same with the other screws as Zeke stepped back.

I shouted, "Z, are you in there?"

I heard a knock on the iron wall. It had to be her. I moved even faster on the last screw, then pulled the iron wall away.

Zahera was trembling, her knees tucked under her chin. She was still in her robe, although it was covered with black soot and grime. I reached out for her, pulled her out. She hugged me with everything she had.

"I think someone else might want to hug you." I turned around and Zeke wasn't there. The front door was ajar.

I stood up, then noticed a crumpled envelope on a table. I picked it up and read the front. *My dearest Zahera.*

I handed it to her. We read the note together, me looking over her shoulder. It was what I would have expected. Short and, yes, even sweet. But it didn't explain his other life. And I didn't bother adding what I'd witnessed at the River Walk. Maybe later. She cried, and I cried with her.

Later, after I'd called Stan, cops showed up in droves. So did Nick. He kept their questioning to a minimum. After a couple of hours, he escorted us to Zahera's place.

There, I unloaded everything to Zahera that I'd kept bottled up inside. In some respects, she was crushed all over again. Slowly, over hours of questions and periods of silence, she understood the dilemma I had been put in. "You had no choice, Ivy. My father played the ultimate guilt card."

She said it was obvious that my intention—trying to keep her out of harm's way—was the truest form of friendship and love. We made our peace and cried more tears, for love lost by death, for love lost by choice. "Someone else's choice," she reminded me with a typical Zahera eye roll. We shared a few laughs and pledged to always be transparent in our friendship.

Fifty-Nine

Zeke lifted his eyes to the mirror and checked out his new look: a thin beard the color of honey, which matched his new hair color on his head. He'd used a wig previously, but that didn't fit his new persona. He pulled a passport from his sports coat and compared the photo to what he was seeing in the mirror. A perfect match. He made sure his new driver's license matched the name on his passport. He was ready to go.

"Tank, you're the best," he said to himself.

He pulled two pictures out of his pocket. He stared at Zahera, who was modeling one of her ultra-sexy dresses. It was a silver number with a slit up the side. *Those legs are amazing*, he thought. A smile came to his face. He had finally admitted to himself that he cared for Zahera far more than he thought he would. Far more than he should. On a couple of occasions, he'd felt a tingle inside and wondered if he was falling in love with her.

He released a deep sigh. He hated hurting her. But it was necessary to create this fake life so he could focus his efforts on working his way inside Udovenko's operation, trying to learn the truth about their new trafficking operation, and gaining the seed money he needed to get his family to a new location where they would always be safe. He was pained by the fact that he wasn't able to find out who was behind the medical lab that was using autistic children as test monkeys and then discarding the spare parts like they were broken electronic devices. It sickened him, in fact. But he knew the FBI would be all over it. They would figure out who was at center of this, eventually.

He wanted to put this scene behind him. Actually, it was more than that. It was his entire way of life that needed to change.

But could he flip a switch and transform just like that?

He looked at the other picture. His son and daughter were playing in the sand on the beach. Damn, they were the cutest. Those heartstrings were made of steel. Nothing could break them.

He tore up both pictures and tossed them in the trash. Then he walked out of the bathroom of the President's Club and headed toward his gate. If all went as planned, he would hook up with his family in about twenty-two hours.

On the flight, he thought about his kids and all the great times they would have. But he couldn't convince himself that he would be satisfied living a normal life, working a nine-to-five job, staring at a cubicle wall for inspiration.

There were too many bad people out there. He knew one day Tank would rise up and call to him. He'd be forced to make a decision then. Would he live his life solely for his two kids, or would he feel that urge to do something for the greater good of society?

He didn't know that answer. He simply stared out the first-class window and took in the view as the sun sprayed rays of orange and purple across the vast sky. It brought him a moment of peace. One of the few he'd felt in the last twenty years.

Sixty

On a certain level, it was heartwarming to hear Cristina's teacher, Candace Foster, speak so glowingly of how much my one and only ECHO employee had developed during her semester of ILA—the modern vernacular for what I'd called English when I was in high school.

"On her first day of class, she was timid, afraid to read anything out loud, afraid to offer an opinion about what we were reading. But after a week of school, I could see a new, more confident person begin to sprout. She was eager to share her thoughts about the reading homework, and by the third week, she was reading a passage from our book of the week. It gave me such joy."

Candy—she'd asked me to call her that when we sat down for our first so-called parent-teacher meeting—wore pink-rimmed glasses. They sat on her high cheeks, which looked like they'd been supplemented by implants. I knew they weren't, because her mother, Maxine Foster, my high school English teacher, had a similar bone structure.

"That's really cool." I nodded, crossing my legs. "What you've done for her—helping her with her dyslexia, allowing her to understand it's not a sign of her intelligence—is awesome. Thank you."

She smiled, and her cheeks swelled. I was sitting across from her at the desk in her classroom.

"It's really all my pleasure. I get so much out of seeing these adolescents grow, especially someone like Cristina, who I know hasn't had the easiest life."

"She told you about her past, her mother, her mother's boyfriend?"

I could see a tear bubble in her eye. "She was sitting right where you were. I had asked her why she thought she had a problem opening up, trusting people. She burst out in tears. I went over there and hugged her. We talked another hour. By the end of that time, she said she didn't want to live her life being afraid, of reading or anything else."

Candy had many of the qualities of what any parent, or guardian, would want from a teacher. She was just like her mother, the woman who literally changed my path in life. If she hadn't taught me twelfth-grade English, I probably would have never gone to college and subsequently would have settled for any old job and any old guy. She had given me hope that I could change the course of my life.

"Cristina's had a tough go, but I'm proud of her. Overcoming a mom with severe addiction and mental issues is tough," I said.

"Boy, don't I know it."

I tilted my head. "Your mom, she was like a rock. She doesn't have those issues, does she?"

She pushed her glasses up the bridge of her nose, her eyes wide for a second. "She's a woman of amazing strength. Like my dad. They've needed to be. My brother—and I love him—but Harrison has been quite challenging."

"How so?"

"Well, he has autism. It's at the severe end of the spectrum."

"I'm sorry. Hasn't been easy, I'm sure."

"Dad's a doctor, knows a lot about the condition, and it still hasn't been easy." She sighed, then her shoulders slumped. It was as though her energy balloon had been popped.

"I've read somewhere that there has been new research in that field. Is there any hope for a cure, or at least some new ways to help treat it?"

"As a matter of fact..." She paused, looked out the window for a long second. Even behind her oversized glasses, I saw eyes that were in pain, eyes that had a story to tell. Would she tell me?—that was the question. I took in a breath, content with her taking her time, to find the courage or just to feel comfortable. But then she drew a straight line with her lips. She was retreating.

"Where were we?" she asked, blinking a couple of times before focusing her gaze back on me.

I wasn't about to give up. "I have this friend. His son, Ethan, has autism. I can see glimpses of hope in him that would take your breath away. So many parts of him are amazing." I took a hard swallow, squeezed my eyes shut for a moment.

She took my cue, continuing the thought. "And there are other times where you wonder if he's really all there, if he understands emotions like joy and love."

I offered a tight-lipped smile. I removed a tissue from my purse and dabbed my eyes. The tears were real. I'd been thinking about the fear that Ethan must have felt during those hours he was held captive. And I knew the torment that Stan had suffered. It had been nearly unbearable to witness, to see this beast of a man—albeit a few pounds lighter than his usual weight—devoured by the emotion of almost losing his son. Yes, his son had autism. Yes, his son was challenging, to the point where he and Beverly might have wanted to give up. But they never did.

I imagined that all parents go through times when they wished their child was different—more of this, less of that. But parents who truly cared didn't walk away. They found a way to get past the adversity and to ultimately see the best in their child. I heard Stan say the other day, with a tear in his eye, that Ethan was his hero. His emotion was real and deep from the heart. But to me, Stan and Beverly were just as heroic. Did they hope that somehow their child would miraculously be cured or at least have his condition improve? Without a doubt. But would they be willing to kill other children with the same condition just to make that wish came true? Hell no. I'd been around so many bad parents, people who either purposely were out to inflict harm on a child—on me when I was young—or who just didn't give a damn. That only made it easier to identify the ones who were at the opposite end of the parental spectrum. Like Stan and Beverly.

But not every child has a Stan and Beverly as parents. Or even an Armand.

"The day before I graduated, your mother told me that she got such joy out of seeing kids grow, similar to what you just said as you've worked with Cristina."

She gave me an *aw-shucks* smile.

"But…" I said with a heavy sigh, "my friend may not see his son reach the same milestone. Too many issues. Too much heartache. I'm just not sure how much more he and his wife can take."

I was becoming quite a good fibber.

"Ivy, but there is hope." She placed her hands face down on the desk. "That research you spoke of, it's years behind what's really going on in the field."

I sat a little taller in my chair.

She licked her lips, as if she were in a struggle—her natural desire to help battling the side of her that told her to stay quiet. She took in a breath, then said, "My father is conducting a research study. Actually, he's doing much more than that. He's refining a surgical technique that might completely alter the neurological connections of a child with autism." She brought her hands together as if she were about to break out in prayer.

"Now? This is happening now?" I asked with excitement in my voice.

"He's made tremendous progress over the last six to twelve months."

"But how has he done something that hasn't been done before and no one knows about it?"

She bit into her lip as a tear escaped her eye and trailed down her face. "Harrison might not have that much longer to live. Not in the way that we could define living."

I nodded.

"If you look at the history of medicine, the biggest leaps in treating conditions were when sacrifices were made."

"By all of the doctors and nurses..." I said.

"And the patients."

I nodded, as if I were getting her line of thinking. "Right, I see what you're saying."

"At their lab, they have a long hallway with pictures of all the kids who have made the ultimate sacrifice. They honor those young boys and girls. Without them, we would not be able to find a cure. And now we have hope."

"Hope," I repeated, fighting every urge not to jump across the desk and slap her.

"I'm sure they're looking down on us right now, happy that their lives could actually mean something."

I stood up and pulled back my sweater to show a small wire and microphone. Her jaw dropped as the door to her classroom opened. A half-dozen detectives and FBI agents swarmed the room. She and I held our gaze for an extra couple of beats as a cop recited the Miranda rights to her, then cuffed her. She began to mumble. A few seconds later, her mumbles grew into an eruption.

She was kicking and screaming, throwing every four-letter word at me.

Drowning her out, I turned and saw Stan walking in the room, Nick at his side. I walked over and hugged Stan. "Thank you, Ivy. I know how hard that was on you."

The room cleared. It was just Stan and me. I sniffled, and he pulled out a handkerchief and offered it to me.

I winced, then said, "Handkerchiefs went out of style about three decades ago."

He stuffed it back into his pocket, and we strolled out of the room. "Have you decided how I'm going to pay off my bet?"

We were in the hallway, and my eyes settled on a map that a class had put together, showing all of their travels during their high school years. An idea came to mind. "I want you and Bev to take a cruise…after you run the Boston Marathon. And it's on me."

"But I should owe *you*. Are you screwing with me?"

I smiled, shook my head. "It's what I want you to do. You guys deserve it. I'll take care of Ethan while you're gone, with a little help from Cristina and Saul. And I bet Zahera will even help out. I know she will."

"Damn, Bev would love that. I've never taken her on a vacation like that."

Now he was getting glassy-eyed. He pulled out his handkerchief and wiped his eyes. "I don't know what to say, Ivy."

"You may be cussing me out tomorrow when I show up on your doorstep for another run. It's time to take your training to the next level."

"Bring it," he said with a smile I'd never seen before.

We walked through the school, allowing me some time to think back to my high school years, and Mrs. Foster's English class that had set the course for my life. The idea that the woman who had changed my life was more than likely in the circle of people willing to sacrifice a child's life just to find a cure for autism…well, it was difficult to comprehend. But after some digging by Stan and Nick, it was plausible.

Dr. Julius Foster was brilliant, but he'd overstepped his boundaries. He was the brainchild of the entire operation: the kidnappings, the fake kidnappings to help infuse funding, and even the trafficking of child body parts. He would be arrested and likely would serve the rest of his life behind bars. His wife, my teacher, might be able to strike a plea deal and serve a shorter term, from what Nick had said. Same with Candy Foster. They deserved punishment, but I also knew that the world was losing two great teachers.

Udovenko, from what authorities had been able to ascertain, had likely retreated back to Eastern Europe.

It was both ironic and sad that, in the end, the man who could offer the gift of life, had taken the most lives in his quest to help his son. I'd seen parents do anything for their kids, even to the point of harming others. Were they just wired differently? Or were most parents just lucky enough to not find themselves in a position so hopeless and despondent to the point of having their core values completely altered?

Zahera had spent the days after our conversation questioning the principles of her father and of Zeke. But she told me something one day that I found insightful. "Love isn't blind, although those who are in love sometimes can't see. And it sure as hell isn't pure. There just isn't such a thing as perfect love. Which makes sense. None of us are perfect. But if there's any quest worth continuing, it's the one looking for that great love. The one that gives us the most hope."

She cried on my shoulder one last time after she uttered those words. And I cried right along with her.

Sixty-One

"**Y**ou first," I said to Saul as a candle flickered between us at the kitchen table.

He stuck a finger in the envelope, then looked up at me. "What if I don't want to?"

"You're going to act like you're ten all of a sudden?"

"But we've had a great night. An incredible meal; we watched a romantic comedy…"

"You just thought that Scarlett Johansson was hot."

He winked. "She couldn't hold your bra strap."

I looked at my chest. "Actually, it's the opposite."

"You're the bomb, Ivy. You're the coolest."

"That's what I was aiming for."

He reached over, put his hand on mine. "You know what I mean."

I did, even if he was afraid to use the L word. We both were. But I had to let him off the hook. "It's been a great night, you're right. So let's end it with a bang and—"

He jumped out of his chair.

"Where you going?"

"The bedroom. You said…"

I clapped out a laugh. "Later. If you're lucky. Now open the letter."

He did. It only took five seconds for me to see the news. He broke out in tears…tears of joy. I was in his lap, my arms squeezing his neck. "I knew you'd do it. You're smart, tenacious, and you've got a cute ass."

A few minutes later, after we'd toasted with glasses of champagne, he stood behind me as I stared at the laptop.

"You going to hit enter?" he asked.

"I don't know if I want to know. Does that make sense?"

"Perfect sense. But you keep wavering. I'd hit enter and see what happens. Keep your expectations low, but leave open the possibility that you could be surprised."

I took another glance at the online form I'd filled out. If I hit enter, the private investigative firm who owned this website would reach out to me to start the process of finding my real parents. They were specialists in the field.

"Okay, here I go." I punched enter.

"How do you feel?"

"Relieved. At least I made the effort. We'll see what happens, like you said. But if I didn't try, I'd always wonder."

He kissed the top of my head.

I reached up and put my hand on his face. "You ready to end the night?"

He splayed his arms, walked in front of me. "But I thought you said…?" He stopped short.

I played dumb. "What?"

"Well, nothing I guess."

I threw off my shirt and ran into the bedroom. "Let's go, Saul," I called out. "It's time to end the night with a bang."

And we did.

John W. Mefford Bibliography

The Alex Troutt Thrillers (Redemption Thriller Collection)
AT BAY (Book 1)
AT LARGE (Book 2)
AT ONCE (Book 3)
AT DAWN (Book 4)
AT DUSK (Book 5)
AT LAST (Book 6)
AT STAKE (Book 7)
AT ANY COST (Book 8)
BACK AT YOU (Book 9)
AT EVERY TURN (Book 10)
AT DEATH'S DOOR (Book 11)
AT FULL TILT (Book 12)

The Ivy Nash Thrillers (Redemption Thriller Collection)
IN DEFIANCE (Book 1)
IN PURSUIT (Book 2)
IN DOUBT (Book 3)
BREAK IN (Book 4)
IN CONTROL (Book 5)
IN THE END (Book 6)

The Ozzie Novak Thrillers (Redemption Thriller Collection)
ON EDGE (Book 1)

GAME ON (Book 2)
ON THE ROCKS (Book 3)
SHAME ON YOU (Book 4)
ON FIRE (Book 5)
ON THE RUN (Book 6)

The Ball & Chain Thrillers
MERCY (Book 1)
FEAR (Book 2)
BURY (Book 3)
LURE (Book 4)
PREY (Book 5)
VANISH (Book 6)
ESCAPE (Book 7)
TRAP (Book 8)

The Booker Thrillers
BOOKER – Streets of Mayhem (Book 1)
BOOKER – Tap That (Book 2)
BOOKER – Hate City (Book 3)
BOOKER – Blood Ring (Book 4)
BOOKER – No Más (Book 5)
BOOKER – Dead Heat (Book 6)

The Greed Thrillers
FATAL GREED (Book 1)
LETHAL GREED (Book 2)
WICKED GREED (Book 3)
GREED MANIFESTO (Book 4)

To stay updated on John's latest releases, visit:
JohnWMefford.com

www.ingramcontent.com/pod-product-compliance
Lightning Source LLC
Chambersburg PA
CBHW021206250626
47155CB00008B/2698